Advance Praise for
REEF ROAD

"The exciting, page-turning intelligence of *Reef Road* cannot be overstated. The clever story will please lovers of mystery, crime, and thriller genres. Author Deborah Goodrich Royce handles the balance of *Reef Road*'s off-kilter story with a magnificent, firm grip. The novel is rife with uncanny connections and flawed main characters with hidden agendas. It's tense with secondary characters, whose impacts are stunning, as events ricochet in a series of strange chain-reactions sprung from perfectly timed twists you'll never see coming."

—CLAIRE FULLERTON, *New York Journal of Books*

"*Reef Road* is magnificent. It feels utterly real, a novel of deeply personal context. It swerves between truth and lies—the lies that lead to an even deeper—and more devastating—truth. Though pure fiction, it reads as compellingly as a mixture of memoir and exposé. It has left me shaken to the core. Deborah Goodrich Royce writes with brilliant understanding of the mystery and occasional grace of trauma."

—LUANNE RICE, *New York Times* bestselling author

"Reading *Reef Road* feels like bingeing a particularly addictive true crime series. Mysteries intersect in this haunting page-turner as Deborah Goodrich Royce explores the ripple effect of violence, generational trauma, and the emotional weight of a case gone cold."

—MEGAN COLLINS, author of *The Family Plot*

"*Reef Road* is a masterpiece. It's a tightly woven and often humorously told thriller that somehow manages to speak volumes about how families pass down trauma. Nothing short of brilliant."

—ANNABEL MONAGHAN, author of *Nora Goes Off Script*

"*Reef Road* is a daunting masterpiece. A plot-driven thriller inspired by a real unsolved murder that you won't be able to put down. This atmospheric thriller satisfies. A stunningly dark read."

—REA FREY, award-winning author of *Secrets of Our House*

"Taut and suspenseful, *Reef Road* reveals how one horrific act of violence can reverberate through multiple lives, even generations. Based on a real-life event, this book will keep you turning the pages well into the night as secret upon harrowing secret unfolds."

—WENDY FRANCIS, author of *Summertime Guests*

"*Reef Road* is a thriller of a roller-coaster ride, an elixir of murder, mystery, and mental instability, built on foundational questions—whether we are destined to inherit or repeat the psychological trauma of our parents, whether we can ever really trust assumptions we make of another, or trust the limits of what we, ourselves, are capable of. Ms. Goodrich Royce is expert at weaving a tale where the interplay among characters rebounds between the real and the imagined, exposing a shocking backstory with current-day repercussions in the process. The backdrop of glitzy Palm Beach, contrasting with staid, mid-century Pittsburgh, reminds us that evil can be found anywhere, unconstrained by geography, education, or social status. Unraveling the characters' motives and psyche, and the plot twists and turns, makes *Reef Road* a perfect book club choice."

—JOAN LUISE HILL and KATIE MAHON, authors of *The Miracle Collectors: Uncovering Stories of Wonder, Joy, and Mystery*

"*Reef Road* careens from a decades-old unsolved murder in Pittsburgh, to a grisly discovery washing up on the shore of the breezy, ocean town of Palm Beach. With expert touch and nuance, Deborah Goodrich Royce weaves the lives of a novelist searching for the truth, a bored housewife, and the menacing figure of a man or two, through the claustrophobic, early days of the COVID pandemic. The result is an asteroid-like collision of deceit, guilt, and greed in an unexpected, stunning climax that will stay with you long after you finish reading. A page-turning, incredible read!"

—BRIAN CUBAN, author of *The Ambulance Chaser*

"Superbly written and elegantly structured, the oh-so-talented Deborah Goodrich Royce brings her unique voice and mesmerizing style to an altogether original novel of suspense. Instantly immersive and deeply felt, *Reef Road* is both intensely personal and powerfully universal. Royce creates a haunting (and surprising!) portrait of a troubled wife—and the relentless writer on the trail of her past. I could not put it down."

—HANK PHILLIPPI RYAN, *USA Today* bestselling author of *Her Perfect Life*

"*Reef Road*, a taut, expertly-crafted psychological thriller, grabbed me from the first page and kept me hooked with its many dark twists. Set in Palm Beach, Florida, during the strange, locked-down days of spring, 2020, the novel alternates between two narratives: an unnamed mystery writer, who is researching the murder in 1948 Pittsburgh of her mother's childhood friend, Noelle Grace Huber; and Linda Alonso, the unhap-pily married mother of two young children. As layer by layer is peeled away, the connection between these two women and the long-dead girl is revealed—and along with it, a powerful rendering of how trauma from one violent act can reverberate for generations."

—VIRGINIA HUME, author of *Haven Point*

"In Deborah Goodrich Royce's propulsive and riveting novel, *Reef Road*, nothing is what it seems. You will keep turning pages into the night, unraveling the threads of two womens' intersecting lives to reveal a shocking act of violence and the devastating reverberations that echo decades later."

—MARY DIXIE CARTER, author of *The Photographer*

"Reef Road paints the unforgettable portraits of two deeply flawed, yet mesmerizing women and how an unsolved mystery seventy-two years ago still haunts them today. Deborah Goodrich Royce crafts an unforget-table thriller full of captivating twists and deeply compelling characters. It is a chilling story of generational trauma and an evocative tale of unre-solved grief exploding into the kind of novel readers will never want to put down."

—JOANI ELLIOTT, author of *The Audacity of Sara Grayson*

"A writer on a mission to solve a decades-old murder. A woman struggling to survive an abusive marriage and protect her children. As these two narrations collide in the most unexpected way, the story takes a marvelously twisty turn. Original, taut, and psychologically complex, *Reef Road* is Deborah Goodrich Royce at the top of her game!"

—WENDY WALKER, national bestselling author of *Don't Look For Me*

"In her novels, Deborah Royce has made herself the 'Queen of Plot Twists' and *Reef Road* has a twist of hand that I didn't see coming. I tore through this book with such delight and anticipation and you will too! *Reef Road* and Royce, publishing's Plot Twist Queen, are not to be missed!"

—ANNIE PHILBRICK, owner of Bank Square Books
and The Savoy Bookshop & Café

Also by Deborah Goodrich Royce

Ruby Falls

Finding Mrs. Ford

REEF ROAD

REEF ROAD

A Novel

DEBORAH GOODRICH ROYCE

Post Hill
PRESS

A POST HILL PRESS BOOK

Reef Road:
A Novel
© 2023 by Deborah Goodrich Royce
All Rights Reserved

ISBN: 978-1-63758-496-5
ISBN (eBook): 978-1-63758-497-2

Cover design by Cassandra Tai-Marcellini and Becky Ford
Interior design and composition by Greg Johnson, Textbook Perfect

Post Hill Press
posthillpress.com

Published in the United States of America

To Carole and Kate

"Our memory is a more perfect world than the universe:
it gives back life to those who no longer exist."

—GUY DE MAUPASSANT, *Suicides*

"In Greek tragedy, they fall from great heights.
In noir, they fall from the curb."

—DENNIS LEHANE

PROLOGUE

THE WIFE

Saturday, May 9, 2020

Two teenage boys burst onto the beach, skirting the *do not enter* tape through the sea grape bushes, surfboards tight under their arms. The sun beat straight down on them, casting no shadows, as if they weren't even there. Despite the closure of the beaches, despite their mother's reminders to do their schoolwork while she went to the store, they could not help themselves.

They were pretty sure the cops who patrolled occasionally would not see them either, because they never did. The police were only looking for cars illegally parked at the side of North Ocean Boulevard. This stretch of beach was grassy and hilly and the water was impossible to see from the road. The fact that the boys were breaking all rules—their parents' and the town's—made their outing all the more irresistible.

The wind was high, the waves were breaking perfectly, and this was Reef Road, famous to surfers around the world. At least, that's what the boys had been told. They had been surfing here for years now, practically since they could walk. Once, they'd gone up to Montauk where the waves, admittedly, were great. But this was their beach and they felt protective of it.

1

They hefted their boards and walked as fast as they could over the frying pan of sand. In their hurry, they did not notice at first the shrieking circle of seagulls down near the edge of the surf. As they got closer, they became aware of dozens of gulls hopping and skittering to and from something that had captured their attention.

Rand, the younger boy—the one whose Palm Beach Day Academy friends called California for his blond curls and speech pattern, peppered with *rads* and *bitchins*—saw it first.

"Bro." He stopped moving, ignoring the burning sand on the soft tissue of his arches. "What the fuck is that?"

"What?" asked Colson—his actual brother and not a metaphorical *bro*—continuing his beeline for the water.

"Dude," Rand said. "Stop!"

"Man, you're such a wuss." Colson paused briefly. "Never seen a dead rat before?"

"That's not a rat, you douchebag!"

Colson ignored him and kept walking.

"*Please* look?"

When his brother sounded like the little kid he used to be, Colson stopped. There was a plaintive note that made him drop his board and approach the seagulls, waving his hands to disperse them.

The seagulls did not like it one bit. Whatever they had gotten hold of, they wanted to keep.

"Beat it!" Colson yelled, kicking sand at them. He watched as one gull almost took off, nearly lifting into the air with the object secured in his beak. But it proved to be too heavy for him and he dropped it.

Both Rand and Colson lunged forward. It was hard to tell who identified it first. Rand's tanned face paled and he turned his head to vomit, avoiding the item on the sand. Colson did not throw up, although he confessed to his brother that he could have.

"Fuck," Colson said, "it's a hand."

"Yeah," Rand agreed, wiping his mouth. "Look," he said, squinting at the body part—the human body part—resting in the sand on their beach. "It's got a ring."

Colson leaned over to peer as closely as he could without touching it. "What the fuck are we supposed to do with this?"

"I dunno, Cole. Call the police?"

"Dude, what do we say? We're not supposed to be here, but we *are* and we found a hand? A fucking *hand*?"

Rand was silent. Both boys stood motionless and stared at it. It was a man's hand, judging from the general shape of it, the short nails, the hair on the knuckles, which looked abnormally black against the blanched quality of the bloated flesh. The end of it, the part that should have been attached to somebody's arm, was roughly severed, like it had been torn off. The ring was a plain gold band.

The seagulls took the boys' stillness for permission and began their recapture maneuvers.

"Arrrggh!" screamed Colson, waving his arms and running a few short steps in all directions to ward off the scavengers.

"You think it's fake?" Rand asked. "I mean, like Halloween?"

"That's really dumb, bro."

Rand paused to pull his hair out of his mouth from the gusting wind. "You think it's real?"

"The seagulls do," said Colson.

"Yeah."

"We can't just leave it. I mean, it's probably *evidence*."

"Well, we can't bring it home," said Rand. "What're we gonna say to Mom?"

This question lightened the mood. Colson started one of his routines that always made his brother laugh: "Yo, Mama," he began, "what's for dinner? We've been out hunting and gathering."

"Can we give you a hand with dinner?" Rand chimed in, one-upping his brother.

The boys cracked up with a forced gaiety neither felt.

"Anyway," Rand said, "I'm not touching it."

"Little One," Colson called him by this diminutive more often than Rand cared for. "You're younger, you've gotta do it."

"Do not. It probably has coronavirus and fell off someone."

"It was a shark, *dummkopf*. He took a taste of this guy and hurled him up."

"You're probably right," Rand said.

"Go find an old plastic bag. They haven't cleaned the beach lately. There has to be one blowing around here somewhere."

"You do it."

"Someone needs to stay and watch the hand," Colson said and started to laugh again. "Just go."

Rand glared at his older brother then headed off to follow his orders. What else could he do? What else could they do? They couldn't very well leave a human hand on Reef Road beach for the seagulls to eat. It wasn't right. Anyway, it didn't take long for him to find one of those long, blue plastic bags that newspapers came in. He picked it up and checked it for holes. He didn't want hand guts dripping all over him.

"Here," he said to Colson when he got back. "I got the bag so you put the hand in it."

"Fine," Colson said. "Baby."

Colson slipped his own hand into the bag and prepared to pick up the appendage in the same way he would pick up poop from their golden retriever. He grabbed the hand through the thin layer of plastic and shuddered at the rubbery-ness of its texture. It gave him the weird sensation that he was actually shaking another human being's hand. Something they hadn't done since COVID.

The good news was it didn't really smell too bad, just kind of fishy.

"C'mon," he said to Rand. "Let's go."

Each boy tucked his board under his arm, cast a wistful glance at the sea, and turned to walk back across the sandy expanse, one of them carrying the day's discovery.

They passed by a woman sitting on the sand, a woman they had not seen before. A woman they did not see, even now. A nondescript woman, dressed in khakis, an oversized shirt, one of those sunblock hats for old people. The kind of woman no man ever sees, especially younger ones.

When questioned later, each boy stated with absolute certainty that no one else was on the beach that day.

4

1

A WRITER'S THOUGHTS

When I look at photographs of Noelle, I try to gauge her expression for signs of what was to come. There are two pictures of her in newspapers, though neither is dated. In one, her hair is parted slightly off center and piled atop her head in a *fräulein*-style braid. I can't tell if one or two braids were plaited to wrap across the crown of her head, but the effect suggests a little German girl in the years before the war.

Noelle's chin in this particular image is dipped down, her eyes look up to the camera, and her smile is slight, lips barely parted. Because the photos I am studying are taken from old newspapers from the weeks and months—even years—after it happened, the pictures are grainy and pixelated.

The upward regard of her gaze allows the whites of her eyes to show underneath the irises, thus lending her an expression that the Japanese— or maybe it is only the macrobiotic practitioners—would call *sanpaku*. George Ohsawa, founder of the macrobiotic movement in postwar Japan, identified this characteristic—the whites of the eyes being visible either above or below the irises from the position of a straightforward look—as a sign of extreme ill health or imbalance, which he attributed to the worsening diets of his countrymen through the influence of Western culture.

This trait, he believed, was an indicator of those marked for death and has been noted by other macrobiotics (I know this because I used to be one) in the gazes of a gamut of doomed historical figures ranging from Rasputin to Marilyn Monroe to Charles Manson. All of them, we can safely agree, qualified as marked for death, although death, in Manson's case, did not happen to be his own.

Ironically, in the photo of Noelle in question, she is looking up at the camera—not straight ahead of her—so she cannot really be called *sanpaku* at all. Though marked for death she was.

In the other photograph that was used by the papers, Noelle is also looking upward, but not in the direction of the camera. She casts her eyes up and to the side—as if to the corner of the room—to an object she sees that is invisible to the rest of us. An angel, I hope. Something good and hopeful and reassuring that her last moments on earth—as horrific as they would be—offered reprieve. Noelle's smile is bigger in this picture— I think I even see dimples in her cheeks—but she is still not fully open to us. She holds something in reserve.

This image of Noelle, however, reveals the girl my mother remembered. She—my mother—did not recognize her childhood friend in the braided girl who resembled a little Greta or Heidi, but she looked at this image and said this was the Noelle she knew. The girl with whom she rode the streetcar, went to school, walked to Frick Park, and, of course, played. They were children, after all. They had been friends since kindergarten.

At the time it happened, the girls had just graduated, my mother said, from playing with dolls to playing records. I like to think of them dancing, but my mother never mentioned it. And I never thought to ask her. Noelle's record player, in fact, featured prominently in newspaper coverage of the events of that night. It was found on a chair next to the table in the kitchen, where Noelle was baking a cake to surprise her parents. Or preparing to bake a cake. It is hard to make out exactly where she was in the process, though the cake was noted to have been chocolate.

Noelle had retrieved the record player, the newspapers said (calling it a Victrola), from the basement where it had recently been stored. A dispute arose in the papers as to who exactly had fetched the Victrola.

Was it Noelle who had lugged it into the kitchen? Or did the killer have a familiarity with the house and know where the family kept this item? Did he go down to the basement after stabbing Noelle thirty-six times, leaving her on the floor near the telephone table in the dining room where she had obviously—and unsuccessfully—fled? Was it he who retrieved the record player from its storage place where Noelle's father said he had so recently put it, and set it up in the kitchen? Her father at one point advanced this theory—that the murderer had moved the Victrola—though I am not quite sure what purpose this action would have served him. Noelle's killer, I mean.

But blood had been found on the basement stairs.

The two undated photos of Noelle must have been taken not long before her death. She was twelve years old when she was killed, and these images show a girl who is roughly that age. Spending time with these pictures, I am reminded of the words of Nancy Mitford describing a photograph of the fictitious Radlett family in her novel, *The Pursuit of Love*:

> *There they are, held like flies in the amber of that moment—click goes the camera and on goes life; the minutes, the days, the years, the decades, taking them further and further from the happiness and promise of youth, from the hopes Aunt Sadie must have had for them, and from the dreams they dreamed for themselves. I often think there is nothing quite so poignantly sad as old family groups.*

The photos of Noelle are indisputably sad, seen through the corrective lens of hindsight. She is alone in them. She is not grouped with her family: her mother, her father, her older brother Matthew. Nor is she pictured with her friends: my mother, Jane Stores, or the others. There is one photo of her girlfriends that I can find, though my mother is strangely missing. She is not among the pallbearers, girls in their serviceable winter coats clustered around the casket, but is somewhere else in the church on the day of Noelle's funeral. Noelle is there, though, in that photo, invisible in her white, wooden coffin.

Life, for Noelle, did not go on. The camera clicked but her life soon ended. The days, the years, the decades did not take her further and further from the happiness and promise of youth. Her promise ended on Friday, December 10, 1948, in the kitchen of her family's modest house in its row of modest houses in the Homewood-Brushton district of Pittsburgh, where she and my mother grew up, for a time, as friends.

2

THE WIFE

Chapter One
June 2019

A lifetime ago—in a time before pandemics and quarantines and losses of a magnitude she had not yet imagined—Linda had whiled away a reasonable amount of time at her local airport. Her mother was ailing in Pittsburgh and needed an advocate at the hospital. Linda, an only child, was the sole candidate for the role. Hence her frequent passages through the self-styled "Airport of the Palm Beaches," which most people just called West Palm. She did not know then—could not have known—how soon the concept of entering an airport would fill her with dread of contamination.

Linda always arrived early at the airport, which, if she hit the north bridge right, was a twenty-minute drive from her house. If she missed the window when the bridge was down, it would add fifteen minutes while the drawbridge slowly rose, allowed waiting boats to pass below, and lowered just as slowly. Slower, it seemed, if she was running late. She drove herself, parked her car in the covered lot, and dashed in unencumbered. She signed up early for TSA PreCheck, printed her boarding pass at home, and never checked a bag, steps intended to expedite her travel from island to mainland and through the halls of the airport. She was nothing if not efficient.

Linda and her family lived on the island of Palm Beach. That famous-round-the-world isle known for glitz and glamour, gates and guards, private clubs that were hard to get into and public restaurants that were even harder—especially in what was known as "the season."

Palm Beach was part of a long string of barrier islands that stretched along the east coast of Florida and up the eastern seaboard, creating an intermediate body of water called the Intracoastal Waterway, a network of canals, inlets, bays, and rivers that continued to Norfolk, Virginia. But, in Palm Beach, the Intracoastal was simply called "The Lake," a shortening of its regional designation as Lake Worth.

Linda's time at the West Palm Airport was usually spent with Starbucks coffee, emails, texts, and a string of calls from home to locate a sock or a pasta strainer for the husband and children she was leaving behind. If it was an evening flight, she might hit the bar at Nick's Tomatoe Pie (spelled just like that, like a digit at the end of your foot)—a pizzeria that ran a length of the corridor on the way to the gates, where travelers stopped to drink at any time of day or night. Linda would not allow herself a drink before six o'clock in the evening. No matter what fissures were beginning to appear in her carefully constructed life, she still had some standards.

Sometimes on her evening travels, she recognized a man at the bar. A tall, sturdy man—one of those guys who looked like he had played football in high school or college. He had a nose that might have been broken and shoulders so wide they looked padded. "Rugged" was the word that came to mind.

It took her a few minutes to place him as a school father from the Montessori her children attended in West Palm. She had only ever seen this man and his wife at the school. She did not know where they lived. The Alonsos—Linda, her husband Miguel, and their two small children, Diego and Esperanza—lived on the north end of the island, the neighborhood-y section favored by young and year-round families. Not on the southern end—the estate section—the area filled with the unoccupied mansions of seasonal visitors.

Sitting at the bar one night, Linda tried to conjure up the faces of this man's wife and children. Redheads, she thought, the wife and two little boys, both boys sprinkled with freckles. The wife probably had freckles, too, but covered them with makeup. Linda cast another glance at the man, looking for hints of freckles. No. He definitely did not have them. She didn't know him—or his wife—well, but she was surprised he didn't recognize her, sitting four feet away. Men usually remembered Linda.

But he never did. Or he gave no signs of recognition. It crossed her mind that he might, in fact, know who she was, but chose not to acknowledge her. Which raised its own set of questions. This fellow never stayed long at the bar, ordered a double whiskey neat, no ice—a committed sort of drink—which he drank standing up, eschewing the stools provided. A committed way of drinking.

She took to watching him, the few times she saw him. She felt almost invisible as she turned her head to look at him or regarded him in the mirror behind the bar. He never looked at her and he never looked in the mirror. She found this something of an oddity, the ability to stand in the presence of a mirror and not gaze into it. But this man was intent on his whiskey and kept his eyes downward, on his drink, on his phone, on his napkin, which he rolled between his thumb and index finger. Then he knocked back his glass, threw down a twenty, and left.

From her vantage point at the bar, she could see him walk to his gate. Chicago. Eventually, she would turn her attention to her wine. Then she would look at herself in the mirror, wondering what it was about her own face that caused this man not to recognize her. Hair still blond with a little help from her hairdresser. Eyes still blue. Had she aged? It was hard to tell. A generic face, Miguel had once said to her. At the time she had laughed, teasing him about his less-than-perfect grasp of the English language. "I don't think you know what it means," she had said. "It's not a compliment!"

"I know what it means," he responded. "It means you're a classic beauty." Then he kissed her, in the sweet way he kissed her then, before things became the way they were now.

One evening, she saw this man with his family. The presence of his wife and sons—freckled just like she remembered—confirmed he was exactly who Linda thought he was. She was making her way down the long hallway toward her gate when she noticed the family in front of her. The man walked all the way to the left, the boys side by side in the middle, and the wife hugged the right. The quaintness of their appearance—parents flanking their little ones—stirred something in Linda. Jealousy, perhaps.

The taller of the boys, the one closest to his mother, was holding a leash attached to a rambunctious beagle puppy. The family came to a stop and Linda slowed her pace. She did not wish to engage with them. Husband and wife had a short discussion before he turned to the men's room. The woman and boys continued on their way and Linda proceeded to follow them.

Suddenly, the puppy strained at its leash and barked its beagle howl at an old lady who was being pushed in a wheelchair. Linda noticed the cat carrier on the woman's lap just as the child lost control of the leash. The dog bounded after the woman and—more to the point—her cat. The boy ran after the dog, the mother ran after the boy, and everyone else paused to watch.

Linda had just a second to step on the leash and she did it. She stopped the dog. She saved the cat. The little boy caught up to his errant beagle and scooped him up. The mother threw a hasty *thank you* in Linda's direction, but she did not really see her, so intent was she on grabbing one child and not losing sight of the other. Like her husband, she did not recognize Linda.

Linda hung back and watched the woman put the dog into the carrier it should have been in in the first place. She watched the aide hustle the wheelchair and its occupants down the corridor. She watched the man return from the restroom and his wife explain to him what had happened. By now, Linda had ducked into the bookstore to observe them from behind a newspaper stand. She watched the woman motion in the direction of where she had just been—Linda—when she stepped on the leash. She watched the woman shrug, dismiss further thought of her, and gather her family on its way.

And so Linda had another encounter with the man at the airport. And once again, only she was aware of it.

3

A WRITER'S THOUGHTS

I grew up under the shadow of a dead girl—a girl I had never met, whose family had not heard of me, a family I would not know if I passed them on the street, nor would they, in turn, know me. Yet the death of this girl long before I was born has clung like pollen to my life.

Noelle Grace Huber was the name used by all the newspapers, though my mother just called her Noelle. She was twelve years old when she was murdered at home on that December night, baking her cake in the kitchen. The same age as my mother. A trail of blood stretched into the dining room, where her parents found her on returning from a night of bowling. Her fingers were nearly severed from her attempts to take hold of the weapon. Her lungs were punctured, as was her skull. Her right side took the worst of it.

But she was not yet dead. The life force in a child is mighty.

Much conjecture was made about the intact status of the telephone table, next to which she was sprawled on the floor. Reporters questioned why the table was still standing. It was a three-legged table, the kind prone to instability. Why had it not fallen over? This led to the proposition that the murderer had stayed on after killing her—listening to the Victrola?—and cleaned up the scene of his crime.

No fingerprints were found on any of it, lending credence to this theory. The mixing bowl for the cake batter, the telephone, the small knife found next to the kitchen sink, all were free of fingerprints, even those of Noelle.

Noelle's father confirmed that the house had been locked when the parents had left earlier, both front door and back. He was equally certain he had pulled down the shade of the window on the back door. The police guessed that someone knocked on that door—someone Noelle must have known, must have trusted, and must have let into the house—because it was found unbolted with the shade raised.

At that point, detectives surmised, this person known to Noelle (but forever unknown to us, since this crime remains unsolved) must have followed her to the spot where she was working on the cake. Was it there that he stabbed her thirty-six times? Or did he begin his rampage in the kitchen and continue it as she tried to reach the telephone? They believed he did not use the knife Noelle was using for whatever she was doing with the cake. It was too light and small, they said, to have penetrated her skull two times, as her skull had indeed been penetrated.

While no prints seemed to be anywhere, blood was omnipresent: on the walls, the floor, the fridge, the basement stairs, along the path from the kitchen to the telephone table.

A Google search reveals her gravestone:

Daughter
Noelle Grace Huber
September 2, 1936
December 10, 1948
A lovely bud of promise to bloom in heaven above

And there is that word again. Promise. It is what we envision *in* our children; it is what we extend *to* our children. In the case of Noelle—the case of the Huber family—both promises remained undelivered.

Noelle's father tried to kill himself after the loss of his daughter. In December 1951, on the third anniversary of her murder, he slashed his own face with scissors. It landed him in the psych ward. He was said to have been distraught at the continued arrests of his son for the murder of his daughter. But no one really knows because police were not permitted to speak with him.

Matthew J. Huber, Jr., was nineteen years old the year Noelle was killed. He worked at the Union Railroad Yard and was at work on that Friday night. At least, he started and ended the evening at work. But a dispute arose as to young Matt Huber's whereabouts between the hours of 7:45 and 10:45, right about when someone was stabbing Noelle Grace Huber thirty-six times.

Witnesses changed their statements, sometimes more than once. Coworkers who swore they had seen Huber at the yard during the hours in question later recanted their testimony. Then one of them recanted his recant. A few said Huber was nowhere to be found in the critical interval. Some noted that Huber was seen later in the evening in different clothing and shoes from those he'd worn earlier in the shift.

Matthew J. Huber, Jr., was arrested four times for the murder of his sister over a period of years, from 1949 to 1954. And only some of those arrests were made by officers of the law. Some were made by others—citizen's arrests—from a cast of characters colorful enough to lend an air of the surreal to the otherwise somber proceedings.

4

THE WIFE

Chapter Two
June 2019

Linda's time in the skies became a strange, disembodied refuge. Sealed in recirculating air, she found herself free of the rat wheel of anxiety that scratched at the inside of her belly—a sensation she had grown so accustomed to that she did not at first notice its absence.

She had not been sleeping at night. The almost-ignorable internal buzz that vibrated in daylight hours picked up its pitch in the dark. If she managed to fall asleep in front of the television, her body would jolt her awake, like an elevator suddenly lurching.

This phenomenon began—not the anxiety, but the cessation of it—on the first of her many flights to Pittsburgh. It was right at the moment when her life with Miguel was becoming strained. Right about the time when their ease with each other had shifted and he—maybe she, too—had begun exhibiting signs of a change. Right about the time when Miguel started going to bed wearing ear buds, playing techno.

Like that movie from ages ago, *The Astronaut's Wife*, in which Charlize Theron played a nice and pretty wife to Johnny Depp's nice and handsome husband. Until Johnny Depp was sent on a mission to outer space and was taken over by an alien who entered his body. Linda couldn't remember how. Somehow, Johnny Depp became host to this alien being and then returned to his wife. Except *he* didn't. It was the alien in Johnny Depp's body. And that was who was lying beside Linda, nodding his head to the thump of techno—an alien in Miguel's body.

Unlike most of the population their age, Linda's parents had refused to move to Florida. Her mother didn't like the heat and her father never said much about it. Linda and Miguel, unlike most of the population *their* age, had ended up there, instead, in the wave of financial services migrations away from New York City.

Increasingly diminished by dementia, Linda's father was no help with her mother's illness. It fell to Linda to manage her mother's care and confer with her oncologists. Linda hadn't told her mother about the difficulties in her marriage and she did not intend to. Telling her father would have been cruel. To him, to her, or both.

It took a minute to realize it when the thing happened. She had already boarded the plane, stowed her carry-on, dropped into her seat, and placed a book on her lap. A symbolic gesture, that last one. She had not been able to read, to concentrate on anything, since whatever was happening had begun. She heard the door close, heard the flight attendant explain the seatbelt, and found herself wondering what she always wondered at this point: Was there anyone on an airplane who did not know how to fasten a seatbelt?

And it was then she noticed it was gone. The nervousness. The agitation that lived in her core. Gone. Just like that, she was able to read. To eat. To nap. She was able to do the normal things people do on airplanes, things she had not done in her own life for months.

It all returned as soon as the plane door opened. Linda battled insomnia every night she stayed in Pittsburgh. Then the same thing happened on the return. As soon as the airplane door closed and sealed her into its vacuum, Linda fell into a dreamless sleep. When the door opened on landing, she tilted off balance again.

Miguel traveled frequently on business and their miles had accumulated into the millions. Linda thought of these miles as Miguel's little prize for her. He had given her pain and, at the same time, offered its balm. Like the Mayan legend that claims that, in the wild, every poison is accompanied by its own antidote within the radius of human vision.

She never stayed long in Pittsburgh. A night or two in a little hotel, now that the family house had been sold. Her dad was in assisted living. Her mother was in the hospital. And those nights were as unsettled as those at home. But once on the plane again, that feeling of buoyancy returned. For a while, Linda was free. Like an astronaut floating in space, her cord to her troubles disconnected.

Linda was not the astronaut's wife, but the astronaut herself.

5

A WRITER'S THOUGHTS

One of the things you discover in researching the slaying of a girl is just how common the slaying of girls happens to be. There is even a name for it. Femicide. People kill females often, especially females they know. It is a phenomenon tragically on the rise during the current quarantine, as females are confined alongside their abusers.

In the years following the killing of Noelle Huber, facts and conjecture were freely mixed and parsed at will in the newspapers. Noelle's death riveted the attention of Pittsburgh and, as an unsolved crime, held onto that attention for years. As late as 1970—twenty-two years after the murder—there was a look-back story in one of the local papers, a roundup of all the unsolved murders the city had seen, Noelle's chief among them. Pittsburgh was called to account for its poor policing and dearth of convictions in multiple murders over a span of decades.

In Noelle's case, there seemed to be no lack of trying, at least on behalf of a group of individuals that sometimes included the cops—but just as often did not. Presiding judges and superintendents of police bemoaned the bungling of the investigation and referred to people we would now call *citizen detectives* as Keystone Kops and amateur Dick Tracys. Randolf "The Rabbit" Anderson and Max "The Wasp" Caverly stood out for their colorful monikers. A "sweater girl"—who turned out to be a pistol-packing reporter—got into the act, as well.

December 10, 1948. People now might characterize that time as an innocent era, which I would counter is patently ridiculous. The Germans had recently incarcerated people by the millions, gassing them and starving them to death. The Japanese had cut a bloody swath through the Pacific Rim while hauling along *comfort women* as convenient, mobile sex slaves. And we haven't even begun to discuss our own homegrown sins, like lynching.

There is no such thing as an innocent era.

But by 1948 the war had been over for three years. Ration booklets had been thrown out or put away. My family stowed theirs in a painted tin where it rested in a pile of photos and strips of negatives, forgotten until dug up by me in my recent spate of research.

My mother was twelve years old at the time of her friend's murder, and my grandmother forty-six. Unusually for that era, my grandmother had had her children late. Equally unusual, she'd had a career. She worked in the bookkeeping department of Gimbels Department Store. She was even given a watch at her retirement, but I don't think it was gold.

The Ritenour—my family—household was small. My grandmother, Betty, my grandfather, Emerson, and their two children, David and Elizabeth. There was a six-year gap between the children, which had once been filled by a brother. He, little Peter, had died of pneumonia at age two after playing outdoors in winter, leaving the age disparity between my mother and David.

My mother had been a spunky child. She often recounted a day when she was still quite small and playing on the front stoop of the house. Unseen by her, some men passed by, chatting, not knowing a child was listening. That night at dinner, when her brother asked for the potatoes, my grandmother refreshed him on manners. "Pass the potatoes, what?" she asked and he, of course, added, "Please. Pass the potatoes, please." When it came to little Lizzie—who was not yet in kindergarten—she tried out what she'd heard from the stoop. In full voice, she asked my grandmother to "pass the potatoes, you summava bitch." This elicited gales of laughter from my grandparents and was all the encouragement Liz needed. As an adult, she was proud of that spark she'd lost. She did not fully realize she'd lost it.

The Homewood-Brushton area of Pittsburgh where they all lived had once been home to industrialists like Andrew Carnegie. By the 1930s, it was composed mostly of attached row houses and small stores that served its residents. One of the early "streetcar suburbs," it had been developed in the late 19th century to allow the working classes to escape the smoke and pollution of the factories and still commute to the jobs they provided.

My grandmother's department store offices were downtown and, as a girl, my mother often went by streetcar alone to meet her mother for shopping or a meal. Liz and Noelle took the streetcar, too, traveling around the city with a sense of freedom.

Noelle had invited Liz that December evening—the night that would become her last—to come over and do whatever twelve-year-old girls did then. Perhaps play records. Liz, at first, said yes. But she changed her mind. I don't know if she asked my grandmother's permission. I don't know if my grandmother would have allowed it. Noelle's parents were going out so my grandmother might not have been comfortable.

It happened in a way that would forever torment my mother. She said yes. She said no. Her friend died. It was too much responsibility for a child to bear.

Jane Stores was invited and declined, as well. Jane and her mother were the last known people to talk to Noelle Huber. Jane took a call from Noelle at nine p.m., and Mrs. Stores picked up when Noelle called again at nine-thirty. She was sure of the timing because she had just sent Jane out to pick up milk and had checked the clock to confirm the shop was still open.

Mrs. Stores's certainty of the hour of the call allowed the police to narrow the murder window further to sometime after nine thirty and before the parents' return at eleven thirty.

6

THE WIFE

Chapter Three
Saturday, April 18, 2020

No one her age was called Linda. It was a common enough name in her mother's generation, but—being born in 1980—she was the only Linda of her own. It was an odd choice. There were no Lindas in her family for whom she was named. Her parents did not speak Spanish; they spoke nothing but English. They had simply liked the name. She is not even sure they knew what it meant. Linda for lovely, Miguel used to say. *Que linda*, he would sing to her, *linda*, touching her face, *linda*, touching her hair, *linda*, cupping her breasts.

It is not hard to understand why she fell in love with him. He was beautiful to behold and her opposite in every way. They were like magnets when the correct sides were pointed to each other—inexorably, unbreakably drawn. They were also like magnets when the wrong sides were facing, impossible to bring together. She just never knew which side was which. And—truth be told—for a long time that excited her.

Miguel and Linda gave their children Spanish names, in honor of his Argentine heritage. She had delivered first a son and they had named him Diego, after Miguel's father, and his father's father before him. Miguel, as the younger son of the family, had not inherited that moniker. His older brother—the Diego standard-bearer of their generation—had died young and never produced an heir, so the name was up for grabs.

He had left their home in Buenos Aires, that brother, in September of 1998—the Southern Hemisphere spring—at the age of twenty-two, on the back of a motorcycle. In the mode of Che Guevara, he and his friend Nico took off to see their continent.

For nearly a year, the family received postcards from Lima, Santiago, Rio. Then Diego and Nico disappeared in the mountains of Bolivia, never to be seen again. Diego's final postcard took ten weeks to arrive from La Paz. Their parents were left broken, each in a different way. Miguel was left feeling betrayed by his brother's flamboyant exit.

That last postcard and its cryptic message—*los quiero, los extraño, volverè pronto*—threw Señor Alonso into a shock of denial from which he never recovered. He carried the card like a cipher whose code—if only he could crack it—meant his favorite son was not dead and would return to him one day. *Love you, miss you, back soon.* The meaning, to him, was evident; the specifics were less clear.

Esperanza, despite the meaning of her name, did not hold out such hopes. She had always struggled with the older boy; Miguel had been her favorite. In the end, she lived years beyond her husband, who died with the postcard in his pocket. Even now, Esperanza lingered, though a festering cancer had eaten increasingly larger chunks of her as time marched on without either of her Diegos, her husband or her firstborn son.

Twenty-two years had elapsed. No bodies had ever been found.

The next child Miguel and Linda had was a girl, exactly two years after their first. She was christened Esperanza, after Miguel's mother, and she was Linda's ray of hope. Espie, they called her, and little Diego quickly became Gogo, from the way Espie said his name.

It could be argued that Linda should have seen a sign in those names—Diego and Esperanza—contained in their very foreignness. As though they hadn't belonged to her and were only passing through. Like butterflies who made their way from continent to continent, from north to south across vast distances, despite their size and frailty. Or in the Alonso family proclivity for disappearance as demonstrated by Miguel's brother, Diego. Linda could have—should have—read more into it. She could have taken a page out of the father's book in his study of the post-card and read the tea leaves a bit more carefully in her own life.

But she had not been careful at all. She had not kept hold of her family.

7

A WRITER'S THOUGHTS

The world has grown silent. More than half of the humans on earth—over four billion souls—have halted their perpetual motion. Those who haven't stopped have slowed. Most of us are at home, whatever home means, a palace or a shack or something in between. We think, dream, pace, breathe, eat, sleep within the confines of our own walls. Or lack of walls, for the less fortunate. It is monastic and inward looking. It is the moment we meet ourselves.

I wander the rooms of my apartment—all three and a half of them—in an effort to avoid that meeting. I open the pantry and stare at the shelves, rip open a package of cookies, and eat them standing up. LU, they are called. French cookies. I buy them—though they are out of my budget (*A little rich for my blood*, my mother would have said)—in the hopes they will make me more abstemious. Less compulsive. More inclined to sit at the table and eat only two. It does not work. I polish off the box and microwave some popcorn. The cycle makes me worry I will run out of food—but not enough to slow me down in eating it.

In developed countries, market aisles have been picked clean of toilet paper, rubbing alcohol, canned goods. The stock market has fallen, risen, fallen again. Businesses en masse are shuttered. In one fell swoop, the world is out of work. The economy has not shut down in this way since the 1930s. People are dying sad, lonely, gasping-for-air deaths in overcrowded hospitals where exhausted medical professionals are forced to decide who gets the ventilator and who gets to die.

On the other hand, the air is growing cleaner than it has been in decades and wild animals are entering vast exurban tracts, exploring areas they have not roamed in a century. This is the yin and the yang of it.

Noelle and Liz were born in 1936, amidst the long and crushing march of the Great Depression. Their families lived in humble houses, but they were lucky enough to have roofs over their heads and the ability to pay for them. My grandmother's bookkeeping job at Gimbels was one of the better jobs of their neighborhood. My grandfather was a milkman and Noelle's father a chauffeur. None of these jobs were fancy, but they were respectable in a time of breadlines. Children like Noelle and Liz survived—even thrived—in a difficult era.

Then the world shifted, as the world will do, and rolled into war.

After years of hardship, citizens across the globe were vulnerable to populist leaders who painted their problems in stark tones of black and white, and offered them someone to blame. Scapegoating, brinksmanship, and the drawing of lines in the sand pushed the world over the precipice into violence. The Depression ended with the advent of something worse.

Noelle and Liz grew up in all this, albeit in America, where the war was at a remove. Yes, there were blackouts and ration books, but the girls were largely unaffected. Pittsburgh was not bombed. They may have turned up their noses to see their mothers mixing dye into greasy, white oleomargarine to spread on their bread instead of butter, but the children led lives of children. My mother remembered being happy.

It was peacetime that Noelle did not survive.

I am reminded of the story of the man who walks away from a plane crash in a forest only to be killed by a falling tree. On the night of December tenth, the tree came looking for Noelle.

My mother did not understand the questions that the investigating detectives asked her. Was Noelle friendly with boys? What was her relationship with her brother? What did she remember about that brother? Did men—or a man—ever approach the two of them? Was there ever anything funny? Anywhere? Anyone? Who?

One of the places the girls passed every day on their way home from school was the old Brushton Primary School. The original school had moved to another location, and, after the war, the building had been repurposed as a refrigerator repair training center for GIs. Liz and Noelle often ran errands for the men—who stood outside and called to them— fetching cigarettes and chewing gum from the local store. The detectives found this noteworthy.

The morning after Noelle's death—before they had heard the news— my grandmother sent my mother to buy bread. When Liz arrived at the bakery, people were talking in hushed huddles. At first, she did not understand. Then, she picked out Noelle's name and began to assemble the facts. "She's my best friend," she blurted to no one in particular, using the present tense, a past tense version of her friend not yet comprehensible. A reporter was in the room and seized his opportunity. He offered her a ride home, which she accepted. He interviewed her along the way and quoted her in the paper.

My grandmother was appalled and kept Liz away from any other reporters. But she could not keep her away from the questioning police.

Jane Stores's mother had no such compunctions. In one of several interviews she gave, Jane was very chatty. Noelle, Jane said, was "big for her age." She added that Noelle's father, Mr. Huber, did not like "boys whistling at her." We know, even if the twelve-year-old version of my mother did not, what the reporters were trying to drag out of Jane. That Noelle was physically mature. That boys noticed Noelle, and that notice had gotten her killed.

My mother has told me the story of a streetcar ride just weeks before Noelle's death. The girls were seated behind a woman and man deep in conversation. Noelle grew distant, ignoring Liz, and turned her attention to the couple. Liz eventually stopped talking when it was clear her friend was not listening. Then Noelle did something that electrified Liz with fear. Fixing her eyes on the woman, Noelle yanked out a strand of her own long blond hair and placed it on the man's shoulder. She then spoke loudly to Liz, saying the man had a hair on his jacket that was not the color of his companion's. The couple left in a huff at the next stop.

My mother always paused at this point in the story and stared off in the distance, seeing—I imagine—the scene play out before her. She would collect herself, shake her head a few times, and laugh. Kid stuff, she would say. Innocent, like the era in which she thought they lived.

At this point I have eaten all the popcorn on top of the earlier cookies. I slip into the bathroom to get rid of it all, knowing I am too old for this, unable to do anything about it.

8

THE WIFE

Chapter Four
Saturday, June 8, 2002

Linda had met Miguel in New York nine months after the attacks of September 11th. She had just graduated from Lafayette College—her first big move out of Pittsburgh—and then she had moved to New York. She had felt proud of her eastward migration from sleepy Pittsburgh to collegiate Easton—which, to her, was practically Philadelphia—and then on to New York City. Eventually, she might even live in Europe. Why not? Then 9/11 came along.

Nothing like the coordinated attacks of that day had ever happened before. Attacks on ordinary people doing ordinary things on a Tuesday, of all days. What could be more ordinary than that? Because of it, they were quickly at war in Afghanistan, threatening the same with Iraq, and Americans were sealing their windows with duct tape against nuclear attack, or anthrax, or who knew what might fall from the sky? In Linda's humble opinion, duct tape did not seem to be an effective barrier to radioactive or poisonous substances.

The way everything was going, it looked like they were headed into World War III. Which she kind of felt in her bones would be worse than World War II because of the types of weapons available. Not least of which was the human body. As far as she knew, apart from the kamikaze flights of the Japanese, people back then did not strap explosives around their torsos and walk into crowded markets to kill and maim everyone in sight. Yet she wanted to stay in New York, no matter how unstable it was.

Linda's mother did not share Linda's vision. Her mother wanted her to come home to Oakmont, Pennsylvania, and get a job as an accountant or something else that was practical and would guarantee a good life for Linda. Linda did not define life in the same terms and did not care for any such guarantee.

As far as school went, she had done okay, but she hadn't had any real sense of direction. At Lafayette, Linda had majored in American civ as a default when her course load didn't add up to anything else that could be clearly defined. All she'd had to do her senior year was pile on a couple extra classes to graduate with that degree. For, while she had a strong vision of herself living in glamorous and far-flung places, she did not have an equally strong vision of how exactly to get there.

One of Linda's roommates—Maddie Cox—hailed from New York. The actual city. Maddie had grown up in an apartment building and ridden the subway to school. Linda pretended this was no big deal, but really, she found it very exotic. She had grown up in a hilly suburb with strip malls and fast-food places and car washes. She tried to stretch her mental familiarity to the concept of corner stores and cafés and urban parks as the only place a person could actually see a flower. And she liked that concept very much.

Maddie Cox had invited Linda to come home with her one spring break and Linda had jumped at the chance. New York City turned out to be a saturated version of itself—exactly what Linda had pictured but more so. Louder. Brighter. Dirtier. Sexier. It was like itself on steroids and she loved it. She resolved to live there after college by any means possible.

Luckily, those means were at hand. Maddie came to the rescue again with a circuitous introduction to a job. Maddie's mother, Bits—that was actually the name she went by—was a designer, meaning she decorated people's houses for large sums of money. Again, Linda pretended to be familiar with the concept of professional decorators. Though, the truth was, the closest she'd come to a decorator was the saleswoman at Calico Corners.

Bits Cox was a close friend of one of the managers at Osborne & Little and, through the wonders of connections, a job was secured. And it was there, at that showroom in the Decoration & Design Building on Third Avenue in New York City, that Linda finally found something that excited her. She loved every variety of fabric, be it damask or chintz or silk moiré. She learned the names of patterns, the application of cording, and fell in love with the word *passementerie*. Why say plain old trim when you could use a word like that?

Nothing she had done was as much fun as going into that beautiful showroom every day, helping decorators find just the right fabrics for their clients to create just the right rooms in just the right apartments. All of it was—to use a word that Bits used a great deal—*aspirational* for Linda. She aspired to have a beautiful apartment. She aspired to have beautiful curtains and sofas and rugs. And *passementerie*. She aspired to be married to the kind of man who could help her have such a life when, to be perfectly clear, her family in Pittsburgh and her job in fabric sales would not provide anything of the sort.

It was in this mixed bag of a mood—fulfilled in her job yet longing for a life that job revealed was possible, fearful of war when toxic particles still floated in the air from the downing of the World Trade Center, excited to exist alone in New York but lonely—that Linda met Miguel.

Miguel had been in New York for two years. He'd come directly from Georgetown—no stops home in Argentina—to work in the investment banking training program in the Latin America division at Citibank. Like Linda, this was a job secured through a wealth of connections. Unlike Linda, Miguel's career had the potential to take him very high. And a wife, she reasoned, along with him.

On that beautiful Saturday in June, Linda wandered down Third Avenue at six o'clock in the evening, when it was still bright but the sun hung low enough in the western sky to only sporadically peek between buildings. Her arms were evenly balanced with two bags from Schaller and Weber—where she could find the German delicacies her mother cooked—and she was enjoying the walk, the heat, the feel of the swinging bags as they rhythmically tapped her thighs. She decided to stop in J.G. Melon's for a bite and, inside, in the dark, at her little table alone, hamburger in her hand, she looked up into the face of the most beautiful man she had ever seen.

9

A WRITER'S THOUGHTS

The coroner's report on the death of Noelle Grace Huber arrived today, ordered through an online link from the Pittsburgh Police Department via the University of Pittsburgh archives. My alma mater. The collection of documents arrived by email, with a polite salutation thanking me for my interest in the Allegheny County Coroner Case Files. Crisp but warm. Professional. They neither know nor care why I am interested. Noelle Huber's death—to them—is ancient history. A historical footnote, if that.

The pandemic rages outside my door—outside all our doors—but inside I keep company with a different death. In the report, it was noted that Noelle was twelve years, three months, and ten days old at the time of her death, she was white, her "social relationship" status was single, and her "occupation" was that of student. The time of the "accident" was reported to have been 11:30 p.m. on December 10 and Noelle was pronounced dead on arrival at 12:28 a.m. on December 11. The cause of death was listed as shock and hemorrhage following stab wounds of head, chest, and upper extremities.

One wound in the left thigh, one wound in the left chest wall, seven wounds in the right chest wall, ten wounds in the right arm and hand, one wound in the right shoulder, five wounds in the left arm and hand, six wounds in the back, five wounds in the neck and head.

I stare at the numbers and make a tally. Thirty-six stab wounds, just like the newspapers said. My mother had said thirty-seven. My entire life, the story of Noelle's murder was framed with thirty-seven cuts to her body, yet consensus agrees it was thirty-six. This discrepancy bothers me. It's like pronouncing a word in your head when you're young that you've only seen written on the page and the mortified feeling you get when you finally hear it spoken and realize you need to relearn it. Debacle. Chimera. *Fleur-de-lys*.

But it is the head business that gets me most. In all the movies I've watched, all the murder mysteries I've read, I have not seen a person stab another person in the head. It is not how it is staged, dramatically. The chest, the stomach, the back, yes. A pistol to the forehead, yes. Back of the head, if it is an execution. But stabbing in the head is a jolt to the system. Mine, I mean. It is not that I cannot envision it; I can picture it all too clearly.

I keep trying to figure out the mechanics of it. A nurse I interviewed for one of the thrillers I wrote explained that you can only penetrate the skull through a narrow selection of entry points. One is the temple, another the eye. The coroner's report does not specify which area of Noelle's head was punctured.

Another puzzle niggles me. How do you extract a knife once you've penetrated a skull? If you stick a knife into a watermelon—not nearly as hard as a human head—you have to hold onto the melon with one hand to pull out the knife with the other. How did the killer manage this feat? How was it that the knife didn't get stuck in Noelle's cranium? I picture her braids again. And then I remember the newspapers said she had washed her hair and was wearing curlers at the moment of her murder.

The optimism of such actions makes me gag.

A small knife already noted—a little paring knife—was found next to the sink, wiped clean of fingerprints. This knife was presumed to have been too small to have done the damage it did. A different knife turned up on Christmas Eve. Two weeks after Noelle's death—according to the newspapers—a large knife was found on a neighbor's roof by the police.

The original cops were adamant that there had been no knife there after the accident. They maintained that they had searched all rooftops near the Hubers' home directly after the murder and confirmed that no knife had been found anywhere at the time of that search. The new knife was much larger—a blade five inches long—and appeared as if from nowhere.

Complicating matters, this roof was inaccessible from the street. The knife would have to have been thrown from street level to the roof-top or left there by someone who had access to interior stairs. Like the smaller knife, no fingerprints were found on this one. No strangers were seen in the neighborhood throwing items up in the air. And this knife was not rusty, affirming it had not been exposed to the elements for long. Mr. Huber, when shown this new knife, said it did not come from his house.

This second knife was not mentioned in the coroner's report. That document concerned itself with the circumstances of the evening, the condition of Noelle's body, and statements taken from family and neighbors. The report was made up of various forms filled out by the coroner, different witness testimonies, and a formal, typed letter submitted by the inspector of detectives. In this particular document, Inspector John F. Rich detailed his interview with the parents at the hospital after Noelle had been brought in:

Matthew J. Huber, Sr., and his wife, Marie Huber, stated that they left Noelle Grace at home about 8:30 p.m. When they returned at about 11:30 p.m., they discovered her body on the dining room floor at the telephone stand with the telephone receiver off the hook. They summoned a neighbor, Walter Whaley of Elcourt Street (533), who removed the girl's body to the hospital in his car. They further said that Noelle had been warned repeatedly not to admit anyone to the house while they were absent. They also stated that they were positive that all the doors and windows were locked when they left home tonight. However, the rear kitchen door was unlocked when they returned home and discovered the body.

At 528 Brushton Avenue, we observed bloodstains on the kitchen floor and walls and also trailing into the dining room to the telephone stand, where there was a pool of blood mixed with vomit. We also saw materials on the kitchen table where the victim was mixing a cake.

Here there is a line typed over with multiple ZZZZZZs—like a cartoon balloon of snoring, as though Inspector Rich were bored—to block out what was written. Then Inspector Rich continued:

A small, wooden-handled paring knife was on the drainboard of the kitchen sink. This knife, along with specimens of blood and vomit, were brought to the homicide office.

We interrogated various neighbors in the vicinity and were unable to find anyone who had heard any unusual noises or had seen any suspicious persons loitering in the neighborhood at the time of this crime.

In company with Lt. Mark R. Moran, we left the home and went to the morgue where specimens of fingernail parings and hair were taken from the dead girl's hands. We also removed a lock of hair from the victim's head for purposes of comparison.

The victim was wearing blue slacks, a red T-shirt, pink panties, and a pink plastic apron at the time of her death.

Respectfully submitted.

And signed.

My mind has fixed on the vomit which, of course, should not surprise me. Naturally she vomited. I vomit all the time without any such provocation.

On December 16—six days after Noelle's murder—the *Pittsburgh Post* ran a bizarre story discussing an old murder from 1909. In that crime, one James Friel, a fourteen-year-old boy, was found with his throat cut, his body bitten, having been sexually assaulted and left in a "haunted house." Police and psychiatrists reviewed this case in 1949 to find clues into the mind of Noelle's killer. A prominent Pittsburgh psychiatrist carefully noted that whoever had murdered Noelle would fall into one of three personality types:

1. The constitutional psychopath
2. The schizophrenic
3. The moron

The coroner ignored these theories.

On Thursday, January 27, 1949, at ten o'clock in the morning, an inquest was held. The mother, the father, the brother, and a small group of individuals were called before the coroner to testify about their recollections of Noelle's last night.

10

THE WIFE

Chapter Five
Monday, March 9, 2020

Reef Road was Pete the mailman's last stop. He followed a daily route that did not bring him to the Alonsos' house before four-thirty or five and he never switched it up.

Linda and the children were already settled in by that hour—Linda cooking dinner, the children playing in the little family room connected to the kitchen. Their house was configured with the kitchen in back, behind the garage, a door between them. Since all the kitchen windows faced the backyard, if someone was watching for the mailman, that person would have to walk into the living room to peer out the big picture window or go into the garage and open the automatic door. Neither of these options was terribly convenient when Linda was preparing dinner and keeping an eye on the children.

Miguel liked to be in charge of the mail. He had accused Linda more than once—not without reason—of mislaying bills when she collected them and leaving them stuffed in odd places. Her car. The bathroom. Her purse. Linda and Miguel engaged in a passive-aggressive competition.

Sometimes, she let him grab the mail when he returned from work. But normally, she got there first.

At the top of the island, where they lived, the land mass narrowed, leaving a short distance, west to east, from lake to ocean. It made this end of the island small and intimate. Separate. Pre-pandemic, there was often a laid-back block-party feeling on Reef Road. Children, dogs, Jeeps, and surfboards filled the street. The neighbors all had deeded rights to a beach cabana on the ocean and most of them also belonged to the yacht club on the lake. People who confined themselves to the southernmost sections of Palm Beach had no idea this neighborhood even existed.

The Alonsos lived in one of those 1960s ranches that had cropped up when the old estates were parceled to pay taxes in the years after the war. They had been lucky to find it. The house was small but sat on a lot ample enough for a pool, a barbecue, a pretty iron table with an umbrella, and a swing set for the children.

Linda always fantasized about dinner *al fresco*, but it was often too buggy to sit through an entire meal in the jungle of their backyard. In the winter months, there was enough of a chill in the evening to ward off mosquitos and allow them to dine outdoors. Otherwise, they waited for those random days when the ocean-to-lake breeze was strong enough to penetrate the vegetation of their gardens and clear the air of mosquitos.

Their house had been fully renovated by a New Yorker who had money to play with before losing everything to margin calls in 2009. His house ended up in the hands of the bank and, after several years, in the hands of the Alonsos.

It was pretty and pale—just the way Linda liked it—in whites and aquas and seafoam greens. The floors were tumbled white marble with a rough and understated surface. The kitchen cabinets were high-gloss white with glass doors to show off her dishes. There were skylights with treated glass, so the house was bright but never hot.

Miguel was involved in every detail of decorating. Linda would have preferred it if the domestic side of their life were her domain. Alone. She would have liked to be able to spontaneously buy a chair or a throw pillow when she was antiquing on Dixie Highway or wandering around the new Restoration Hardware in West Palm Beach. But Miguel had a finger in every pie.

"It's our home, Linda," he would say. "Why would you want to choose something without my input?"

Which was a bit overly dramatic as far as Linda was concerned. It wasn't as though Miguel ever even disagreed with her, so he could have stepped back and had some faith in her taste. She'd worked as a decorator for years after she'd left Osborne & Little. Before the kids came. Miguel could have granted her some dominion in this area of their lives. But he did not. Linda increasingly chafed under the yoke of his control.

Today, Linda had taken the children to the pediatrician after school. With driving and waiting and two full sets of well checks, it was after five by the time she got home. Clicking open the garage, she pulled in and helped the children out of their seatbelts. Diego was in a booster seat by then while little Espie was still in a car seat. Linda decided to stretch everyone's legs and walked the two of them down the short driveway to the mailbox. Surely Pete had been there by now.

"Mama, let's do alley-oop with Espie," Diego said.

"Ayeoop!" Espie squealed. She loved it when her parents each took one of her hands and lifted her up, swinging, with the cry of *Alley-oop*!

"Gogo, you're not really big enough to do it with just Mama." Linda tried to say it gently, knowing Diego considered himself quite big. "When Daddy gets home, we can all do it. With you, too, if you like."

This was a complicated lure for Diego. He loved to be swung through the air by his parents just as much as Espie did, but he liked to present himself as too grown-up for such babyish pleasures. Which of his longings took precedence depended on the day.

"Okay, now, Gogo, please hold Espie's hand for a minute while Mommy opens the mailbox."

Diego took his charge very seriously and held onto both of his sister's hands with enough force to make her squirm.

"Oooww! Gogo stop it!"

"Gently, Diego," Linda said.

"Well, I just don't want her to run in the street 'cause she's a baby."

"Not a baby!" Espie wailed.

"All right, you two," Linda intervened as she stuffed a wad of envelopes and catalogues into her oversized bag. "Espie, give me your hand. C'mon, let's go inside. Mommy needs to make dinner."

They entered through the garage and Linda pressed the button to close the door behind them. Once in the house, she forgot about the mail in her hurry to start cooking.

Chicken Milanese was everyone's favorite. The children had a mixed bag of palates. Gogo ate like an adult and proudly challenged himself to try everything that was put before him. Linda could serve him his chicken with arugula salad on top, just like it was meant to be eaten. Espie, on the other hand, was much more tentative about food. She did not care for new tastes, didn't like many vegetables, and Linda struggled with whether or not to prepare "nursery food" for her that was different from what the rest of the family was eating.

Miguel did not approve of nursery food because his mother had not served it. He maintained that he and his brother ate whatever the parents ate. Linda found out this was not entirely true from Mimi, the Alonso's all-around retainer. She had coddled the boys with toast soldiers and tapioca for years, and Miguel had been a horribly picky eater until the day he left for college.

It was not worth challenging his memory of facts, however, so Linda just navigated the difficult dance of figuring out on a nightly basis what she could make to satisfy everyone. Something Espie would put in her mouth and Miguel would find more appropriate than chicken fingers and mac and cheese.

"No mail tonight?"

She jumped at the suddenness of Miguel's voice right behind her. His kiss grazed the nape of her neck and he paused just a second to bite her. Not hard. It was a gesture that once would have filled her with desire. Now it only served to disgust her. Then he moved off to greet the children.

Linda thought about pulling the envelopes and catalogs out of her purse, currently discarded on one of the stools under the counter. She thought about handing him everything, allowing him to separate it all into regimented piles, the way he did.

"No mail today," she said, surreptitiously wiping the back of her neck before she resumed chopping tomatoes.

11

THE WIFE

Chapter Six
Monday, March 9, 2020

Miguel drank too much that night. Not at dinner. He never drank at the table. He prided himself on his self-control in front of the children. And "control" was the operating word. Their nightly ritual—from dinner to bath to books to bedtime—was as choreographed as a Broadway play.

That night, like all others, Miguel settled into the large upholstered chair in the children's room, Espie on his lap, Diego tucked beside him. Espie wore footed pajamas in white with yellow daffodils, reminding Linda of springtime at home. Diego wore stretchy, blue, two-piece pajamas with red double-decker buses all over them—a souvenir from London.

Espie had her right thumb firmly stuck in her mouth, index finger curled over her nose, favorite stuffed monkey clutched in her left hand. She stared at the pages of the book in a sleepy trance. Gogo anticipated turning the pages because he was a *big boy* and could read (sort of).

Miguel theatrically read *We're Going on a Bear Hunt* exactly three times. His dramatic interpretation included bear roars and renditions of squelching mud and swishing grass. Everything about his reading was always the same except the timing of his delivery. In what he claimed was an effort to strengthen Gogo's abilities to read and to pay attention, Miguel sped up and slowed down to keep Gogo on his toes. If Gogo missed a beat and turned a page too slowly, Miguel abruptly stopped and let out a small sigh in a show of indulgent exasperation. Linda was mortified when she saw her son's cheeks turn red and his brow furrow in redoubled concentration, willing himself to master the next turn of the page.

After the third reading—never two, never four—Miguel placed the book on the table next to him and stretched in a pantomime yawn.

"No, Daddy!" Espie cried, as she did every time. "One more! Pwease!"

"Espie," Gogo seized the opportunity—also like every time—to lord his superiority over someone, "Daddy can't read to us all night. He has things to do."

Things to do. It disturbed Linda to see her baby boy seamlessly parrot her husband's condescension. This was when Linda swooped in and scooped up Espie to put her in her bed with a tickle and a kiss. Miguel did the same with Gogo. Then they switched places.

True to form tonight, Miguel kissed the children on the tops of their heads. Cheek kissing he reserved for adults on both cheeks; his children he kissed atop their freshly shampooed heads. Next, he turned on the little chick nightlight, ostensibly for the benefit of Espie. Gogo insisted he was too big for nightlights but was always extra careful to remind his parents to put it on for Espie's sake.

Pausing at the door, Linda said her usual, "Sleep tight. Don't let the bedbugs bite," to which Gogo responded, "Gross!" and Espie giggled. And, just like always, Miguel said, "*Buenas noches. Que sueñes con los angelitos.*"

Then Miguel and Linda left the children's bedroom.

Linda headed for the kitchen, and Miguel went to their bedroom to change into his favorite black Armani sweatpants and an ironed, white T-shirt. She had tried to tell him multiple times that his style choices were a little too Euro-centric for Palm Beach, more suitable to Miami.

Maus & Hoffman was the store she had tried to direct him to, but the colorful aesthetic favored by the locals was lost on him.

Miguel entered the kitchen and stopped to watch Linda clean up. It made her self-conscious to have someone—anyone, really, but especially Miguel—oversee her work habits. With a sigh—meant to be heard by Linda but in a way that Linda was supposed to think she was not meant to hear it—Miguel walked over to the liquor cabinet. As though the desultory way in which she wiped the counter could bring a sober man to drink.

Miguel made a show of selecting what he would have. Linda knew he would pick vodka. He always picked vodka. He selected the bottle of Tito's, poured a rocks glass two-thirds full, and added ice from the bucket Linda had refilled earlier. He crossed the room toward Linda while he swirled the glass, making little clinks. He took a sip and winced with pleasure. Then he took a longer drink.

"*Querida*," he said. "Are you using the organic cleanser? I noticed that Manuela keeps buying Fabulosa. Have you spoken to her?"

"Yes," she answered. "And yes. Yes, this is Meyer's. And, yes, I told her to stop buying Fabulosa."

"Just asking, Linda. You don't need to get so snappish when I ask a question. I care about our health."

"Well," she said, placing the cleanser under the sink and walking over to toss her cleaning rag into the laundry basket, "I don't mind you asking, but you asked the same thing yesterday."

12

A WRITER'S THOUGHTS

I tried to go to the post office today. Five autographed copies of my latest book were due to readers who had entered and won a *bookstagram* contest. Writing is writing, but it is also all this other stuff, like *bookstagram*, that it never used to be. A writer can't just write books anymore, not if she wants to sell any. In the middle of this pandemic, the selling of books has become an even more cumbersome task.

Making use of plastic bags, I packed my latex gloves, mask, hand sanitizer, a pen—heaven forbid I use the germy post office implement to write my labels—and set off. The coronavirus drill is familiar by now: Drive where you're going without your gloves and mask, don them to exit the car, and wear them in whatever public facility you need to enter, which has been reduced to grocery, pharmacy, and post office. You can't enter a bank anymore, or a restaurant, or a store, or a gym. On exiting, reverse the process to strip off the gloves in a way that turns them inside out and immediately toss them into a trash can, preferably one you don't have to touch. Then carefully disinfect your hands with hand sanitizer. Finally, remove your mask.

The post office door was open, but the place was deserted. I called out a few times, "Hello?" but no human appeared to weigh and ship my packages. It had a *Twilight Zone* feeling of abrupt abandonment. I took my parcels back out the door, followed the prescribed steps to disinfect myself, and got back into my old Ford Focus.

At home, I am faced with time and the devils that dwell there. In the past, there is my mother, Noelle, her murder. In the present, there is my dog, my writing. The future does not bear considering.

I grab a bowl of cherries—it's still early in the day and I'm still eating fruit—and scan the news before settling in to write. Today, a massive Navy ship has arrived in New York to serve as a floating viral hospital. A field hospital has gone up in Central Park to do the same. I watch the ship—*Comfort* is its name—as it motors into New York Harbor past the Statue of Liberty. A sense of siege overwhelms me.

I turn my attention to Noelle.

At the time of her murder, Matt still lived at home. He was supposed to have been at work at the Union Railroad Yard that Friday evening. The testimonies from his coworkers conflicted. One fellow, Marvin D. Tanner, was used as Huber's official alibi. Huber claimed to have spent time with Tanner, drinking coffee with him at the yard, during the critical hours in question. Tanner corroborated the alibi. Then he later retracted his statement, saying he had "gone out on a limb" as a family friend. In truth, he added, he had not seen Huber on the premises of the railroad yard between 7:45 and 10:45 on the night in question.

The superintendent of the Pittsburgh Police claimed six witnesses contradicted Tanner and validated Huber's claim to have been at the railroad yard all evening. The names of these witnesses were never made public.

What complicates matters is that some of the questioning, even some of the arresting—let us not forget that Huber was hauled in four times over the course of six years for the murder of his sister—was done by individuals who were not actually working with or for the Pittsburgh Police Department. The key players were as follows:

1. Randolf "The Rabbit" Anderson. A self-styled private detective, Anderson apprehended Huber multiple times until 1954, six

years after Noelle's death. After being sued by Huber for "malicious arrest," Anderson was cleared of the charges. Anderson had a dark past of his own with a conviction for passing counterfeit money. He claimed that solving Noelle's murder would help him clear his name by doing "something good" with his life. That, and he was hoping to earn a presidential pardon for doing it.

2. Max "The Wasp" Caverly. A private detective and former cop, Caverly performed one of the citizen's arrests of Huber. But he took it one step farther in charging Huber's parents, as well as Marvin Tanner—Huber's erstwhile alibi from the railroad yard—with being accessories after the fact. Caverly, too, was subsequently sued by young Huber. And, like Anderson, he was later cleared of the charge of "malicious arrest."

3. Officer Dick Richards. Richards was, unusually for this crew, a real cop. Richards arrested Huber in April of 1949—the first such arrest—and was immediately suspended by the department for ninety days for having done so. Part of the problem was the manner in which he had carried out his mission, enacting his arrest with a backup player who was not an officer of the law. In fact, she was a blonde in a tight skirt and sweater with a gun holstered to her right hip, described by the press as a "pistol-carrying girl reporter." Richards claimed she was a "sworn deputy" but refused to give her name. After his suspension, Richards withdrew his charges against Huber, saying that "circumstances in the past few days have proven conclusively to me that Matthew A. Huber, Jr., is not involved in this crime. I am going to withdraw the charges at once." And that was the end of that.

4. Police Superintendent Charles R. Jeffries. Jeffries was in office at the time of the murder and for several years thereafter. He continually came down hard on all forces pursuing young Huber and loudly bemoaned the amateur "citizen detectives" who were interfering with the police investigation, doing more to help the real killer elude detection than to solve the crime.

5. Police Superintendent Mark W. Jones. Jones replaced Jeffries in 1953, whereupon he reopened the case, ordering a new "top-to-bottom" investigation of everything that had taken place on the night of the murder and in the ensuing five years.

I try to picture them all. A few of them have their photos in the papers, but mostly the reader is given only repeat images of Noelle and her brother, Matthew. Noelle, of course, is seen in the same two pictures, with braids and without. Matt is seen in various stages of being apprehended. Sometimes he is looking at the camera, sometimes away. Sometimes he is wearing a T-shirt and leather jacket, like James Dean. Occasionally there are pictures of the father or the cops. A particular image stands out of the officers examining the kitchen of the Huber home right after the murder.

From my earliest memories, I have known my mother's friend was murdered. But this raft of supporting details has only recently become accessible to me. It is as though a black and white sketch I've looked at all my life has burst into brilliant color. During my childhood, the snippets my mother revealed were brief. In my young adulthood, she filled in more detail. But my mother's imprint of her friend's murder was that of the twelve-year-old child she'd been at the time. A large part of her was frozen in 1948. What I have access to now with the internet, the coroner's report, and books I have been able to track down that mention Noelle Huber's murder in the context of a corrupt and lawless Pittsburgh has given me a deeper understanding of what really happened.

Or maybe my understanding is no deeper at all, but I simply see more puzzle pieces strewn across the table. That and the fact that my DA friend got the case reopened several years ago.

13

THE WIFE

Chapter Seven
Monday, March 9, 2020

Linda waited for Miguel to fall asleep after reluctantly yielding to him in bed. She did not think of it as making love anymore. There was a keyed-up energy to it all, like they were skirting at the edge of mania. It did not quite dip into rage, but it no longer qualified as love. Linda and Miguel were walking on the edge, all right. The edge of what, precisely, she did not yet know. But she had the growing sense it would be revealed to her. That she was a player enacting her part in a play that was not of her making.

In a similar way, the world seemed to be teetering on the edge of something unknown. Or, at least, something unremembered. There had been earlier pandemics far in the distant past. But none of them really believed it could happen to them. She didn't. Her friends didn't. Still, she could hear the drumbeats any time she turned on the television news.

Linda never watched the news around the children. She did not want to frighten them. Some of her friends kept the television on all day and their little ones were having nightmares, asking questions her friends could not answer. What worried Linda more than the questions children asked was the ones they didn't.

She remembered her own childhood when her parents had begun to fight. Her father came home later and later each evening, eventually skipping dinner entirely. Linda would sit with her mother at the table, trying to swallow her meal, as her mother swirled ice water in her tumbler. Linda knew it wasn't water her mother was drinking. She saw her trips to the dining room liquor cabinet. But Linda never asked questions. She would not have known, first of all, that she had the right to do so. She would not have known, secondly, what to ask.

Palm Beach had grown unseasonably hot for March. The mosquitos were thickening to the point where she could no longer allow the children to play outdoors. In the middle of a sunny day—a time when mosquitos traditionally hid out in the shade—Linda had seen them covering Espie's soft little arms and legs. She didn't know what upset her more, the sight of the insects on her daughter's flesh, or the sight of herself swatting at her child with barely controlled hysteria. Everything was on the edge now.

Linda listened in the dark to the hum of the air conditioner and the slap of palm fronds against the roof. Her newfound insomnia had introduced her to things that go bump in the night. Plus, the rising heat had brought with it wind that was blowing incessantly, making her feel a bit mad.

When Miguel's breathing became deep and regular—he was not a snorer—Linda waited another fifteen minutes, staring at the clock with the illuminated face on her bedside table. Only then did she slide out of bed, carefully lifting the sheet so as not to pull it across Miguel's body. She went over to the bathroom, reached inside to turn on the light, and shut the door quietly. Should Miguel wake and miss her, she hoped he would see the strip of light under the closed bathroom door and assume she was in there.

Down the hall, little plug-in nightlights guided her passage. In the living room, the big plate-glass window allowed streetlamp glow to reach inside. In its dull light, all of her crisp whites and blues were washed in sepia tones, rendering the room a negative of itself. At least she would not step on a toy as she made her way in the dark. Miguel refused to live in a playroom. Every night after the children went to bed, Linda returned all their toys to their bedroom.

She went through the kitchen, which smelled lemony fresh from her after-dinner efforts. Here, her way was brightened from the various appliance clocks, beaming at her in small blue digits. She reached under the counter to the stools and felt around for her purse. When she found it, she carried it with her the final leg of her journey.

The double doors to Miguel's office were kept closed. Linda had to use two hands and a push from one bare foot to get the door on the right to detach from the door on the left. At the tell-tale squeak, she held her breath and listened to the house.

There was nothing but the buzz of the refrigerator and the clunk of the automatic icemaker on a never-ending cycle of production. Where all the ice went, she did not know.

Miguel was not following her.

Inside the office, she gently closed the doors behind her. If for any reason Miguel came into the kitchen for a glass of water, there was still a chance he might think Linda was in the bathroom.

She did not turn on a lamp. In the ambient light from the window, which was barely enough to see, Linda set her purse on the desk and extracted the pile of mail, shuffling through the envelopes, one by one.

Then she found it.

A letter from a bank that was not their own. She flipped it over and, using the letter opener Miguel kept in a shiny polish—the one with the boar tusk handle from his grandfather's collection—carefully sliced it open. Extracting a single sheet of paper, Linda walked closer to the window to look at it with the aid of the moonlight.

Congratulations Mr. and Mrs. Alonso, we have approved your home equity loan in the amount of $2,000,000.

She touched that number for luck. Then she carefully slid the letter back into the envelope, pulled a book from the shelf, and slipped the letter inside. She made sure she lined up the book with its neighbors and wiped the shelf with her sleeve. Before leaving, she took a good look at the title so she might easily find it later: *Tropical Plants and How to Love Them*.

Miguel would never even glance at it.

14

A WRITER'S THOUGHTS

Today dawns dark, as it usually does for me. I wake early. Four a.m. Three. If it is before five, I try to read in bed and lull myself back to sleep. After five, though, the game is over and I get up to make coffee. Sometimes I can sneak out of the room without waking the dog, who snores at my feet. But it's not very likely. The prospect of food and an outing when darkness still reigns is too enticing to miss.

Cordelia is a standard poodle named for one of King Lear's daughters. The good one. Because my Cordelia is a much better daughter to me than I ever was to my mother. She is big, though. Too big, really, for a small woman like me. A small, middle-aged woman to boot—a woman without her former supply of estrogen to keep her bones rubbery and avoid a brittle break should a dog knock her down.

When Cordie was a puppy, she was a lot for me to handle on a leash. But she is a smart girl and responded like a champion to obedience school. Really, she trained me. Our walks have been a source of delight for both of us. She is older now. Ten. Her lustrous black coat has gone grey around the muzzle and she is getting stiff. We don't take long walks like we used to. Plus, the heat of Florida has grown oppressive. I can only imagine how hot it feels to Cordelia, no matter how short I keep her trimmed.

I check the clock and see it is 4:30. Morning enough. I give up the illusion of sleep and slide my feet as quietly as I can to the floor. Cordelia stirs, so the two of us go out into the black dampness of a Florida night. Despite the current curfew, we will walk a little way. We listen—or I do since Cordie is growing deaf—to the sounds all around us. Frogs croak, crickets chirp, and something else—the distant sound of water. Almost imperceptible, but there. The endless beating of surf on the ocean side. The gentle lapping against seawalls and pilings on the lake side.

I take a gulp of humid air as Cordie stumbles. It is the second time she's done this. I stop, give her a pat, touch her paws, palpating for an injury I cannot see in the dark. She does not react, so, reassured, I turn my attention from the dog walking next to me to the girl who exists in my mind. Noelle Huber was, of course, killed at night. I wonder if there is a study of the likelihood of murder by time of day.

Home again, coffee in hand, I pursue this question on the internet. *The Atlantic* magazine, in an article dated Nov. 19, 2012, says that, particularly when you are older, you are 14 percent more likely to die on your birthday than any other day of the year. While in certain geographical areas, you are 13 percent more likely to die after receiving a paycheck. And, if you are human—if?—you are more likely to die in the late morning, say, eleven a.m., than at any other time.

But those statistics—odd as they are—apply to dying of natural causes, not to being stabbed thirty-six times in your home. A most unnatural cause to be sure.

To that point, the *New York Times*, on Nov. 27, 2018, reminds us that the most dangerous place for women is in their own homes. More than half of all female homicide victims in 2017 met their fates at home at the hands of someone they knew. "Of the approximately 87,000 women who were victims of intentional homicide last year around the world, about 34 percent were murdered by an intimate partner and 24 percent by a relative."

Mother Jones, on April 25, 2013, backs this up: "You are more likely to be killed by someone you know than by a stranger, and you'll probably be at home when it happens." They add that "between 2005 and 2010, 60 percent of all violent injuries in the country were inflicted by loved ones or acquaintances. And 60 percent of the time, those victimizations happened in the home. In 2011, 79 percent of murders reported to the FBI (in which the victim-offender relationship was known) were committed by friends, loved ones, or acquaintances."

The *New York Times*, in the previously cited story, goes on to say, "Domestic violence against women and girls is rooted in societal norms about men's authority to exert control over women."

Finally, I find what I am looking for. The United States Department of Justice's website offers insight into the occurrence of violence as measured by time of day. Apparently, incidents of violent crimes increase by the hour, starting at six a.m. and rising up to nine p.m. and then begin to decline until the following morning. That is, if the perpetrator is over eighteen years old. If that person is under eighteen, his actions reach a peak at around three in the afternoon. Right after school, it would seem.

I don't know the exact time Noelle Huber was attacked, but it was sometime after that last phone call to the Stores house at 9:30 p.m. and the Hubers' return home at 11:30 p.m. Statistically, the US Department of Justice puts 62.3 percent of violent crimes at ten p.m. and 55.9 percent at eleven p.m. In every way, Noelle's murder conforms to statistical probabilities.

I also don't know how long it took to kill her. I hope it was fast but fear it would have been impossible, given the number of stab wounds, her trajectory from the kitchen to the telephone table, and the fact that she was still alive when her parents found her.

Digging further into the timeline of the night in question, the disappearance of all fingerprints becomes complicated. Surely there were fingerprints somewhere in the house belonging to the family members who lived there: Mr. and Mrs. Huber, Matt, and Noelle. But exactly where those fingerprints remained and what was wiped down was never clarified. I called the Pittsburgh Police Department and spoke to a detective in homicide, requesting the police report. He called me back the next day to say my request had been denied. No explanation was offered.

There is the theory that the killer stuck around after stabbing Noelle to clean up after himself. But there was another window of opportunity for someone else to tamper with the scene of the crime. According to newspapers, a conspicuous time lag existed between the moment a neighbor saw Mr. and Mrs. Huber return to the house at exactly 11:30 p.m., and 11:51 p.m., when two other events occurred simultaneously. The first of these was Mr. Huber's call to the police station to report the stabbing of his daughter. The second was Mrs. Huber running out the door screaming.

The fact that the Hubers did neither of those things when they first arrived home and waited twenty-one minutes to scream and call the police triggers a number of questions. What happened in those intervening minutes? Did the Hubers engage in a cleanup? And, if so, why?

Sororicide is what you call it when you kill your sister; fratricide is doing the same to your brother. Wikipedia says, "There are a number of examples of sororicide and fratricide in adolescents, even pre-adolescents, where sibling rivalry and resulting physical aggression can get out of hand and lead to the death of one of them, particularly when a potent weapon is available or when one is significantly older than the other and misjudges his/her own strength."

Matthew Huber, Jr.'s, whereabouts between the hours of 7:45 and 10:45 p.m. on the night of Noelle's murder remain unclear. Then there was the matter of the change of shoes and shirt mentioned by some of his coworkers. What is more, a shirt was later found in a garbage bin behind the Hubers' house.

This shirt—a white button-down splattered with stains—became the subject of lively disagreement in ensuing hearings. Police Superintendent Charles Jeffries told the jury that the stains were iron rust. But Dr. Coleman Watts of the Mellon Institute, after performing a hydrogen peroxide test on the markings, determined that the white shirt was covered with blood. The origin of that blood, however, was indeterminate. It could have been animal or it could have been human, according to Watts.

The shirt was consistent with a brand and style young Matt Huber had regularly purchased from a particular haberdashery downtown. In early days, Huber acknowledged that the shirt could have been one of his. Later on, he flatly denied having said it and further denied ownership of the shirt.

15

THE WIFE

Chapter Eight
Sunday, April 19, 2020

At eleven a.m. on a Sunday morning, Linda picked up the phone to
call the police and report her family missing. Why she had not called
the cops the day before, the day it had actually happened, was an act
of omission that would come back to haunt her. Under the microscope
of hindsight, it was clear what Linda could have—should have—done.
Instead, she had spent hours puzzling over how precisely one called the
police to report a day-old tragedy.

Did one look up the general office number and ring the front desk?
Or did one simply dial 911? And would this really qualify as the type
of emergency that 911 was equipped to handle, especially during this
pandemic? She thought of 911 as the place to turn for crises that had
some immediacy. *Help, there's a man outside my window! Help, my child
is choking on a carrot! Help, my family disappeared twenty-four hours ago?*
It did not seem to meet the criteria of urgency.

Linda, who had, in actuality, awakened at five a.m. the day after the
disappearance, had waited six more hours to place the call. Once she did,

once the officers came to see her—in what would be another miscalculation—she told them she had just woken up.

Two cops came to the door—a man and a woman—wearing masks and latex gloves. They slipped blue paper booties over their shoes before entering the house. Linda started to don her own mask, but the female officer asked her not to.

"Ma'am," she said, "if you don't mind, since we're masked, would you please leave your face uncovered?"

"Of course." Linda complied and ushered them in.

The woman entered first, holding out her badge for Linda to see. "I'm Officer Jones."

The man followed on her heels, holding his badge up, as well. "I'm Smith."

"Would you like anything to drink?" Linda offered.

"No, thanks, ma'am," Officer Jones replied, pulling out a tablet and a stylus. "Why don't you tell us why you called?"

Linda gestured to the furniture in the living room. "Won't you sit down?"

"New protocol is to stand," Jones answered again. "Because of COVID-19."

"Ah." Linda backed away a few paces.

"You want to tell us why you're concerned?"

"Yes. It's my husband. And my children. They've been gone since yesterday morning."

"Yesterday?" asked Smith.

"Yes. He took them—Miguel, my husband—to the surfing beach at the end of our road. Not to surf, though. I mean, my son, Diego—we call him Gogo—he's only five. And my little girl, Espie, is three."

Linda paused.

"Ma'am?"

"They left around eleven. My husband wanted to go earlier. I tried to hurry them. But Gogo was reading. And Espie was playing with her toys. Her monkey and her little stuffed animals."

Linda turned to look at a family photo, perfectly framed in sterling silver and sitting on a glass end table.

"Is that them?" Officer Smith asked.

"Last Christmas," Linda said. "So then I made breakfast. French toast. I called the children into the kitchen at eight. Maybe it was eight-thirty. They ate well. They bickered a little, normal stuff. By that time, it was already too late to get them out the door by ten. They weren't even dressed."

"Do you know why your husband was in a hurry?" asked Officer Jones.

"No, I don't," Linda said and looked at the cops, who waited for her to go on.

"Anyway, by the time I got everybody into clothes they could agree on, it was close to eleven. Maybe ten forty-five."

Jones looked up from her iPad to ask, "What were the children wearing?"

"Turquoise shorts and a flowered top for Espie—red and purple flowers—with short sleeves. And red shorts and a navy polo for Gogo. They both wore sneakers. Oh. And purple hair ribbons. Espie loves ribbons."

Officer Jones noted these details.

"Before they left, Miguel asked for more supplies in their backpacks. More snacks. Sweaters. It seemed weird but it wasn't worth fighting about. I gave them each a couple juice boxes. Cheddar Bunnies. Apple slices. That kind of thing. And sweaters. A purple one for Espie and a navy one for Gogo. But I found it strange at the time. Not alarming. Just strange."

"Why's that?" Officer Smith again.

"Well, the beach is so close. And it was hot. And they were supposed to come home for lunch. But, with Miguel, there's no use in questioning him."

Jones stopped typing. "What do you mean?" she asked.

"Just that my husband is…well, we don't actually live in a democracy in this household. Anyway, they didn't come home for lunch. By around one…wait, was it two? I'm not sure, but at some point in the afternoon, I

62

got worried. Maybe unsettled is a better word. The quesadillas had been ready since twelve-thirty and they were getting cold and hard. Plus Espie still naps in the afternoon and her schedule was going to be off."

Linda hesitated again, but neither officer spoke.

"So I walked over to the beach myself. To look for them. I went up and down a few times but there was no sign of them. It occurred to me they might have come home by a different route and we may not have passed each other walking. So I came home to see if they were here."

"What time would you say that was?" asked Smith.

"Maybe two thirty? Or three? First, I walked around the house to see if they were in back. On the swings or something. We keep our doors locked. Most of our neighbors don't, but we do. I thought Miguel might have forgotten to take his key with him and they'd be waiting outside. When they weren't there, I went around to the front and came inside.

"But they weren't here either. I went into the children's room and I…I just sat on my son's bed. I remember looking around. I saw Espie's monkey. Her favorite thing. Then I felt around under Gogo's pillow and found his scrap of blanket. He likes to think he's a big boy—he's five, did I say that? But he can't get rid of that blanket. He doesn't even let me wash it."

Linda wandered over to one of her clean, white chairs and unceremoniously lowered herself onto it.

"And there it was," she continued, "in the room. His security blanket. It wasn't with him. And that's what got me. Espie's monkey and Gogo's blanket were here in their room. These things that were supposed to make my kids feel safe were here, safe and sound. But where were my children?"

Linda looked at the two cops as if she expected an answer.

"What did you do then?" asked Jones.

"I…I should have called you then. I know. But I fell asleep. On my son's bed. I didn't actually mean to. I only meant to wait there for a little bit."

"You fell asleep?" Smith asked.

"I guess I did. I mean, I know I did. The next time I was aware of anything, it was dark outside. It took me a few minutes to remember where I was. And why. When it all came back to me, I jumped out of the bed so fast I twisted my ankle on a toy on the floor. Hard. I limped down the hall. I looked in our bedroom, the guest room, the bathrooms. But there was no one. And something just took me to Miguel's office and then...I..."

Linda started to cry.

"I just had this feeling...I didn't want to go in there. I don't like that room. Everything in it is made from the skins of cows and the tusks of boars and who-knows-what-all from his family's ranch in Argentina. It was maybe ten thirty by then. I switched on the light and looked around. Everything looked perfect. Nothing had moved. But I felt pulled to the safe in the closet. I knew what I would find. What I would *not* find."

Linda's crying escalated. "Do you mind if I go get some tissues?"

Officer Jones waved her off and Linda walked down the hall to her bathroom and sat on the toilet seat. She grabbed a few tissues, blew her nose, and took a look at herself in the mirror. She pressed her hair down with her hands, retied her ponytail, and returned to the living room.

"Where was I?" she asked.

Jones consulted her notes. "And then I knew what I wouldn't find," she paraphrased.

"Their Argentine passports were missing. All of them. I realized they'd left the country to go to Argentina. And I can't follow. Americans are not allowed to fly into Argentina now, because of the pandemic. But my children are dual citizens. And then I screamed."

Linda dropped her head and pressed her eyes with the heels of her hands.

"Mrs. Alonso," Smith said, "If your husband did try to board an international flight with your family, he would have had to show a letter at the airport from his spouse granting permission to fly out of the country with minors."

"Yes. Maybe," Linda said. "But those checks are spotty. Anyway, he could have forged one."

"So let me get this straight," Smith continued, "You discovered all this yesterday? At approximately ten p.m. last night? And you waited thirteen hours to call the police?"

"I...I...this fatigue came over me. It was like I was drugged. I collapsed on the floor in front of the open safe and fell asleep. It was the children, yes. But there had also been so much stress between my husband and me."

Once again, Jones looked up from her tablet. "Stress?"

"We'd been fighting. I'd found some paperwork a month or so ago. Should I go get it?"

"Sure," said Jones.

Linda left the living room to retrieve the letter she had so carefully hidden in the bookshelves. She returned, holding it in two hands. "He was borrowing money," she said. "I had questioned him about it. He didn't like that and we fought. Multiple times."

"What do you think that has to do with this?" Smith asked.

"It's a lot of money." Linda thrust the letter at the officers. "Two million dollars."

Jones peered at the piece of paper. Smith did as well. Neither of them touched it.

"Mind if we take a look around the house?" Smith asked.

"Of course," Linda said, waving them in the direction of the hall that led to the bedrooms. "Anything that might help you find my babies."

"Thank you. We won't disturb anything. Just take a quick look. You'd be surprised. People usually leave a clue."

"Do they?" Linda asked.

The cops traversed the living room and made their way to the bedrooms. First the children's room. They spent the longest time in there, stopping to look at things, touching nothing. They briefly scanned the guest room.

In the master bedroom, they paused to look at the bed, piled high with crisp, white sheets with white, embroidered edges. It resembled a wedding cake.

"Did you make your bed when you got up this morning, Mrs. Alonso?" Jones asked.

"I didn't actually sleep there," Linda replied. "Remember I told you I fell asleep in my husband's office. On the floor."

"You say you fell asleep after returning from the beach for," Jones swiped her iPad to consult her notes, "at least seven hours in the middle of the day?"

"I guess," she said. "Yes."

"And then, after touring the house, you fell asleep again for, what would you say? Another twelve hours? Assuming you were up for an hour from around ten to around eleven?"

"I guess so."

"Do you normally sleep that much?" Jones asked.

"I've had trouble sleeping lately."

"Do you take anything to help you sleep? Medications?"

"Sometimes."

"Did you take any last night?"

"Yes," Linda said. "I remember now that I did. I took two sleeping pills. And I normally take only one."

"Where do you keep your medications?" asked Smith.

"In the medicine cabinet in our bathroom."

"So, you walked into the bathroom, took two sleeping pills, got into bed, and went to sleep."

"Yes. Wait. I'm sorry. No. I mean, I didn't get into bed. I'm not sure what I said before. I'm so overwhelmed right now. I don't know when I took them."

Officer Jones swiped the tablet backward to correct Linda's earlier statement. Or to make a note that Linda was contradicting herself.

"May we open the medicine cabinet?" Smith asked.

"Of course," Linda answered and both cops moved into the bathroom.

"Is this them?" Smith emerged holding up a prescription bottle. Linda looked at it and saw the real name of the product, zolpidem. It made her think of a fortune-teller's name.

"Mrs. Alonso? This prescription for Ambien is in your husband's name, issued on the thirtieth of March. Dosage is ten milligrams. You say you took two?"

"Yes. I usually take one. And maybe I only take five milligrams. No wonder I slept."

Smith opened the bottle and counted the pills. "Twenty-six pills gone in a pretty short time."

"Mrs. Alonso," Jones said, "do you have any reason to believe that your husband may have harmed himself?"

"Did you check the garage?" asked Smith.

"What?"

"The garage. Did you check it to see if Mr. Alonso had taken the car?"

"It never occurred to me. I mean, after I'd found the passports missing, why would I check the garage?" Her hands started to shake.

Officer Smith nodded and went to check the garage.

16

THE WIFE

Chapter Nine
Tuesday, March 10, 2020

Six weeks before Linda's children disappeared, before their disappearance was even a speck in Linda's mental range of possibilities—though what would have seemed possible about the pandemic that was closing in on them?—Linda had gone to Publix. In the dairy section, she ran into her friend, Devon, accompanied by her little girl.

"Hey, Devon," Linda said, turning to Espie and Gogo. "You remember…" Linda could not remember the child's name.

"Emma," offered Gogo.

"Right," Linda said. "You guys remember Emma?" Obviously they remembered Emma better than she did.

"Hi, Emma," Espie said shyly.

Emma just blinked at them, a lollipop in her mouth. Linda contemplated the germ-spreading possibilities of a public lollipop in light of the virus she had been hearing about on the news.

Linda and Devon made small talk, wondering where the world was headed. Then they moved in different directions—one to yogurt, one to cheese—saying they should get the children together soon.

"Oh," Linda said casually, turning to Devon. "You're a chiropractor, right?"

"Yes. Are you having an issue?"

"I was just wondering. I'm having some pain in my back."

"Come in," Devon offered. "You can call my office or just text me for an appointment."

"That'd be great," said Linda. "I'll text you."

They met two days later, a day before the lockdown. Devon offered Linda a gown from the cabinet. "I'll be right back."

Linda put it on and looked around the room. There was a laminated diagram of muscle, nerve, and sinew that made her think of the butcher, and a hanging plastic spine, complete with movable discs. As Linda reached out to touch it, to play with its rubbery discs, Devon returned. "Please," Devon said, indicating the examination table, which Linda settled upon, face down. Devon placed a heated blanket over her.

"That feels good," said Linda. "Thank you."

"Tell me what's troubling you," Devon said as she ran her fingers gently down Linda's spinal column.

"I have this pain in my back. Really more the side."

"Turn over," Devon said, picking up Linda's head and turning her neck in various directions. "Have you done a sonogram or CT scan to have a look?"

"I don't think it's internal."

"Do you have an idea what it is?"

"Actually I do. I mean, something happened."

Devon lifted her hands from Linda's body and stood silent. Waiting.

"Last year," Linda said. "My husband. He…we fought. I think he broke my ribs."

Devon took a deep breath. "Listen," she said, "I can do something with the laser to promote healing and relieve pain. But I'm obliged to inform you of services that are available. Counseling. Places where you can seek safety."

"Safety? It's not like I'm…" Linda trailed off. "It only happened once."

"Do you want to talk about it?"

"I...I guess I do."

Devon walked over to the chair and sat down.

Linda sat up on the table, hugging the blanket around her. "It was about a year ago. Not quite. I went out one night and came home late and I shouldn't have woken him up. But I did."

"And that would be a problem because...?"

"Well, Miguel is just...you don't really know him but he's...he likes control."

Devon waited.

"I'd been out driving. Just driving. I took his car—his Porsche—and put down the top and put on the radio and I just drove south. That was all. To Boca or Ft. Lauderdale or I'm not sure which. And, yes, I'd had a few drinks. And no, I shouldn't have done it. But that was all I did. Honest. I took the ocean road and it was beautiful and I just felt free and I guess I needed that."

"You don't normally feel free?" Devon asked.

"No," Linda answered. "Miguel is...I feel scrutinized and observed and...there's no other word for it...controlled."

Again Devon waited.

"So I came home and I guess I was reckless because I woke him up. He was groggy and it took him a while to focus. Maybe he'd been drinking, too."

"Do you and your husband drink heavily?"

"Heavily? No, no more than anyone else."

"I don't drink," Devon said.

"No more than most people," Linda corrected. "I realized it was late, too late, and that it would be hard to explain where I'd been. So I made up a story about going to the movies with my friend, Ana. But I guess she'd called while I was gone so it all went south from there. Miguel knew I was lying but I was lying for no good reason. I mean I hadn't done anything. But it would be hard to convince him of that at that point since he'd caught me in a lie already."

Devon glanced at her watch.

"I'm sorry. I know I'm rambling. I do that when I get nervous."

"Linda, I'm not sure why you're nervous with me right now."

"No, I know. I just…it's hard to tell this story. I'll speed it up. He… um…he asked me where I'd been and I was just angry or reactive or I don't know what, but I told him I'd been with another man."

"Why would you do that? If it wasn't true?"

"I know! I mean, I don't know. I just did. And his face screwed up in a way that scared me and he crooked his index finger and motioned me to come toward him. I did and he slapped me. Hard. And when I fell to the floor, he started kicking me."

"Jesus, Linda."

"And he just kept it up until he stopped. I tried to crawl to the door, to get out of there. But he started crying and begged me to stay. He held onto me there on the floor. He said he was sorry. Said it wouldn't happen again. And that's it. That's what happened."

"Has it?"

"What?"

"Happened again?"

"No," Linda said. "It only happened that once."

But Linda—and Devon—knew that a single act of violence may seem to be an isolated incident with a beginning, middle, and end. But it didn't work that way. Like a stone thrown into a lake, its ripples continued outward, in ever-growing circles to the point where an observer might not be able to trace the movement of the water's surface to the original impact from the tossed stone. But, even unseen, that connection existed.

17

A WRITER'S THOUGHTS

A single act of violence does not end. Noelle Grace Huber was murdered seventy-two years ago this year, but, for me—for others like me—it never ends. I never met her. I never met her family. I never met her suspected murderer/brother—though he is still alive. Who knows? It could happen. He still lives in Pittsburgh. Outside of Pittsburgh, actually. Not in the area where my mother and father migrated when they left the changing neighborhood of Homewood-Brushton as newlyweds. My family moved north, to a little town called Gibsonia, to raise their family. Matthew Huber moved east to raise his. To another little town called Oakmont.

I've even found his current address.

Members of the Ritenour and Huber families—minus Noelle, of course—left the city of Pittsburgh in the 1950s and '60s, the period known as "white flight." When white folk were abandoning urban America for its surrounding suburbs because they didn't want to live near Black folk. Some of them believed Black families might bring a neighborhood down. Although one could reasonably ask what sort of uplifted neighborhood they all thought they were living in when little girls were being killed in their kitchens.

It turns out that Homewood-Brushton happened to have been racially mixed already. At the time of Noelle's murder, in fact, a white woman in a nearby house was quick to blame a Black man. The woman in question, a Mrs. Meredith West, had traveled from Philadelphia to visit a friend in Brushton, where she happened to be on the night of December 10. She spoke to multiple newspapers after the incident, claiming to have seen "a tall, slim Negro fleeing from the scene of the crime." She added an enigmatic coda to her interviews, saying she was willing to help the police but that she would only do so when she was ready. "I'll do it in my own way," was exactly how she put it. I shudder to think of the number of tall, slim Black men who were hauled in and interrogated based on Mrs. West's observations. No tall, slim Black murderer was ever revealed to have existed.

And why twelve-year-old Noelle would open her door—when repeatedly advised not to do so by her parents—to an unknown man of any race begs a host of questions. An elaborate theory Mr. Huber advanced involved Noelle's phone call to young Jane Stores. When Noelle called the Stores' residence for the second time, it was nine thirty p.m. and it was Mrs. Stores who took the call, having just sent Jane to the store to buy a quart of milk.

Mr. Huber put some thought into this theoretical chain of events. He wondered if, at some point after that phone call, Noelle heard someone knock at the front door. Not the rear door—the door that had been found unlocked with the shade partially raised—but the front door. Might Noelle have gone to that door, thinking it was her friend Jane coming to see her on the way home from her errand? Might she have opened that door to a stranger, believing she was opening it to Jane?

The next question would logically be, then, who relocked the front door? If a stranger pushed his way into the house by way of the front door, if that stranger stabbed Noelle thirty-six times and departed by the back door, leaving that door unlocked, would that stranger have returned to the front door to lock it? There is never any mention of blood on or near the front door or tracks of blood leading in that direction.

Surely, if you stab a person thirty-six times, you would have blood on your shoes (remember the witness testimony that young Matt Huber was seen at the railroad yard in the later evening in different shoes than he was wearing in the early evening). And, even if the intruder locked the door behind him right after forcing his way inside, still having clean shoes at that point, would he have waited to start stabbing the girl until she had run into the kitchen?

A variation on the theme of the front door—also put forth by Noelle's father—is that Noelle might have heard something out on the street, farther away from her house. She may have thought Jane was not necessarily at the door but somewhere on the block. Noelle may have opened the front door and walked out to the street to look up and down it for Jane. At that point, this stranger may have snuck into the house, unseen by Noelle, and hidden in wait for her return. Noelle would have then locked the front door behind her herself when she came in. And then, this stranger could have sprung upon her in the kitchen.

18

THE WIFE

Chapter Ten
Saturday, April 25, 2020

Miguel's car—a 2015 Porsche 911 convertible, black on black, purchased new the year Diego was born—made Miguel, in Linda's view, look like a drug dealer. The flashiness of it was probably the reason they were still on a waiting list for the club. They'd been accepted as members of a sort—provisional members—but they seemed to languish in that place long beyond the normal length of time. Linda wondered if Miguel had driven a different car, or worn different clothes, or been a little bit less of a peacock in other ways, they might have been upgraded from provisional status long ago. Still, they had not been officially rejected.

They spent a fair amount of time at the club, swimming with the children, dining, boating. It was there that they docked their boat—an impressive, thirty-two-foot Boston Whaler. Miguel loved to fish the Gulf Stream, which ran closer to land in Palm Beach than anywhere else in Florida. The boat was also bought brand spanking new by Miguel the year Diego was born. Both car and boat were the gifts Miguel had given to himself to celebrate that milestone. To Linda, he gave a Van Cleef & Arpels watch, so she was not left out of the prizes.

While not an ostentatious boat—nowhere near as showy as Miguel's car or the much larger boats that studded the docks of the club—the Boston Whaler Outrage was still an expensive piece of equipment. From its purchase price to its maintenance costs, it was a big load for the Alonsos to carry.

The day after the children's disappearance, Officers Smith and Jones entered the Alonsos' garage in search of Miguel's car. And lo and behold, there it was. Linda's car, on the other hand, a practical 2017 Volkswagen Golf SportWagen in her favorite sparkling white, was not. The fact of the missing vehicle—specifically the one that had the children's car seats strapped into it—lent credence to the theory that Miguel had absconded with the two of them.

Linda did not know how to create a new normal. The world had closed. Just like that. Without her babies, the world may as well have sealed itself up around her. She did not care. She could not muster the slightest interest in news of the pandemic other than to see its perfect symmetry to the ruin of her own life. A cosmic staging of an exterior reality that mirrored her interior state.

She lay for hours—days—without moving. In her white bed in her white bedroom in her white house on Reef Road. The pristineness of it mocked her, teasing her with a false sense of purity. Of cleanliness. Of order. Like the world around her where microbes lurked unseen on the palm of a clean-seeming hand, the kiss of a blemish-free lip, the sole of an innocent-looking shoe. Linda and Miguel had maintained a shoe-free household, the memory of which surged like bile to burn the lining of her throat. What a laugh. What a colossal joke that they had fostered some illusion of protection from outside forces when it was forces inside that were staging formations against them.

One week ago. Only a week. Seven days since she'd had a life with her family. Each ensuing day unfolded, taking her farther from physical solidity and hurtling her deeper into untethered reaches. Weightless and weighted, like rocks.

Linda's inertia pressed on her like weights on a scuba diver. As she lay on the sofa or the bed or the floor of the children's room, she pictured herself in a wet suit, a heavy belt strapped around her middle. In her mind's eye, though, Linda's imaginary suit was studded with weights from her toes to her nose.

And at that image, around and around in her head went the song, *Head, Shoulders, Knees and Toes*. Before her eyes loomed the image of little Espie trying to maintain the increasingly frantic pace Gogo would set whenever they sang that song. Of the way they all would laugh until sometimes Espie ended up in tears. Of the way Linda would have to rein in the speed of their singing to allow Espie to keep up, touching the body parts in question and remembering the order in which to move her hands.

The hands of a loved one—even after that person was gone—always stayed with you. Linda remembered her mother's hands from her last days in the hospital, pierced by needles held down by tape. The bruises that would form on her paper-thin skin and blacken in a pool around the punctures. The fact that they would not let her mother wear her wedding and engagement rings, rings they cut off her fingers, rings she had not taken off since the day she had married Linda's father, even in the dreary years of their separation so many years before. The indelible impression left on the ring finger of her left hand from a lifetime of wearing those rings.

Linda thought of her children's hands. At age three, Espie's were still baby fat with little dimples where her knuckles lay beneath. At five, Diego was beginning to have the hands of the boy he was becoming. Not quite as sinewy as they would eventually be, but the dimpled knuckles of babyhood had yielded to a bonier form.

Linda thought of Miguel's hands. Of the use he made of them that night when he had struck her. She looked at her own hands, empty of any purpose. No baby to hold, no toddler to comfort. Useless appendages weighted down like the rest of her.

Linda's mind traveled to the stuffed monkey sitting down the hall, patiently waiting in front of its teacup on the table. Her mind moved on to see Gogo's blanket tucked so tenderly under his pillow. Almost worse than the children's absence was the useless presence of these objects.

19

A WRITER'S THOUGHTS

The heat takes permanent hold as Florida bumps up to summer. Gusts of humid air move from west to east, not the normal direction of our breezes, which usually come in across the ocean. When there is wind, there are not supposed to be mosquitos. But now, we have ones that are Jurassic-sized, banking in the current, landing skillfully on my arms, my ankles, any skin exposed. Maybe they are inland swamp mosquitos, flying here from what is left of the Everglades to have their day in Palm Beach, now that the crowds are gone. In the suspended animation of this pandemic, dolphins have returned to Venice, wolves to parts of France. Maybe the fauna of Florida are reclaiming their own, as well.

I eat ice cream in honor of the weather. The bulimic's favorite treat.

I think about what it would be like to be in Pittsburgh now, in the middle of the quarantine. Cold. Isolated. Lonely. I think about Noelle Huber's brother, still there, ninety years old and alone, now that his wife has died. Is he lonely? I wonder if he misses his sister. Seventy-two years dead is a long time gone. Do you miss someone differently if you killed them than if you didn't?

Home, alone, and—yes—lonely—myself, I search Google for that answer. *Does the murderer miss the victim?* is the query I eventually form.

Among the myriad sites and images that pop up in response to my question (none of which are actual answers to my question), a photograph appears of the rear end of a gray Chevrolet with a bumper sticker that reads, *Someone I Love Was Murdered*.

I contemplate driving around with such a label. Which makes me think of my mother, who has been dead for seven years now. My mother did not sport such a bumper sticker on her car, but she hardly needed to. She was the living embodiment of its sentiment. As loudly as those words on the Chevy shout out the reality for that car's driver, my mother's life screamed the story of what had happened to her friend. And, I would argue, to her. Not in the same way, I am fully cognizant of that fact. But a murder does not have only one victim.

Noelle Huber's murder at age twelve changed the life of Liz Ritenour, her friend. The anxiety she carried affected every decision she made. It made her a fearful, overprotective mother. It caused me to absorb her fears and, perversely, to rebel against them and take wild and stupid risks, feeling great fear as I did. But doing it nonetheless.

It affected the way she handled her old age. Staying in her house in Gibsonia, locking the doors, setting the alarm, asking a male neighbor to record her outgoing answering machine message, for fear that someone might rightly guess she lived alone. Someone like Noelle's killer. The killer who was never found, who was possibly Noelle's brother, who—in the end—outlived even my mother.

To my knowledge, Matthew Huber never contacted my mother. Never called her on the phone. Never Google-stalked her in the way that I have done him. To my knowledge, he did not know my mother existed. And he certainly would have no awareness of me.

I live not far from the Lake Trail, around the corner from Publix. Which is convenient since I shop a lot for food. You might take that to mean I like food. Actually, I kind of hate food and the hold it has on me. Food and I have an exceedingly messed-up relationship.

My apartment is on a narrow street called Oleander Avenue, named after the beautiful—and poisonous—flower. You would think it would be lined with flowering oleanders, but it is not. The vegetation on the road is piecemeal. A straggly palm tree here. An overgrown gardenia bush there. Scrubby grass. Dirt. I don't have a garage but keep my car on the street and my bike in a little, covered lean-to in the backyard. It being Florida, I always need to bring a towel out to wipe the bike for moisture and spiders.

The Lake Trail represents a wonderful bit of civic-mindedness on behalf of the city's planners. It stretches from the end of Worth Avenue, just below the middle bridge, and—with a few breaks along the way—continues all the way north to the top of the island with a promontory overlooking the cut. The cut is where boats, large and small, pass through to the ocean in a roiling current. Mostly pleasure and fishing craft, but we have our fair share of commercial vessels and even a cruise ship or two—those destined for the Bahamas—that make their way through the cut to and from the bigger docks of West Palm Beach.

I walk early. My routine is to go out first with Cordie, at most for a few blocks. Then I bring her home, feed her, and get her settled in the cool of the air conditioning before I take off again.

By the time I go back out on my own it is seven, a time that is still not fully light in Florida. Coming from the north, I am continually surprised by the nearly equal parts of day and night that exist as one approaches the equator. Florida is subtropical—not fully equatorial—so there is still some seasonality to the weather and hours of sunlight. But it is more subtle here than farther north.

I remember past travels—in the days when the world could travel, when I still traveled, when I was not so glued to my house, my chair, my prescribed walking path—when I spent time in the Ivory Coast and Papua New Guinea. In those tropical regions, the sun sets at six p.m. and rises at six a.m. three hundred and sixty-five days a year. Always the same. Always hot. And always with those enormous fruit bats hanging from the trees, biding their time until nightfall.

Why don't we have those bats in Palm Beach?

In the pandemic, bicycles are only allowed on the trail before eight a.m. and after four p.m. The town is trying to reduce human-to-human contact without fully closing the trail. I follow the rules because I don't want access to the trail to be taken away entirely. I also follow the rules because I am a rule follower.

Sometimes, in the late afternoon, I take my bike all the way north. Once I near the yacht club, I am forced to leave the trail since the waterfront there is taken over by boat dockage. Cutting in, I continue up the road instead of the trail, past Angler, Seagate, Dolphin Roads—all Florida-sounding names—and come to my destination.

Reef Road.

The street where Linda lives. The street from which her husband and children have disappeared. The street with the famous beach. The beach where the surfers flock. The beach where Miguel took the children. The beach where Linda goes, day after day, in her pointless pursuit of relief.

If she only asked me, I could tell her there is no relief.

When my mother died, I cried less for who she was than for who she could have been. I ascribed to her the qualities she might have had, had her friend not been murdered that night. Had my mother not bailed on her friend to leave her alone and vulnerable. Had someone—anyone— paid attention to the broken bird she became and done something to help her when she still could have been helped. Had my father not eventually left her. And me.

Spunk is the first of the qualities my mother might have retained. Back when she was little Liz swearing at the dinner table, she had possessed a boldness that Beth, the adult she became, did not. I remember my mother cowering in the house when someone came to the door.

"Go!" she would say. "You answer it. Tell them I'm not at home."

"Mom," I would counter, "this is dumb. I can see from here it's the neighbor. No one's going to hurt you."

I would add that last part to make her feel bad for her phobias. To let her know that I knew she was damaged. To let her know I was embarrassed by her. Because it is true. I did not want to have *that kind* of mother. I did not want to be *that kid*. I did not want to come from the family I did, with some string attaching us all to a dead girl.

But she was, and I was, and I am, tethered to the knife that killed Noelle. And here I am, alone. Always alone. But now, the world joins me.

The days go by, one to the next, with fuzzy divisions between them. It is April 26, the middle of a Sunday in the middle of the quarantine in Palm Beach. We have been home—the collective *we*, not the personal *we*, since my household is me and my dog—for about six weeks now. Of course, how are we to know if this is the middle or just the beginning to this saga? We can safely assume it is not the end, but where exactly we are in the lifespan of this new situation in which we all find ourselves, no one knows. Nor do we know where it will lead us.

Today's forecast is rain. But I need to get out of the house so I'm going to risk it. I let myself out the back door, armed with my supply kit—mask and gloves, tissues and hand sanitizer—and head for my bike. If I'm fast, I can get up to Reef Road and back before the heavens open. The sky is blackening, though it is only two in the afternoon. I wipe off the bike, swing my leg over and go, skipping the Lake Trail in favor of surface streets.

Pedaling up County Road, I glide under the magical canopy of banyans that run for several blocks and sweep in a wide arc over the road, allowing in only the most dappled light. Right now, though, with rain coming, it is as dark as night under the trees. I pass the ornately tiled gateway—all that is left of the old Stotesbury estate—*El Mirasol*—on my right, and the houses of a development called Phipps Estates on the left, which replaced the old Phipps family estate when it was razed and sold off in parcels. Only a private garden and its ghosts remain.

I think about my mother, Liz, who changed her name—at least her nickname—as an adult, to Beth. Both are diminutives of Elizabeth, but, I suspect—in my mother's case—moving from who she was as a girl to who she wanted to be as an adult was the goal. To shake loose a few ghosts of her own. Alas, she did not succeed.

If my mother had wanted to leave her past behind, why did she never leave Pittsburgh? My father was a salesman for a highway equipment company. Surely he could have found a similar position in a new town? Put his foot down and forced his wife to make a fresh start? I often wonder if my mother was more marked by her childhood than any of us. Actually, I don't wonder that at all. I know she was. I think our psychic scars run as deep or as shallow as the precipitating events that cause them. A childhood splinter leaves no trace. A gash made falling off a bicycle down a steep slope in the North Hills of Pittsburgh leaves something more.

McCandless Township, just north of Pittsburgh, is where I fell hard from a bicycle while visiting my cousins. It is where the Iroquois Nation once lived. It is where George Washington once visited, accompanied by his guide, Christopher Gist. While the Iroquois left a few artifacts and George Washington left a history, I left no mark on McCandless, despite the mark my fall left on me.

I am a stranger here, too, though I have lived in Palm Beach for fifteen years. I am not social. I do not attend the galas or luncheons I read about each morning in *The Shiny Sheet*. I have never been on a committee or been asked to donate a weekend at my country house for an auction. I don't buy ball gowns, high heels, or *minaudières*, though I do like that word. *Minaudière*: a small, hard-cased clutch purse that typically features decorative embellishments.

I have no need of those things. I am not part of anything. I am an outsider. I am, in fact, a *minaudière*, encased in my own hard shell.

But who, really, isn't? What mark do most of us leave? Noelle left her headstone, two pretty pictures, and a trail of grisly newspaper articles about her demise. She left her killer, too, but he will leave no visible trace because his identity will never be known.

But, ah, those invisible traces.

My mother outlived her friend by decades, but what did she leave behind? Me, a childless writer. A troubled, childless writer, I might add. I will leave my books, that much is certain, but will anyone read them? Will they disappear from library shelves in coming years, to be replaced by whatever it is that will evolve in their stead? Will there even be library shelves? Libraries?

I mentioned the fact that Noelle's case was reopened in recent years. How, you might wonder, do I know that? I, who am not a member of the Huber family? I, who am tangential to every story I tell? It turns out that it helps to be a writer.

In researching one of my books—my tenth—which dealt with an unsolved murder (do they all?), I spoke with Seamus O'Haney of the New York Prosecutors Training Institute. In my initial letter to him requesting an interview, I mentioned the murder of my mother's friend and the effect it had on her—and me—ever since. I quoted A. O. Scott's review of the film *Mystic River* from the *New York Times* on October 3, 2003:

> *At its starkest, the film, like the novel by Dennis Lehane on which it is based, is a parable of incurable trauma, in which violence begets more violence and the primal violation of innocence can never be set right.*

"And that's it, isn't it?" I said to him later, when we were face to face. "Violence begets more violence, and the primal violation of innocence can never be set right."

"It was the brother," he said.

I stared at him for a beat. "How do you know?"

"When you stab someone thirty-six times, it's personal."

Noelle's story had aroused something in Seamus O'Haney, enough to make him reach out to the Pittsburgh Police Department. His call jogged some collective memory there and sent them to the old reports. On top of the reams of material about his multiple arrests for the murder of his sister, things we all know by now, a new fact emerged. New to me, at least. Matt Huber was a flasher. He had a documented history of arrests for exposing himself to women.

This information raised everyone's eyebrows. In fact, it got the detectives so interested they sent some rookies downstairs to the property room to look for evidence. When they found a box of clothing stored away from the night of Noelle's murder, their interest reached a crescendo.

Seamus was pretty excited at this point as well. It was quite an opportunity for law enforcement. If they could get some genetic identification from this material, it would result in a sixty-year-old DNA conviction. Pretty heady stuff for a bunch of cops and a prosecutor. Convictions are what they live for. Convictions offer conclusions. Convictions allow people like my mother to sleep at night. People like me, too.

And so the case was reopened. The fabric was delivered to the FBI laboratories in Quantico, Virginia. Matthew Huber—by then an old man—was given a polygraph test—and Matthew Huber failed it. He was brought in several times for questioning.

In one session, Huber's wife, who had accompanied him, broke down and screamed, "You didn't do this, did you? Tell me you didn't do this!"

Judging from her reaction, the cops were beside themselves with certainty that he did, in fact, do this. What wife says something like that if she knows in her bones that her husband could not have done it? That is what Seamus said to me, anyway, when he gave me a progress report.

In the end, though, the fabric turned out to be irretrievably degraded. There was no DNA to be found on it. The case was dropped again, after Matthew Huber was brought in for this fifth (and presumably final) round of questioning in the death of his sister. Did he do it? I don't think we will ever know. I know what I think, but would I ruin someone's life for it? His wife's? His children's? His grandchildren's?

I see that I have arrived at Reef Road. The sky looks ominous. I continue a bit farther north, battling rising winds, to the entrance to the beach and struggle to stow my bike in the bushes. Will I wait out the coming storm here? Huddled like a stray cat as the grasses whip my face? I don't know if I have much alternative now. There is nowhere else I can make it before the deluge.

For a moment I allow myself to consider the epic finality of being struck by lightning on a day like this at a time like this in a world like this. It would be a climactic sendoff, worthy of one of my novels. Or maybe it would just be overwrought. And I feel I am not quite finished yet. Although, at that thought, I do realize that little Noelle Huber might not have felt she was finished either. No one actually asked her. But Cordelia is home alone. Who would know to check on her if something happened to me? No one is who. And what would become of her? Nothing good. So, not today, I say. As if anyone is asking me.

If—when—the rain comes, I will get through it. I've gotten through worse before. Instead of focusing on the prospect of getting wet, I decide to think of Linda.

20

THE WIFE

Chapter Eleven
Sunday, April 26, 2020

Linda sat on the sand at Reef Road beach, looking up at the blackening skies and trying to root herself into the earth. Which was not working. It was about to rain, and rain hard from the looks of it. Still, she could not muster the energy to get up. She had drifted here, clutching Espie's monkey and Gogo's blankie to her chest.

On Monday, April 20, the day after Linda called the police, those same cops found Linda's car in the long-term lot at Miami International and impounded it. Records of tickets on Delta Airlines had been located by one or the other of them, confirming that three Alonsos—Miguel, Diego, and Esperanza—had flown to Buenos Aires from Miami on the evening of Saturday, April 18. One week and one day ago. The night Linda Alonso was wandering around the house and sleeping, her children had left this country for a country where she could not pursue them due to pandemic lockdowns. Which rendered her utterly powerless.

They would have had to quarantine—they would be quarantining still—but that would pose no problem. They would all be at the gracious

Alonso apartment on Posadas Street in the Recoleta district—a beautiful old, practically Parisian neighborhood—poignantly named after the Convent of Recollection. Linda always loved that detail. Eva Perón was buried in a cemetery nearby.

Naturally, Linda had her mother-in-law's phone number. She had been dialing it for days, but no one picked up. Which was surprising. Esperanza Alonso employed a married couple who lived in. They had worked for her for years. Especially now that her cancer had advanced to the point where it was surely the end (although they had wrongly predicted her death more than once), Mimi and Hector would be there with her.

In spite of COVID-19, Linda was certain they would have stayed on in the Alonso apartment. She knew they had family in the country— in Viedma, Patagonia, where the Alonsos had a ranch—but Hector and Mimi would not have left their mistress alone right when the going got rough. That was not how it was done in old-fashioned Argentine culture. The lady of the house and her lifelong servants had a bond that was familial. So it did not make sense that the phone rang and rang.

Maybe her mother-in-law had asked them not to answer. Maybe the family was stalling for time before they…before they what? What would be their next move? They held all the cards. They had the children. There *were* no other cards. What leverage did Linda have at all? Local police would not be much help in this cross-border domestic squabble.

In idle moments—all moments were idle now—Linda went down the internet rabbit hole of international child abduction.

The Hague Convention had a multinational treaty to address this very issue. In any country that was a signatory—and most civilized countries were—there were protocols to "provide a uniform means of safely securing the return of children wrongfully retained by a parent in a country different than the habitual residence of the children, and to leave all custody determinations to the country that is the habitual residence of the children."

The worry about Argentina, it seemed, was that they were extraordinarily slow in processing these claims. Years could go by—and often did—while the stateside parent petitioned for the return of the children and Argentina, willfully or not, dragged its feet.

Linda felt a shuddering touch and looked up, half-expecting to see her children standing next to her. Around her, the grasses switched back and forth in the mounting winds, flicking against her like a horse's tail. Above, the sky dropped down with fast-moving dark clouds that seemed to crash into the surf, which was hurtling itself upward to meet them. A storm was imminent now.

She squinted to see better and realized someone was out there, riding the wild waves. A man in a wetsuit was actually surfing. As the air grew heavier with gusts from all directions, Linda was riveted to see what the man might do. Indeed, if he would survive. He crested one last wave then hauled his board up the beach, leaning hard into the wind and nearly falling when it changed direction. It was when he was practically upon her that she was able to see his face. He was unmasked, as was she, both having believed themselves to be alone.

Her heart stopped. It was the man from the airport. The father from her children's school.

"Hello," he suddenly said, startling Linda out of her trance. She realized she had never heard his voice, which was pleasantly low.

"Hi." Linda scrambled to her feet.

"The weather's really coming in," he said.

"It is."

"Michael Collins," he offered his name, but, in the time of COVID, not his hand for shaking. "Like the Irish freedom fighter?"

"Linda Alonso," she said. "Don't your children go to Flagler Montessori? In West Palm?"

"They do," he said, furrowing his brows. "Yours?"

"Yes." She waited to see if he would show any signs of recognition, either from school drop-offs, school parties, or the half dozen near-encounters they'd had at the airport last year.

Michael Collins studied her intently without revealing whether he remembered her.

Linda looked just as closely at him. He was a large man, handsome in an ex-athlete kind of way. He was obviously Irish from the name—and had the green eyes to prove it. She thought of Liam Neeson playing Michael Collins in the movie. This guy clearly didn't think she knew who Michael Collins was.

"You know this beach is closed," she said.

"Yeah, well, I'm a cop, so…" he laughed a little, which softened him.

"Am I going to be arrested?" She surprised herself with her easy banter, given her current situation.

"Well, that all depends. I'm in the homicide division, so, unless you killed someone…?" He laughed again. "Can I give you a ride?"

"Um, sure. It's not far." Linda accompanied him to his car, which turned out to be an old, tan Jeep Wagoneer with the fake wood sides.

"Nice," she said, pointing to it.

"Yeah, I let my surfer side win over my cop side for this one."

"Right," she said. "Not very cop-like."

"Wanna get in the back seat?" he asked. "Keep more distance between us? I'll put on my mask."

"Okay," she said and opened the rear passenger door while he stripped off his wetsuit and attached his surfboard to the top of his Jeep. Inside, she could see he had the requisite amount of children's junk strewn everywhere: balls of all kinds (golf, tennis, soccer), smashed goldfish crackers, racquets, dog-eared books, spent water bottles. And, stealing a glance back at him, she could see he had the requisite amount of buffness for a surfer/cop.

He pulled a white T-shirt over his head and slipped a mask on his face before he got into the car and slammed the door behind him. Linda donned her mask, too.

"You have two boys, right?" she asked as he started the engine. "I remember them. Freckled? Like their mom? Turn here."

"That's right," he said, turning onto Reef Road. "You know my wife, Maeve? They're all up in Chicago now. They were there with my dad when this all hit and then…we thought it was best to stay put."

"Good idea."

"What do you have?"

"A boy and a girl. They're in Argentina. With their dad."

"Sounds like we're in the same boat."

"Kind of. This is me. Right there on the right."

He spun into her driveway. "Nice house."

"Thanks." Linda sat still, unsure if it was okay to get out. He was a cop, after all. She felt like she needed his permission.

"I guess none of us knows when our families will return," he suddenly said.

"No."

"Plus, my dad. He may not make it," he said. "Maeve is really good with him. I think he secretly likes her better than me."

"I'm sorry."

"Yeah. Well, here we are," he said, telegraphing her dismissal.

"Thanks for the ride." She opened the door. "I appreciate it."

Linda stepped out of the Jeep at the exact moment the heavens broke, soaking her to the skin in an instant. She ran up the driveway, stumbling once from the wind, and punched in the garage door code. She ducked down to squeeze under the rising door before it was fully open. Once inside, she turned around to look at Michael Collins. She could barely make out his face through the driving rain, but she could see him lift one hand in farewell. She raised a hand in return, then pressed the garage door button to close it, waiting in her cold, wet clothes and soggy face mask until the door dropped down completely. Only then did she turn to run inside.

She realized, as she did so, that she hadn't mentioned their encounters at the airport. Well, she wouldn't be seeing him again anytime soon.

21

THE WIFE

Chapter Twelve
Wednesday, April 29, 2020

The days of solitude steamrolled over Linda. She felt increasingly beset by a crawling sensation deep under layers of skin. She tried to ignore it, but it moved around. To an arm or the back of a calf, the bottom of a foot that made her tear off a shoe and scratch until her skin was raw.

They'd been paying Manuela to stay home because of COVID. Little by little, Linda's unclean house became the focus of her thoughts. Her family had been gone eight days now. Her only companions were the microscopic insects ever present in her rugs and bedding.

Linda dragged herself up to wage war.

Armed with a battery of products, including Fabulosa—the cleanser Miguel abhorred—she was struck with the realization that Manuela did not yet know that Linda's family was gone. That Linda was alone in the house. The last time Manuela had been there, everything had been normal. How and when would she tell her what havoc the pandemic had wrought in their household?

Linda bent with more vigor to her scrubbing.

Cleaning normally made her feel better, although the odds of that happening now were slim. Still, no one cleaned the way Linda's mother had taught her. Certainly not Manuela. Every Saturday morning of Linda's childhood after the age of ten, she and her mother had cleaned the house.

It was not a big house, but it still took a chunk of her time to clean it. And the loss of her freedom on Saturday mornings was keenly felt. While her friends were riding bikes to the park, Linda was dusting and vacuuming and washing the louvered blinds with a Murphy's Oil Soap-soaked rag wrapped around the head of a spatula. She would never forget that back-forth motion of soaping each slat of wood, making sure to go up and down vigorously at either end. This week, she would bring the house on Reef Road to her mother's level of sterility.

Did she mean to use that word? Sterile as in clean or sterile as in unable to bear children? That thought ricocheted her mind back to her newly childless state, and she had to sit on the floor for a moment to combat the nausea that overtook her. Surely, she was living a dream. Surely, the events of the recent past—death-delivering microbes, family dispersal, global shutdown—were just chapters in a nightmarish book she had somehow picked up in the dead of sleep. But she knew this was not true. Her children were thousands of miles away in another country. A country *she* was unable to visit until some aspect of this pandemic shifted gears, the possibility of which seemed increasingly remote.

Señora Alonso was dying, though she had appeared to be at the point of death more than once. But she could not live forever. And the Alonso estate was not insubstantial. The sole remaining son stood to inherit a great deal. The family had had factories in the south before the Peróns nationalized industry and incurred the loathing of the upper classes. But the Alonsos cozied up to subsequent governments, particularly the military leadership that overthrew Isabel Perón in 1976. The year Diego was born, and two years before Miguel's arrival.

Linda never could tell if Miguel's mother liked her or not. Linda had married her favorite son. Señora Alonso was unfailingly polite, but there was a chill to her kindnesses. A repetitive motion kind of feeling that those kindnesses did not emanate from any real affection for Linda but only from an overdeveloped sense of etiquette.

Señora Alonso had asked Linda to call her Mother—even Mama—in the early years. But the words lodged in Linda's throat. Miguel's mother was a very formal woman, the opposite of Linda's. Linda's mother's way of dressing up was to wear dressy pants and a sweater. Señora Alonso's way was to wear a Chanel suit. And she had a closet full of them. Even at her sickest, she would put together a wool skirt and silk blouse with a pair of flats as her only concession to the backache caused by chemo. Only once did Linda see her mother-in-law unable to get out of bed. And then, her maid, Mimi, had helped her into a quilted silk bed jacket over a Porthault nightgown and tied an Hermès scarf over her head.

Linda could sometimes use the word, mother, when she spoke to Señora Alonso, but she always said it in English. And she added the last name. Mother Alonso, she called her, like Miguel's mother was an abbess. Linda's inability to use terms of endearment with his mother had not escaped the notice—or disapproval—of Miguel.

Linda began the cleaning project on Monday. By Wednesday, she was in it so deeply she was barely aware of the itch that had prompted it to begin with. She had tackled the task with more fervor than she'd felt for anything lately. She worked in a methodical fashion. First, she did the living room, bedrooms, and Miguel's office. Top to bottom she cleaned, even washing the insides of windows with white cider vinegar, just like the mirrors. She dusted and polished. She laundered and ironed sheets. She vacuumed. Then she attacked the rooms that really required elbow grease: the bathrooms and the kitchen. These she wiped down with rags and brushes, scrubbing floors on her hands and knees.

After two days of heavy work, she was ready for the garage, the last of the interior spaces. She pictured her house as a snake shedding skin. What would be left of the Alonso household after Linda was finished with it would be the same, but not the same. The dust, debris—even the skin cells that dropped from their bodies—would be gone. It felt like a sacrament of purification and she was illogically hoping it would yield some sort of transformation of her circumstances. Like she was feeding the hygiene gods and they, in turn, would spit up her children.

Linda put Miguel's car out in the driveway. Hers was still at the police lot while they continued their investigation. She left the big door open to air out the fumes while she washed the walls with bleach and the windows with vinegar. She threw a bucket of sudsy water onto the floor and was kneeling to go at it with her scrub brush. Just as she started in on the corner, she heard a voice behind her.

"Wow," the voice said, followed by a low whistle. "You're some cleaner. You remind me of my mother."

Linda looked up to see Michael Collins standing in the doorway of her garage, his mask dangling from one ear. The sun was behind him so it was hard to see his face, but she could tell he was wearing a suit and not his surfing clothes.

"Hi," she said, rising up from the floor. "Are you, um, can I…?"

"I'm just on my way to the office and I thought I'd stop by and see how you're doing."

"Really?" Linda was conscious of her present sweaty state. She could feel the knees of her jeans, wet and stuck to her skin. Her hair was halfway out of her ponytail and pasted all over her face. She gave it a swipe with her forearm and asked, "Would you like some coffee?"

"Nah," he answered. "I don't want to bother you. Just checking in. Any word on your family?"

Linda tilted her head. No news had broken about her family situation.

"The precinct is small," he said. "I heard what happened."

"Oh." She wondered if that was ethical. Were cops allowed to discuss their cases with other cops? Did they have confidentiality rules, like doctors? "Well, no. I haven't heard. I mean, they found his car at the airport. My car, I mean. They found a record of the airline tickets."

"Yeah, I heard that. Anyway, that's why I stopped."

"What about your family?" she asked sharply. She did not enjoy feeling like a charity case: the woman who'd misplaced her children.

"Still north," he answered. "No one is really traveling yet. I wouldn't want them on an airplane."

"Gotcha. Keep 'em safe," she snapped. Regretting her tartness, she added, "Please come in for a cup of coffee. It would be nice to have someone to talk to."

Michael Collins looked at his watch, then his car, then at her. "Sure. I have time for coffee."

And like a good working-class kid—like Linda—he hesitated before walking over a freshly scrubbed floor. "May I?" he asked, pointing down, before stepping into the garage and putting on his mask.

Linda couldn't help but laugh. It was what her mother always taught her to do and clearly this Michael Collins had a similar sort of mother.

"Come on in," she said. "I haven't actually washed this floor yet."

22

A WRITER'S THOUGHTS

When Noelle Huber's father slashed his face with a pair of scissors, it was December of 1951, three years after his daughter's death. Newspapers of the day reported that the Huber patriarch had performed his act of self-mutilation in despair over the continued arrests of his son for the murder of his daughter. They also reported that detectives tried to gain access to Huber while he was hospitalized under the care of a psychiatrist. His attending doctor was said to have denied access to the patient, citing his mental condition. "He is a very sick man," was his precise wording. Supporting that claim, Huber was reported to have been "tied to the bed" for the duration of his stay. Who leaked these salacious details was not mentioned.

That was then.

Here, now, in Palm Beach, in this time of worldwide confinement, I think about Mr. Huber in his hospital room. And I can't help wondering what he knew; what drove him to take scissors to his own face. There is no way around it—it was an act of extraordinary violence. Not your usual suicide by pills. I also wonder if he was actually trying to kill himself or to do something even worse, something that would cause him to visibly suffer for the rest of his life, to give himself a set of exterior scars that were as ugly as those inside.

Here is what else I wonder: Was it, in fact, a Shakespearean tragedy of family dynamics of incest and murder and denial that drove the father to rend his own flesh with the shears? Was it the brother who killed the sister? Was it the parents who cleaned up? Were Mr. and Mrs. Huber acting on a primal instinct to protect the living child since it was too late to save the dead one?

I wonder, too, how much the doctor knew. After taking scissors to his own flesh, did Matthew Huber, Sr., unburden his soul to his psychiatrist? More cynically, I wonder if Mr. Huber was aware of the fact that the doctor was obliged to keep the secrets of his patient.

According to encyclopedia.com:

The concept of 'doctor-patient confidentiality' derives from English common law and is codified in many states' statutes. It is based on ethics, not law, and goes at least as far back as the Roman Hippocratic Oath taken by physicians. It is different from 'doctor-patient privilege,' which is a legal concept. Both, however, are called upon in legal matters to establish the extent by which ethical duties of confidentiality apply to legal privilege. Legal privilege involves the right to withhold evidence from discovery and/or the right to refrain from disclosing or divulging information gained within the context of a 'special relationship.' Special relationships include those between doctors and patients, attorneys and clients, priests and confessors or confiders, guardians and their wards, etc.

The Oath of Hippocrates, traditionally sworn to by newly licensed physicians, includes the promise that 'Whatever, in connection with my professional service, or not in connection with it, I see or hear, in the life of men, which ought not to be spoken of abroad, I will not divulge, as reckoning that all such should be kept secret.'

It is a beautiful thing, this oath. It makes a person feel safe in the care of a doctor. It enables a person to say things that a person might otherwise withhold.

23

THE WIFE

Chapter Thirteen
Wednesday, April 29, 2020

Linda held the garage door to the kitchen for Michael Collins. After he'd made the reference to the Irish revolutionary, she could not decouple his first name from his last. She waited for a moment, pushing the door wide, then realized he would not be able to pass by her without coming into much closer contact than the suggested six feet. He would, more likely, brush by her body with his own. This reminded her that she probably smelled from days of heavy housework.

She jerked away from him. "I'll run and get my mask. Just come in."

"Sure," he answered.

Rather than grab the squashed mask she already had in her pocket, she went into her bathroom and stole a look in the mirror. As she furiously ran a brush through her filthy hair, she considered Michael Collins's behavior. Like at the airport last year. Did he really not recognize her then? It was more than believable, judging from the wreck she was now. But normally she garnered quite a few looks from the men she passed in public. Men saw her; they didn't ignore her. She was *visible*. She grabbed a lipstick, then paused. She was covering her face anyhow. It was ridiculous to make such an effort at being presentable. She tossed the lipstick into the drawer.

Back down the hall she went, a clean mask firmly in place, slowing her breath so that the mask did not move in and out from her mouth like a bellows.

"Hi," she said as she reentered the kitchen to find him standing near the doors to Miguel's office. Out of habit, Linda kept those doors closed. Michael Collins appeared to be examining them.

She busied herself making coffee with the Nespresso machine. "Do you like espresso or cappuccino? Miguel—my husband—he likes cappuccino, so I'm pretty good at making it. Actually, it kind of makes itself."

"Espresso for me. I hate milk. Sugar, though, that's another story." His voice, like everyone's voice in a mask, had a muffled quality. But his eyes were crinkled from smiling.

"How many?" she asked as she held the tongs over the sugar bowl.

"Three," he laughed. "I hang around too many Cubans at work. I cut back, though. Used to take four."

"Wow!" Linda laughed as she dropped the cubes into his coffee, stirred it, and handed him the cup. "Should we go outside? I mean, so you can take your mask off and drink it."

"Sounds good."

For the second time, Linda started to hold the door for him, then made the same readjustment to put some space between them. She crossed the patio to put up the table umbrella for shade.

"Here, let me do it," he offered, setting his cup on the table. The coffee sloshed in little bursts each time he turned the crank on the mechanism.

"I'll hold that," she said and picked up the cup. She handed it back when he finished, then moved to the far side of the table. "I'll sit over here. Then we don't need the masks."

"So," he said when his face was fully visible, "how are you?"

"If I'm not mistaken," she said as she took off her own mask; now she regretted skipping the lipstick, "you've asked me that already."

"Well, under the circumstances…" He waved his hand in a self-explanatory gesture.

"My kids are gone. I can't even reach them on the phone. I haven't talked to them in eight days." Linda got up to grab something skittering across the grass. She held it up and squinted at it. It was an empty packet of Cheddar Bunnies, Espie's favorite snack.

"They're only three and five," she continued, shoving the wrapper in her pocket. "And, the worst of it is, they don't have their special things. A monkey. A blanket. Well, a piece of a blanket. So," she now waved her hand in the same self-explanatory motion, "under the circumstances, I'm pretty crappy."

"Has your husband ever done anything like this before? Anything to make you think he might be capable of it?"

"No. Well…no."

"Anything going on in your marriage? His work? Your finances?"

"We've been married for a while. We have two kids. The usual stress."

"The officers who took your statement the other day said your husband had borrowed a large sum of money recently?"

"Is this an official police visit, Mr. Collins?" Linda asked.

"Michael, please. I thought I might be of help," he answered. Then he added, "Mrs. Alonso."

Linda narrowed her eyes. "You can call me Linda. And yes. He borrowed…well, he was approved for a home equity loan for two million dollars. I don't know if he actually got the money."

"Have you tried calling the mortgage company?" he asked.

"No one is answering the phone. I'm guessing with this shutdown they're working remotely."

"The timing of all of this is pretty convenient." Michael picked up his espresso and sipped it. "So many threads that are difficult to trace right now."

"That must be cold," Linda said. "I can heat it up."

"Nah, I never drink it too hot anyway. Not down here in the heat," he said. "It's funny, though. I mean, his timing was pretty amazing."

"Maybe he was planning it."

"The pandemic?"

"Taking the kids."

He twirled his face mask around his left ear. "He flew out of Miami?"

"It's the only way you can go from here. I mean, it's the logical way."

"And *were* things good, Linda?"

Linda looked at him, sitting on her terrace, drinking coffee, and conducting some kind of police questioning. "No, Michael," she finally said. "Things were not good."

24

A WRITER'S THOUGHTS

Mysteries move in many directions, some of them blind alleys. In fiction—both written and projected onto the screen—some of these blind alleys are called MacGuffins. According to Wikipedia, "a MacGuffin is an object, device, or event that is necessary to the plot and the motivation of the characters, but insignificant, unimportant, or irrelevant in itself. The term was originated by Angus MacPhail for film, adopted by Alfred Hitchcock, and later extended to a similar device in other fiction."

Hitchcock, at a lecture at Columbia University in 1939, explained a MacGuffin as follows: "It might be a Scottish name, taken from a story about two men on a train. One man says, 'What's that package up there in the baggage rack?' And the other answers, 'Oh, that's a MacGuffin.' The first one asks, 'What's a MacGuffin?' 'Well,' the other man says, 'it's an apparatus for trapping lions in the Scottish Highlands.' The first man says, 'But there are no lions in the Scottish Highlands,' and the other one answers, 'Well then, that's no MacGuffin!' So you see that a MacGuffin is actually nothing at all."

A MacGuffin is not to be confused with a red herring, which leads us in the wrong direction. A red herring is equally engaging but takes us where we are not actually aiming to go and sets us up to form a false conclusion. An example might be a pair of ladies' stockings found in a bedroom by a wife after her husband has been home alone. She may conclude that her husband has had an affair with another woman. The truth may be something entirely different, such as her husband might like to wear ladies' stockings himself. And—if it is a red herring—the ladies' stockings may draw attention away from the husband who is hiding in the closet with a gun, ready to shoot his wife.

The question is, how do you know which it is?

On February 20, 1953, more than four years after the crime, there was a newspaper story about a renewed investigation into the mystery surrounding a cap found in a barrel in the backyard of the Huber home in the early weeks after the murder that had subsequently been lost. Several other pieces of evidence had gone missing as well.

The cap was originally discovered by Randolf "The Rabbit" Anderson (the self-styled detective who had arrested young Matt) on the day the Huber parents were moving home after vacating the house postmurder. For reasons unknown, the actual Pittsburgh Police Force had not discovered this item in the Hubers' backyard.

This cap was the type used by truck drivers at the time and bore a metal license, issued in 1947 by the state of Illinois. A search with the Illinois Secretary of State traced it to a driver from Peoria. Pittsburgh homicide detectives worked closely with Chicago police and the owner of the cap was tracked down. But his claim of never having been to Pittsburgh checked out.

The story of the cap came up again at this later moment when the new superintendent of police, Mark W. Jones, ordered a fresh "top-to-bottom" investigation. This time, both of the senior Hubers and Matt, Jr., were asked to take lie-detector tests. Apparently, in the past, at the suggestion of some of the citizen detectives, Mr. Huber, Sr., had agreed to the test. But then he suffered his nervous breakdown and his attorney advised against it.

Later that spring, on March 5, 1953, Mabel Jefferson popped up in the news. Five years before, the year Noelle was killed, she had been in eighth grade at Baxter Junior High, one year ahead of my mother and Noelle. Mabel, who was Black, was involved in a "slay for pay" plot in which a white man masterminded a scheme to rid himself of his nagging wife by hiring a group of Black killers. Mabel, smeared in the papers as a "reefer smoker," was called their "dope-using contact girl." Her parents simply called her incorrigible. The thing that tied Mabel to Noelle was Mabel's claim, in this news flurry, that she had walked home from school with Noelle on her last day alive.

The stories of Mabel and the cap luridly emblazoned headlines in the late winter/early spring of 1953. Were they MacGuffins? Red herrings? Neither clue led anywhere. As far as I can tell, neither the cap nor the girl was germane to the story of the killing.

In life, many stories are not tidy. Clues don't often mean anything. Murders aren't always solved.

25

THE WIFE

Chapter Fourteen
Wednesday, April 29, 2020

"You look like you want me to go." Michael set down his espresso cup on the patio table. "And I need to get to work."

Linda laughed. "Is it that obvious? It's just that, once I start cleaning, I'm kind of hell-bent on finishing."

"Got it," he said, rising. "Anything you need me to lift or move? My mother always had me picking up couches and tables for her."

"No. I mean, no…"

"C'mon. I'm really good at it."

"Okay, well…if you insist. Back in the spare bedroom, there's a big dresser I can't really get the vacuum under."

"Allow me to be of service," he said as he placed his mask on his face.

"That's very kind." Linda put on her own mask and led him into the house. In through the living room—where she paused to pick up the vacuum—down the hall, and into the guest bedroom.

"Nice," he said when they entered the room, all done up in shades of green. Such pale sea greens that it was like being submerged in the ocean. "Get many overnight guests?"

"I'm sorry?"

"Friends and family? Do many people stay in this room?"

"Not really, no," Linda said as she busied herself plugging in the vacuum. That task required pulling out the little plastic outlet protector, one of the many she had placed in electrical sockets around the house when her children were smaller. She'd never gotten around to taking them out. Espie, at only three, probably still couldn't be trusted not to stick something into one. At the thought of Espie, Linda's throat filled with bile and she dug her fingernails into the edge of the plastic cover that seemed to be glued in place.

"Here, let me," Michael leaned over her in a way that—if she were to be a stickler—she would say was not socially distant at all.

"I'm fine," she said, tasting the sourness rising up from her stomach and wishing this guy would keep his distance for any number of reasons. Not the least of which was that she was right now practically puking. "I can do it."

She dug harder until she drew blood. "Shit," she said as she stuck her finger under her mask and into her mouth, retreating from the outlet in defeat.

Michael easily pulled the cover off the outlet right next to the one she'd been battling.

Linda pointed to the dresser. "Could you?"

"Certainly." He picked up one end, then the other, and shimmied it away from the wall.

Linda switched on the vacuum and ran it back and forth over the carpeting where the dresser normally sat. The distinct sound of an object getting sucked up the hose came out of the machine. "Ugh!" she said as she switched it off.

"I'm really good at that," he offered.

"Don't tell me. You used to do it for your mom?"

"That's right," he said, laughing.

Linda moved out of the way so Michael could kneel down on the rug and get whatever it was that was in her vacuum hose out of it. Which he did in short order. He *was* good at it.

He stood up and reached out to Linda in a way that made her think he was about to grab her face and kiss her, through his mask and hers, too. She felt both appalled and thrilled. Then, just as fast, he withdrew his hand from her ear.

"Look!" he said, like a hired magician at a children's party. "A quarter behind your ear! Heads or tails?"

But Linda could see that it was not a quarter faster than Michael Collins could see the same thing. She was speechless as she watched the coin circling over itself as it rose in the air in perfectly executed arcs, like those of a flying ace.

"Okay, if you're not going to pick," he said, still laughing. "I'll take tails."

He caught the coin in his right hand. He flipped it onto the back of his left and covered it with a little slap. "Ready?"

She looked into his green eyes, over the blue of his paper mask, and found herself thinking how well he matched this room.

He lifted his hand off the coin. He paused. He leaned in closer to get a better look. He picked it up and turned it over. He stared at it and turned it again. "What is it?"

"Um, let me see." Linda took it from him and walked over to the window.

The center of the coin was gold, with a surrounding rim of silver. One side read, *Estado Plurinacional de Bolivia*. On the other side, it read, *La Union es la Fuerza*, across the top. In the middle it said *5 Bolivanos*. And at the bottom it held a date. Specifically, a year. It was possible, she thought—in fact it was likely—that Michael Collins had not seen the year. Linda looked at the coin for a very long time. She did not look at Michael Collins.

"Take any trips to Bolivia lately?" he asked.

Linda made a split-second decision. She set the coin on the windowsill and pulled the mask off her face. She took six short steps to where Michael was standing. She reached up with both hands to gently remove his mask from the loops over each of his ears.

She dropped both masks to the floor and held his face in her hands. His cheeks were rough to the touch, like he hadn't shaved in a while. She looked straight into his eyes, but she was not asking his permission to do what she was going to do next. Her look to him was, in fact, the opposite. She was letting him know that she was taking charge of this situation. That they were moving beyond COVID and coins and spouses and children who happened to be out of town, for good reasons or for bad.

She had to stand on her toes to kiss him and that is exactly what she did. And the moment her lips touched his, the moment she slipped her tongue into his mouth that still tasted of sugared coffee, Michael was released from his motionlessness and kissed her back.

They ripped at each other's clothes and at their own as they fell onto the floor, eschewing the nicely made bed in the pretty, sea green room. They rolled and they clawed and they kissed and they fucked and—when it was over—Michael fell asleep.

Linda waited to hear where his breathing would go. Would he snore? Or just breathe deeply and rhythmically like her husband?

When it turned out he was gently snoring, she got up as silently as she could, crossed over to the windowsill, picked up the Bolivian coin, and quickly took it out of the room.

26

A WRITER'S THOUGHTS

For decades, Dominick Dunne was the de facto mouthpiece for those of us who have survived the murder of a loved one and subsequently turned the idea of murder into something of a life mission. Those of us whom the podcast, *My Favorite Murder*, has so aptly dubbed, *Murderinos*. Those of us who have made murder—not the committing of it but the endless nitpicking over it—our *raison d'être*.

In the early 1980s, Dunne's daughter, Dominique, was a young actress in Hollywood. She'd had a prominent role in *Poltergeist*, a film written by none other than Steven Spielberg, and her future looked bright. Until, that is, John Thomas Sweeney, her obsessive ex-boyfriend, killed her outside her West Hollywood apartment on the night of October 30, 1982. More precisely, he strangled her that night. Dominique did not actually die until five days later when her family took her off life support at Cedars-Sinai Medical Center.

The ensuing trial of Sweeney, a well-known Los Angeles chef, was nearly as disturbing as the murder. The judge granted Sweeney enormous benefit of the doubt. So much testimony regarding his past violence was kept from the jury that, in the end, he was only convicted of voluntary manslaughter and misdemeanor assault. After serving a short sentence of three years, he resumed his restaurant career having hardly missed a beat.

Appalled by the meager consequences Sweeney was dealt for killing Dominique, the Dunne family could not resist making mischief for him. They handed out fliers outside of Sweeney's first restaurant post-prison that read: "The food you will eat tonight was made by the hands that killed Dominique Dunne." Dunne continued to stalk Sweeney wherever he tried to relocate himself until Sweeney changed his name and disappeared.

Dunne, in the six-degrees-of-separation game, was considerably closer in relationship to his daughter, Dominique, than I am to Noelle Huber. But Dunne's vocation (and avocation, I might add) are illustrative of what becomes of any of us who are tangential to extreme acts of violence. We end up fixating on it. Or, if not exactly fixating, we end up with a heightened awareness of the violent proclivities of our fellow humans.

Digging in the Dunne archives on the internet, I discover a murder that occurred—at least the lead-up to it occurred—several blocks from my apartment. *Power, Privilege, and Justice* was a television show hosted by Dunne in the early 2000s, each episode devoted to a specific crime in a specific region. *There's a darker side to the lifestyles of the rich and famous, and writer Dominick Dunne explores real-life cases in which high-profile personalities discover they can't buy their way out of trouble* was its tagline.

This particular murder took place on January 16, 1987, in Atlanta, when Lita McClinton Sullivan, a beautiful and soon-to-be-divorced Black woman, opened her door to a flower delivery and met, instead, death by gunshot. It happened to be the very day when Mrs. Sullivan's divorce would be finalized. It also happened that shortly after her murder, a collect call was placed from a pay phone in the Atlanta area to the home of her almost-ex, James Vincent Sullivan, a white man, who resided in the famous "ham-and-cheese house" in Palm Beach.

"Ham-and-cheese" is not the actual name of the house—an enormous 1928 Maurice Fatio-designed mansion overlooking the Atlantic Ocean in the estate section of town. Its name has changed over the years to reflect its changing ownership, but the "ham-and-cheese house" is its affectionate local moniker because of its façade of alternating horizontal stripes of red brick and white coral keystone.

James Vincent Sullivan, working-class-born, lived in this house with Lita, his elegant and patrician wife. James had grown up in Boston and was smart enough to attend Boston Latin, a rigorous public school. Lita had grown up in the Black establishment of Atlanta. James worked for his uncle in a liquor distribution business in Macon, Georgia, and was lucky enough to inherit that business when his uncle died, making him an instant millionaire. He was subsequently lucky enough to land himself a well-educated and well-bred wife.

From the start, Lita's family did not like James. But for whatever reason—who can say why someone succumbs to a con artist?—Lita fell in love with him. Trouble began immediately. For one thing, James was a notorious skinflint. People said they were surprised to shake Lita's small and elegant hand to find her skin unexpectedly rough. They suspected James was too cheap to hire help and made Lita clean the house herself. It is hard to know if this was true or if embellishments were added after the fact.

James worked heartily to thrust himself into the fulcrum of Palm Beach society. He acquired the historic mansion and learned to pilot an airplane. He got himself invited to events at the toniest private clubs. In 1983, he worked on the mayoral campaign of Deedy Marix, who went on to serve three terms, throwing a fundraiser for her at the ham-and-cheese house. Sullivan even managed to wangle a seat on the prestigious Palm Beach Landmarks Preservation Commission, a small group that presides over the aesthetic integrity of the island's residences and public buildings.

While Sullivan's star rose, his wife was frustrated. Palm Beach, in the early '80s, was much more color-conscious than her native Atlanta. Unlike Groucho Marx, who famously quipped that he refused to join a club that *would* have him as a member, Mrs. Sullivan had little interest in beating on the doors of one that would *not* welcome her. So, one fine day in 1985, Lita packed up the car and drove home to Atlanta, where she began proceedings for divorce. Which would have been final two years later if Mrs. Sullivan did not meet her demise from the bullet of a hired assassin.

The saga dragged on. Sullivan married twice more: first to Suki, a Korean, who eventually sued him for divorce, citing cruelty and "abusive frugality," and then to a Thai woman with whom he disappeared from the country for years. Finally, the McClinton family lawyers received a call from a woman named Belinda Trahan. Trahan claimed her then-boyfriend, Phillip Anthony Harwood, was paid $25,000 by James Vincent Sullivan to kill his wife, Lita McClinton Sullivan. Sullivan was caught in Thailand in 2002.

James Vincent Sullivan is currently serving a life sentence for hiring the hit man to kill his wife. But their money—his and Lita's—has never turned up. The McClinton family is still looking for it in money havens like Switzerland and Liechtenstein. In a way, Sullivan won. He may be rotting in jail, but he has kept the money to himself. I think we can safely call this a Pyrrhic victory.

27

THE WIFE

Chapter Fifteen
Tuesday, May 5, 2020

The border to Argentina remained sealed. The town of Palm Beach did, too.

Linda sat in her house on Reef Road, repetitively dialing the telephone number of the Alonsos in Buenos Aires. She held her breath as the phone rang on, wagering bargains with God. She would breathe when someone picked up. But no one ever did. God did not care if she breathed or not.

Why were Mimi and Hector not answering? No matter how bad things got with Señora Alonso, one of them was always with her, doing everything for her. Linda remembered Mimi dashing to the bakery in the predawn hours to pick up *medialunas*—delicious Argentine croissants. Mimi would have baked them herself if she could have done them half as well as the bakery. But Señora Alonso wanted *medialunas* from the bakery. They were better than Mimi's.

Could they all be in the country instead? Linda had called that house multiple times, but no one answered there, either. She pictured them there, way down in the Patagonia. Well, not all the way down. Only as far as Viedma, about six hundred miles from Buenos Aires, and not at its farthest south—the Tierra del Fuego—a frozen, arctic land.

Miguel's parents both had deep roots in the region. The family lore was that they did not meet at home but had met in 1967—just after a military coup—in Buenos Aires. Diego, his father, was a law student at the University of Buenos Aires, and Esperanza, his mother, was visiting her cousins in the city. One night, at a party at a house in the Recoleta district—where they would live for the rest of their lives—young Diego met Esperanza. It was Christmas, the hot season, and Esperanza was dancing with a naval officer in the garden. Diego spotted her when he stepped outside for a cigarette. As the sound of the orchestra floated out the open doors, he was struck—so the story went—by this bold young woman alone in the garden with a man. Diego decided to cut in, Esperanza met his eyes, and the rest, as the family told it, was history.

They married six months later, in the wintry month of June, in the *Catedral Nuestra Señora de la Merced* in Viedma. It was a modest affair, as such affairs were in those days, with a Saturday morning wedding. The bride and groom skipped lunch at Esperanza's parents' and took the long train ride to Buenos Aires to spend one night at the Alvear Palace Hotel. Diego resumed classes on Monday.

Esperanza, like her name, had filled the Alonso family with hope for a nursery filled with babies. But babies did not come. One year passed. Two. Five. After nine years, Esperanza had no hope. Neither did anyone else.

And then, following another military coup, a miracle happened. Baby Diego was born in 1976, Miguel in '78. Two beautiful and bouncing boys, each the picture of their father. Diego, the first, was saddled with the mantle of the name. Miguel, the second, was given a name less freighted with expectations. The Alonsos reveled in their good fortune.

Some thought it too good to be true.

28

THE WIFE

Chapter Sixteen
Thursday, May 7, 2020

The contours of an affair, once begun, are as irresistible to trace as the contours of a lover's body. Linda quickly found she could not keep her hands off Michael Collins. Nor could she keep her mind off visions of the time they spent together during the time she was not with him. She found herself aching for him in the day. Not the kind of emotional ache she felt for her children that emanated from the regions of her heart. No. This ache came from a lower place. Linda found herself so sexually aroused as she went about her day that—on top of the grief and anxiety she felt for her missing children—her mind ricocheted among a feverish array of non sequiturs at a pace that made her dizzy.

Three weeks had passed since the disappearance of Linda's loved ones. One week had passed since she'd first had sex with Michael. It was hard to make that math look good. To see herself as a virtuous mother and wife. Linda found alternating ways of explaining it.

She flattered herself with the rationale that, in so quickly bedding Michael Collins, she was only seeking physical release from her pain.

Michael did not mean anything to her. His body did not replace the bodies of her children. Maybe his body replaced that of Miguel, but Michael did not create whatever problems the Alonsos had been having in their marriage.

At other times, she looked in the mirror at the face of a harlot staring back at her. What kind of woman would do what she had done? Would do what she was *continuing* to do on a nightly basis? Because—yes—Michael and Linda were actively, repeatedly meeting.

He came back the very next night after their encounter in the guest room. Just as the sun was setting, Linda heard the doorbell ring. She peeked out the living room window and there was his jeep, surfboard resting on top of it. When she opened the door, he stood for a moment saying nothing, then he held up an object in his hand. Linda squinted to see it. It looked like a hair clip, the tortoiseshell kind with teeth on both sides that you use to fasten a bun.

"I found this in my jeep," he said, shoving it at her. "Is it yours?"

Linda knew it was not hers—that he was using it as an excuse to come see her—but she peered at it just the same. She had been pacing the house all day, trying to come up with a reason to see him, and she was relieved he had beaten her to it. He had obviously gone surfing after work because he was wearing board shorts and a long-sleeve T-shirt. His hair was wet, his feet were bare, and he smelled of salt and sweat.

"Do you drive without shoes, Michael?"

"Sometimes. When I'm not going far."

"Is that legal?"

"You could perform a citizen's arrest."

This made her smile.

"Is this your hair thing?" He held it out again. He must have known it belonged to his wife. Even Linda could remember seeing Maeve with those things in her messy red bun.

"Let me see." She took it and moved to a lamp in the living room to look closer at the kind of clip she never wore. Turning to him, she said, "Why don't you come in for a glass of wine?"

"I don't know," he said, looking back at the street, while his body leaned into the door.

"Somebody following you?" she asked.

"You never know." He pulled the door closed behind him, fastening the lock with a click.

He crossed the floor in his tanned bare feet, leaving tracks in the pile of the fluffy, white rug. He took the clip from Linda and turned her to face away from him. Using his fingers like combs, he brushed her hair up off the nape of her neck. The lightness of his touch made her shiver. He twisted it around in the style of his wife's and closed the clamp to hold it. Linda felt the little teeth scrape along her skull and shuddered once again.

Then he grabbed all of it, hair and clip together, and pulled her head back until her neck bent as far as it could. She felt ready for Dracula to fly in through the window and bite her. Naturally that did not happen. Unnaturally, Linda led Michael Collins to her bedroom and the bed she shared with her husband. It was that easy to cross the next barrier in an ever-collapsing string of them.

29

THE WIFE

Chapter Seventeen
Monday, May 11, 2020

Linda was distantly aware that the first stages of Florida's reopening began today. She saw pictures in *The Shiny Sheet* that still clattered onto her driveway. Maybe it was yesterday. Was this the time of year when the paper cut back to weekend only? She could not remember. It did not matter. Restaurants were setting out tables, six careful feet apart; masked and gloved waiters were wiping them down between patrons. She would not be going to a restaurant. She had not ventured much beyond her house and her daily walks to the beach. But the opening of restaurants surely signaled that the world would open soon. Including the airways to Argentina.

She'd had a FaceTime call with a lawyer in Boca today. "Attorney for the Child," he had billed himself. José Mercado was his name.

"What makes you think your husband—he's still your husband?" Mr. Mercado began.

"He is. But he took the children without telling me. And he had recently borrowed money."

"A home equity loan, you say?"

"Yes, but…"

"And you don't know if he has drawn on those available funds?"

"No, but…"

"Mrs. Alonso." Mr. Mercado said this as a full sentence. A patronizing, paternalistic sentence. "Why don't we give this a little time?"

If there was one thing Linda could not abide, it was the royal *we*. Miguel used it. This guy sounded just like him.

"Thank you," she said. "I'll get back to you."

She would not be getting back to him. She would handle this herself. As soon as the skies opened, she would board a plane to Buenos Aires and find her children. For now, to calm herself, she decided to walk to the beach. She threw on a floppy hat, grabbed her mask and house keys, and let herself out the front door.

She did not get far. There, in her driveway, was Michael Collins, standing tall in all his cop glory. Now that she saw him on a regular basis—now that they were technically lovers—she was amazed she had not. pegged him immediately as an officer of the law, back when they passed each other in the airport. He had that rumpled quality—there was really no other way to describe it—like he'd slept in his clothes. Or maybe, now that his wife was away, he *had* slept in his clothes.

"Linda," he said.

"Michael," she replied.

"I was hoping to ask you a couple questions."

"As in two?" she asked.

"As in a few," he answered.

"I was on my way out for a walk."

"I can walk. If you're inviting me."

Was she inviting him? Did she have a choice in the matter?

"Do you mind if we go to the beach?" she asked. "I know it's still not legal."

"It's as good a place as any."

They walked to the end of Reef Road. She kept her mask in her hand. He kept his dangling over one ear.

"Aren't you afraid that's going to fall off?"

He looked over at her but kept walking. "Well," he said, "my ears are pretty big. And I may need to put it on in a hurry. And I'm a little bit lazy. And I've got another one in my pocket."

"You've thought it through," she said.

"That's what I do," he said, coughing a bit as he said it.

"Are you sick?" she asked.

"Just allergies."

"Do you want to start your questions now?"

"Do you mind walking in peaceable silence for a bit?"

Linda laughed. "Like *The Peaceable Kingdom*?"

"Pretty much."

"Are you religious?" she asked.

"In a way, I am," he answered.

"Is your wife?"

"No," he said. "My wife has her issues with God."

"Should I ask you to elaborate?" Linda asked.

"Probably not," he said, just as they arrived at the cordoned-off path through the tall grasses that led to Reef Road beach. "After you," he motioned around the barrier tape. Linda passed him and got the slightest whiff of his aftershave.

"You smell like a lemon," she said. "I didn't notice that before. *Myrsol*?"

"How'd you know?"

"My husband wears it."

"My wife told me it was something of an inside secret." He laughed. "She gave it to me."

Linda wondered if his Irish wife had really given him that obscure Spanish aftershave. Or had he simply seen the bottle of *Myrsol Agua de Limòn* in her bathroom, on Miguel's side of the counter, and purchased a bottle himself? Had he taken Miguel's? Linda tried to recall whether she'd noticed the bottle on the bathroom counter this morning.

"So this is where I surf." He interrupted her thoughts.

"I've seen you surfing here."

"Shall we walk a little way?" he asked and turned south to set off along the hard-packed sand at the water line. "Do you know our proximity to the Gulf Stream around here?"

"Closer than anywhere else on the east coast, I think."

"That's right," he said. "Forty or so miles out. But the outward ripples of the current come much closer than that. A couple miles. Sometimes closer."

Linda stooped to pick up a shell, larger than the ones that usually washed up on this beach.

"A Florida fighting conch," Michael said. "You should throw it back. It's still alive."

"Why's it called that?" she asked as she arced her arm back and gave the conch a good spin. It landed about ten yards into the ocean with a plop.

"The males sometimes fight," he explained. "You're laughing at me but it's true!"

"Okay," she said. "I think I believe you. Maybe."

"I made it up," he said.

"I knew it!"

"No. I really didn't. They fight."

"Now I don't know what to believe."

"Solving a case can be like that," he said and coughed again.

"You sound like a philosopher. You also sound sick. Are you sure you're okay? You're being careful?"

"I'm okay," he said. "Do you fish?"

"Fish? A little. My husband fishes a lot. He has a Boston Whaler he takes out to the Gulf Stream."

"Do you ever use the boat?"

"I can drive it. But not really. I don't go out on my own."

"Not ever?"

"What is this about, Michael? Is this one of your official questions?"

"Something washed up on this beach over the weekend. I took the call. It came into my department. Homicide."

30

A WRITER'S THOUGHTS

Apparently sharks barf. This is of interest to me for a variety of reasons, not least of which is the fact that I, myself, am no stranger to barfing. We have a long and checkered history, barfing and I. Sharks vomit for reasons entirely different from those of a bulimic woman, and they eject a fascinating array of items when they do so. Far more interesting than anything that's ever come out of me.

According to a site called The Verge, about ten years ago a marine biologist named Austin Gallagher and his team hauled an eight-foot tiger shark onto his boat in the Florida Keys. They did this sort of thing all the time in order to tag them with satellite trackers. Gallagher was straddling this particular shark mid-measurement when he saw "a huge plume of feathers explode on the back of the boat."

It is common knowledge—among those who know about sharks—that sharks barf, so it did not come as a total shock to Gallagher. But he was particularly thrilled to be in such close proximity to a shark who was in the act of doing it. Sharks vomit primarily under stress. But—get this—they don't just vomit up food or whatever other objects they've been gobbling in the sea (bones, turtle shells, feathers, and the like). Sometimes they regurgitate their entire stomachs! This has been recorded on film and I have dutifully watched it on the internet. It is a well-known shark phenomenon. And when they do it, they mostly just swallow the stomach back down after it has had a little clean-out. That sounds more familiar to the likes of me.

Why do I do it? Would that I could answer that question. And here, I must point out the happy and unusual opportunity to be able to use the subjunctive in English. We don't often do it. Would that we did. *Murder though it have no tongue, will speak,* is an example of the subjunctive taken from Shakespeare. *Hamlet,* to be precise.

Now back to regurgitation.

My mother was undone by the murder of her childhood friend. I was undone by a childhood with my mother. My mother, in her impaired state, raised me to be impaired. I know, it doesn't seem fair to always blame the mother. But we do, don't we? I didn't have children, myself, so I dodged that bullet.

To that point—the point of my childlessness—I never made a conscious decision to not have children. To not marry. To not enter into the stream of life that most girls grow up thinking they will someday enter. There simply came a point when I realized it had all passed me by. But it was not until those opportunities were far in my rearview mirror.

I grew up in the American suburbs in the 1960s and '70s, where there was nothing but houses and houses filled with children. But we were an anomaly with only one child in ours, and maybe that is one of the reasons I never had children. I had never become accustomed to them.

My mother, in her fixation on Noelle, her murder, and her still-on-the-loose murderer, was always overprotective. That is too mild a word for what she was. She was smothering. Her attentions to me were not so much affectionate as they were possessive. Like she'd lost something valuable to her and did not intend to lose its replacement. It had cost her dearly once, and she wasn't about to pay that price again.

So while I felt an intensity of energy directed from her to me, it never felt like what I imagine you would call "love."

Once, I tried to attend a pajama party. It was junior high, I was thirteen, and a group of girls from our block invited me when we were walking home from school. Maybe we weren't walking together, and maybe I was tagging along too closely, and maybe they were just being polite. However the invitation came about, I chose to see it as sincere.

My father was not in town. My mother took a pill right after dinner and made her way to her bedroom. I told her I would lock up the house. She trusted me enough by that age to relinquish this duty to me. The routine was always the same: Start at the front, make your way to the back, checking all the first floor windows and doors. This was before the ubiquity of house alarms—something that would greatly alleviate my mother's anxiety—so it rested upon us to seal up the house like a tomb.

Only that night I cheated. I slipped out the back door and made my way to Debbie Stubinsky's house next door. I rang the bell.

"Hi!" Debbie said with surprise when she opened it. She was dressed in bell-bottom jeans and a tie-dyed shirt that hinted at an American flag. My jeans were too high waisted, my shirt was a plaid button-down. Plus, I had tucked it in in what I could now see was not a cool move.

"Hi," I said, searching for more words. "Thanks for inviting me."

Other girls had made their way to the hall, dressed just like Debbie, and were studying me like a specimen. I tugged a little at my shirt, but it wouldn't budge from my jeans.

Debbie, who had talked of becoming a nun after a stirring viewing of *The Song of Bernadette* in sixth grade, made a visible decision to put her saintliness to work. "Come in!" she said, a little brighter than seemed natural. "Guys," she said to her friends, "look who's here!"

As if they hadn't seen me.

The evening progressed pretty well as far as I could tell. Popcorn, a movie, confessions about boys they liked. I didn't contribute much to the conversation. But I hadn't embarrassed myself either. Closing my eyes as I lay on the makeshift bed on the floor—everyone had a sleeping bag but me so Debbie's mother had found a pillow and blanket—I indulged in a fantasy future. Debbie and I would become close. The other girls would accept me. In time, they would invite me to their houses. At first, to accommodate Debbie. But later, because they liked me.

I was drifting in this happy trance and did not hear it at first. One of the girls had to touch my shoulder. Then she started to shake me. And it was worse than I could have imagined.

"Noelle!" my mother screamed from somewhere in the vicinity of our house. "Noelle! Noelle! Noelle!"

I did not speak. No one did. I rose, hesitated, then made up the bed as carefully as I could. To make it look like I had never been there in the hopes they'd forget this had happened. I did not say goodbye to Debbie or any of the other girls. No one said goodbye to me. They were all sitting up by then and someone had turned on a light.

That was the part that killed me. If only the light had been left off. Maybe they would not have known it was my crazy mother screaming for her long-dead friend.

I slipped out the door, ran across the Stubinsky lawn and my own, vaulted the steps of our porch, and grabbed my mother by the arm, harder than I probably should have. We made our way into the house, in through the front door she'd left gaping wide. She locked it herself this time.

None of the girls ever mentioned the incident to me. None of the girls ever spoke to me again. Even sainted Debbie.

And she never became a nun.

Mostly I just stayed home with my mother, a precursor to the children who would come later—Linda's generation of children—who were kept at home, indoors. Children who came after Etan Patz, the little boy who disappeared on his way to school in 1979. But my mother did not need an Etan Patz to convince her that children weren't safe. She knew it before anyone else did.

My father was a salesman for a highway-equipment company, so he was always on the road. Ironic, given that we would now diagnose my mother with agoraphobia. She hardly left the house. My grandmother did the grocery shopping for us. She indulged her daughter's weaknesses and I can't say I blame her. She was, after all, quite present at the scene of the crime that caused them. She saw what little Liz had gone through. She knew that her daughter had been afraid to even go to the bathroom alone for many months after the murder. It may have been longer. And she, as Liz's mother, had taken on the responsibility for her daughter's well-being. Or lack thereof.

A maid came once a week to clean and run other errands. Dry cleaners. Pharmacy. Hardware store. Aggie was her name—short for Agatha—and her kind, if distracted, presence probably kept me as marginally sane as I was. Am.

My father, on the other hand, was rarely home. I don't think he could bear to be cooped up in those four walls with his family, and he, unlike my grandmother, abdicated all but financial responsibility for any of us. When he was occasionally home, he dropped names like Johnstown and Bethlehem to us at dinner, important-sounding names of important-sounding places that were part of the wide territory he covered.

I was suitably impressed. I was aware of the Johnstown flood of 1889, when a dam built for a fishing camp for wealthy industrialists burst, sending a forty-mile-an-hour, sixty-foot wall of water into the towns below, killing thousands in its debris-filled path. And I thought he was speaking of the same Bethlehem I'd heard of in church. The fact that my father spent time in both of those places made him seem rather unreal to me. Mythic. A status he retained in my eyes even after he left us without a word. I kind of understood it.

My mother was not mythic. And I did not have the vocabulary to understand that she was simply tragic. Her way of controlling the uncontrollable was to control me. My way of rebelling against her control was to lose control of myself. ABC Freud, right there. Not so complicated at all.

As for marriage and children? You could analyze that one any way you want. But, really, no one ever asked me. And here I live now, in Florida, having become *a woman of a certain age* who lives with her dog. I have become the voyeur that I did not want to be, the passive observer of life that my mother wanted me to be. To protect me. To keep me safe from sharks.

But there are always sharks in Florida, and items that sharks throw up sometimes make their way to the beach. In Florida, *murder though it have no tongue, will speak.*

Just like in Denmark.

31

THE WIFE

Chapter Eighteen
Monday, May 11, 2020

Michael's words knocked around the walls of Linda's brain like a pinball. How long did she stand there digesting what he said? What *had* he said? Something was found on the beach. Something turned in to the cops. To the homicide department.

And Michael Collins let her take all the time she needed. Time was on his side now, not hers. He stood near her, kicking his toe in the sand like a surfer without a care in the world, when what he really was, was a cop who cared very much where this whole thing was going. Was, in fact, manipulating where it was going.

"My wife's coming back soon," he finally said. "With my boys."

"That's great for you."

"Yes. I haven't felt like myself with them away."

"Is that supposed to be some sort of excuse for what we've done?" she asked.

"I just…"

"Are you saying you're sorry?"

"Of course I'm sorry. I've hurt my wife."

"She doesn't need to know. She won't be hurt if she doesn't know."

"I don't know, Linda." He stopped kicking the sand and faced her. There were speckles of brown in the green of his eyes—like stones at the bottom of a clear lake—easier to see now that they were out in bright sunlight.

"What are your boys' names?" she asked.

"Sean and Timmy. Timmy stands for Mortimer."

"Mortimer?" She looked out to the crashing waves. "That's kind of unusual."

"It was Maeve's grandfather's name. It means dead at sea. Morte. Mer. I didn't like it."

"But she got her way."

Michael reached out and grabbed her by the shoulders, turning her to face him. "Linda, do you expect to see your husband again?"

"Yes, of course. I may have to fly to Argentina, but I'll get my children back."

Abruptly, he let go of her and strode toward the entrance to the beach. He coughed some more and talked as if to himself, not slowing his pace to allow her to easily catch up with him. At times, she found herself nearly running.

"We have a conundrum," he said. "We have your husband and kids flying to Argentina on Saturday, the eighteenth of April. We have their passports all checked out. We have their flight all checked out. We have security cameras IDing them getting off the plane in Buenos Aires with a whole bunch of pictures of their nice little faces in their nice little masks. We have your car turn up in the airport lot in Miami. Everything checks out neat and tidy."

He spun around to face her. "And then we have something come up out of the blue. Out of the ocean there. And it turns out it's not tidy, at all."

He turned to continue walking, leaving the beach and heading down North Ocean Boulevard to Reef Road. Neither of them said anything for a while. They walked in silence, though it could no longer be called peaceable.

"In fact," Michael suddenly blurted, "it causes some confusion as to who, exactly, might have gotten onto that plane with your kids last month and who, exactly, might have gone out on a boat right about the same time."

Linda stumbled, but Michael did not slow down to assist her.

"And then we have you," he continued. "You call the cops and tell your story. You run into me 'accidentally,'" he made air quotes with his fingers, "and tell your story. You ask me to have coffee and move a piece of furniture. And a coin turns up from Bolivia. Dated 2017. Three years ago. And then you come on to me. Hard. And then, when you think I'm sleeping, you get up and move that coin. We have a conundrum, Linda."

They continued up her front walkway and stopped in front of the door.

"Come in, Michael. Please," she said. "Just to talk."

"It's over, Linda."

32

A WRITER'S THOUGHTS

There was a turning point in my childhood when my mother could possibly have gone down one road or another. I say possibly because I will never know if she really pivoted at that moment or not. In the end, it played out the way it played out. I don't have a parallel universe outcome at my disposal for examination.

The day in question, we had gone to visit my cousins, who lived in McCandless Township. These were the children of my mother's brother, David. We did not see them much. Given the six-year age difference between our parents, given my mother's reclusiveness, given the fact that my father wasn't often around—with all those givens, family visits were a rarity. Dave was always kind to my mother, but I did not sense a closeness.

They lived on a big hill, which was common for Pittsburgh. They kept a pony, which wasn't common at all. A year before this visit—the last time we had seen each other—my cousins were outside with their new pony. My dad, in town for a brief appearance, accompanied us to their house. There, he ignored my mother's misgivings and pushed me out the door, encouraging me to play with my cousins. This was easier said than done.

They were all years older and I was an oddball, at best. They were nice to me; I would never suggest they were not. But they did not know what to do with me. I am sure they had heard from their parents, Dave and his wife, Darlene, the saga of my mother's trauma. I am sure they had been instructed to always treat me well. And they did. But our encounters were awkward.

On that day, though, the prospect of the pony excited me. Never having been on a pony (imagine my mother's thoughts on that!), I decided to give it a try. Not knowing quite how to manage it, I stood in the yard to observe. This was my default position, to keep to the sidelines and watch.

The oldest of my cousins, Becky, was pulling her brother, Joe, from the pony's back. The pony was fitted with a blanket. I did not see anything I would have recognized as a saddle, so there wasn't much for Joe to hold onto. Nevertheless, he resisted.

"No!" he cried to Becky. "I don't wanna get off!"

"C'mon!" she panted, yanking him with both hands.

I couldn't really see what Joe was doing, but it looked like he was squeezing his legs around the pony. It also looked like the pony didn't like it.

"Becky, stop!" he yelled.

"Get off!" she insisted.

Becky was older by two years and she was just then at the moment of early adolescence. This made her much bigger than Joe. And a good deal more disagreeable. I would have put my money on Becky winning the fight.

Becky gave Joe a mighty tug which proved to be the clincher. He fell off sideways, kicking the pony on his way down. The pony—whose name I still had not learned—leapt in the air and ran away. Joe scrambled to his feet and hit his sister, who, in turn, clocked him hard across the face. Just as Joe was gathering himself for another go at Becky, I was consumed by a piercing pain in my back. It took my breath away by its intensity and the fact that I had no idea what it was.

Becky and Joe stopped fighting. They both turned to look at me, gasping.

"Mooooom!" Becky called out, turning her head to the house but pointing her finger at me. "Twinkles just bit her!"

Twinkles. Even in my anguish, I found it a stupid name.

We left in a hurry after that and I was on penicillin for a while. And for more than a month, when I held a hand mirror to look at my bare back in the medicine cabinet mirror, I could track Twinkles's toothy circular bruises as they went from black to green to yellow.

But this was not the pivotal incident for my mother. My mother, in fact, handled the pony bite better than expected. The precipitating event happened a year later, on our next visit to her brother's. I mentioned the hill. It was a very large hill. Being from the region, I was familiar with hills, but this one was impressive.

After the fiasco with Twinkles the prior year, I felt more embarrassed and uncomfortable than usual. Becky and Joe weren't even home when we arrived; obviously, I concluded, avoiding me. My father was not with us for this visit. Which made what happened even worse. There was no one to get hold of my mother and talk her off the ledge.

The adults sat in the living room, my mother chatting with Dave and Darlene. I was reading in a corner until Darlene urged me outdoors. I grudgingly got up, found my bookmark, and stepped out the door. It was raining. Why adults thought a lone, bookish child would be happier outside in the rain than in a chair with a good book, I could not have said. I made my way around the house, over the scraggly grass, and past the post where they used to tie Twinkles.

Twinkles did not appear to be in residence anymore, but no one had explained her disappearance. She probably bit the wrong person. I found the garage door open and several bicycles flung on the floor. They appeared to have been thrown where they lay, collapsed in odd poses, a tire turned backward, upside down on a pile of wood. One of them was pink, with long, sparkling streamers coming out of the rubber caps at the ends of the handlebars. It must have once belonged to Becky, but it looked too small for her now.

I do not know why I got on that bike. Why I took it out to the road and pointed it down the hill. I do not know why I panicked midway, forgetting entirely the concept of hand brakes and furiously pumping my feet backward in an effort to apply nonexistent foot brakes. I do know that I fell hard, tumbling down the hill, entangled with the pretty pink bike. When I finally came to a rest, I was a bloody mess and the bike was broken.

I sat for quite a while at the bottom of the hill in the rain. And when I got up to find my cousins' house, in my confusion, I went to several others first. I was gone a very long time. And that was the part that got my mother. Her level of worry was already high by the time I hobbled up the driveway, dragging the mangled bike behind me. Had my father been there, I think she may have been able to keep it together. Without him, there wasn't a chance. When we left that day, it was for the last time. I would hear my mother on the phone with her brother or Darlene from time to time. But I never saw my cousins again. And, once again, it was all my fault.

33

THE WIFE

Chapter Nineteen
Monday, May 11, 2020

Linda took the proverbial bull by his proverbial horns and reached one hand up to touch Michael's face and one hand down to touch him somewhere else. And she did it fast and hard, kissing him as she did so, right there in front of her house, in full view of the neighbors.

"Jesus, Linda," he said, pulling away from her.

"Come in, Michael," she said again. "Please."

"I…" he hesitated, glancing toward the street.

But Linda had felt his erection the moment she touched him and knew he would stay.

"Okay, fine," he said, when he realized the same thing, and pushed his way into the house.

Linda closed the door behind him. He slammed her against that door harder than she had expected and they dropped to the cold marble floor. They didn't even make it to the rug. Everything about sex for Linda and Michael was rough and raw. She tried to keep it going as long as possible. To avoid further topics of conversation. To avoid him leaving.

Eventually they were both spent. Michael groaned himself to his side and reached down to rub a knee.

"Are you hungry?" she asked.

"No."

"Want a drink?" she tried again.

"No." He sat up and reached around for his clothes. "Listen, Linda..."

"Oh boy, here we go." She stood up and grabbed her dress, slipping it over her naked body. She picked up her bra and panties and held them in her hands. "What's going on, Michael?"

"You need to tell me that," he said as he pulled his pants over the undershorts he'd just put on. "I think you're the only one who can."

"What washed up on the beach?"

"A ring. Actually, a partially decomposed hand wearing a ring." He yanked his button-down shirt over one arm, then the other, and worked the buttons, top to bottom. He did not look at her. "A wedding ring engraved with an inscription. Initials. I can't tell you any more than that."

"What are you even talking about? A hand? A ring?" She laughed a little as she said it and threw her underwear in a misguidedly dramatic gesture. It didn't go very far and landed limply next to her. She kicked it out of her way as she crossed over to the liquor cabinet. "Well, I'll have a drink, even if you're not."

Her hands shook as she poured a shot of vodka into a crystal glass. A wedding present, she remembered. From Miguel's parents. She shuddered and topped up the glass. "Sure you don't want one?"

"I'm working," he said as he finished buttoning his shirt.

"Is that what you call this?"

"You started it."

"You sound like a five-year-old." She laughed and knocked back a good swig of the vodka.

"You don't even know me, Linda. And I don't know you."

"I know something about you, Michael. I know you're a cheating husband to your wife, Maeve."

"That's a low blow."

"I call it as I see it."

"Stop it. This isn't going to help you."

"No one is going to help me. Not that extradition lawyer. Not the regular cops. And it seems not you."

"I'm sorry, Linda, but I've been doing this a long time. And something doesn't add up."

"Maybe you should stop doing math and go back to police work and help me find my husband."

"Maybe you should stop being a smartass and try to help your own case."

"Case?"

"This is real. You need to come in for questioning."

"Are you arresting me?"

"I'm just saying you're going to have to come into the precinct at some point and you're going to have to come prepared." Michael coughed. "You might want to talk to a lawyer."

And then he coughed harder. The hardest he had coughed so far today, and she realized he had coughed quite a bit. He launched into a wracking coughing jag from which it took him a few minutes to recover.

"I think you're sick." Linda said. "I think you might have the virus."

"Nah," he said. "Just a tickle in my throat."

34

A WRITER'S THOUGHTS

*D*eus *ex machina* is a nifty literary trick, if you can pull it off in a way that doesn't seem contrived. The *Oxford English Dictionary* definition is concise: *A power, event, person, or thing that comes in the nick of time to solve a difficulty; providential interposition, especially in a novel or play.* In classical Greek drama, where it was created and often employed, the gods would appear in a clumsy machine coming down from Olympus to wrap things up, resolve pesky plot points, and allow the audience to feel that things were as they should be in a world where things often were not.

No gods appeared to save Noelle Huber. No gods appeared to avenge her death once it happened. No one paid the price for stabbing her thirty-six times while she was trying to bake a cake. Even when the case was reopened in recent years, when the detectives got so excited about hauling in the brother again and scoring a sixty-year-old DNA conviction, the gods had something else in mind. A dead end. A blind alley. A MacGuffin or a red herring or a worthless pursuit of justice in an unjust world.

My mother could not get over Noelle's murder. She feared that she, herself, was always in danger at home because home was where her best friend had met it. Danger, that is. It is ironic, indeed, that my mother ended up confining herself—and me—inside the four walls of our house even though she found no safe haven there.

Due to her age at the time of the crime, my mother did not know how seriously Noelle's brother was considered the prime suspect as her killer. For the same reason, she also did not know that there had been allegations of impropriety between Noelle and Matt. It would have been incomprehensible to her.

Combing through the digital archive of newspaper coverage of the murder, I find the article where Matt, himself, acknowledged that he'd had unnatural sexual relations with his little sister. And I find the one when he later denied it. My mother would not have read these newspapers at a contemporaneous moment. Her mother would have protected her from such salacious material. But the cops alluded to it, albeit obliquely, when they questioned little Liz about Noelle.

I am going to say what I think happened.

I think that, at some point in the months before the killing, Matt Huber seduced—or coerced—his pubescent sister, Noelle, into engaging in some variety of sexual intimacy. I don't know what kind. And it may have happened more than once. I think Noelle may have had diametrically opposed feelings about that seduction. Or coercion. On the one hand, I think she was aroused by it—we are animals, after all, creatures of base instinct and physical reactions beyond our control. On the other, I think she was disgusted by it—we are human, after all, sentient beings with evolved consciousness and a sense of a moral compass. And, finally, I think she was ashamed of it—we are psychologically complex and fragile beings and it is a well-known fact that children usually blame themselves for the bad things that happen to them.

In the months preceding her death, I think Noelle was living in a state of profound psychic turmoil. I think the weird hair she placed on the coat of the man on the streetcar was a tiny glimpse, for my mother, into Noelle's confused psyche.

On the night of Friday, December 10, I think Matt Huber left the railroad yard and returned to the house, knowing his parents would be out, knowing Noelle would be alone, hoping for a bit of quick action before slipping back to work. I think he came to the back door and Noelle let him in. I don't know why he did not have a key. Maybe he did have a key and he let himself in and raised the blind later to make it look like Noelle had peeked out the window to let in someone else.

Once in the kitchen, I think Matt tried to initiate something with Noelle. I think he touched her or made a verbal suggestion. And I think Noelle said no. I think her moral compass and her sense of shame overrode her libido and her sense of desire. I think she threatened to tell their parents. I think Matt knew there would be severe consequences for what he'd done to his twelve-year-old sister. I think a big fight ensued and, at some point, I think Matt snapped. I think his initial impulse was to shut her up. And he had impulse control issues, from everything else we know about him. I think he grabbed a knife and went at Noelle. I think he savagely killed his sister in a fit of blind rage over her threats to expose their secret. I think he panicked even more when it was done, when Noelle lay battered and bloodied on the floor. I think he changed his clothes, disposing of the shirt in the bin behind the house. I don't know where his shoes went, but he changed into new ones. I think he went back to the railroad yard and pretended he'd never been gone.

I think Mr. and Mrs. Huber came home and, seeing their daughter nearly dead and having some insight into what may have happened in terms of their son, made the Sophie's Choice to save one child when they'd lost the other. I think they spent twenty-one minutes cleaning fingerprints where they could. And then I think they paid for it for the rest of their lives.

I think the entire evening and everything that followed it was a large and consuming snowball that—once it started rolling downhill—gathered human detritus into itself, including my mother by proxy.

In terms of the peculiar assistance from the police and officials of Pittsburgh: I think the father, being a chauffeur, must have driven some influential people around town. The Huber family ended up with a very important lawyer—politically prominent and, no doubt, expensive to retain. The family also had the support of the mayor and the superintendent of police. I think that Pittsburgh was playing by its own rules in those days—partly corrupt, partly lazy, partly myopic—and these prominent folks simply liked Mr. Huber, their driver, and did him a favor when asked to do so and called the law off his son. I don't think they—the prominent politicians and lawyers—ever imagined that young Matt Huber could have killed his sister, Noelle. I think they thought they were just helping a guy they knew and liked. A guy who needed—and they believed was worthy of—that favor.

I think Noelle's father could not bear to live with what he had done, what they all had done, and descended into a black despair. My mother said she saw him a few years after Noelle's murder and he had become an old man, stooped over, his hair gone white. He looked vacantly at my mother and muttered, "You fought like little Indians. Now one Indian is gone." My mother didn't know who he meant.

Only one person did not deteriorate from the carnage of that night, and that person was Matt Huber. Not only did he *not* deteriorate, he thrived. He married. He procreated. He picked up a few more arrests along the way for exposing himself to girls. And he went on to live a long life. He is still alive today.

But this is only what I think. Matthew Huber, Jr., has never been convicted of anything. And we are, in the United States of America, innocent until proven guilty, let us not forget.

Deus ex machina can be considered lazy storytelling. To have an unlikely event or person appear out of the blue is just not believable. But I would counter by saying who, in fact, would have believed that this entire year of 2020 would have happened in the way that it has? Who would have believed a global pandemic would overtake the world? Who would have believed that American cities would end up in a chaos of rioting and violence and under partial military rule?

Some may have, but most would not.

Nassim Nicholas Taleb came out with a book in 2007 called *The Black Swan: The Impact of the Highly Improbable.* The *New York Times* has called it one of the twelve most influential books since World War

II, and it has sold more than three million copies. That figure gets my attention as a writer.

Taleb's area of study is randomness, probability, and uncertainty. He uses the example of a black swan to illustrate the fact that improbable events and realities pop up to surprise us just when we think we have it all figured out. The example goes as follows: Hundreds of years ago, Europeans were familiar with swans, and they knew what swans looked like. Swans were white. All of them. They had seen them, after all.

And then those Europeans traveled out into the big, wide world, eventually landing on the continent of Australia. Where they found black swans. And, just like that, the impossible—a black swan—was not impossible at all. It was merely something that a particular group of people happened not to have seen before.

But—and this is a big but—the book concentrates on the extreme impact of rare and unpredictable outlier events.

Because there is always an impact.

35

THE WIFE

Chapter Twenty
Tuesday, May 19, 2020

And then Michael Collins vanished.

Linda's time with him eight days prior—a day rife with potentially pesky problems for her, she would be the first to admit—was the last she had seen or heard from him. The intervening days passed in a slow drip of simultaneous monotony and terror. Boredom was a part of it—yes—considering the ongoing cincture that was winding tighter and tighter around her life, squeezing her brain of all but the most rudimentary functions. Taking in and excreting food. Sleeping, although not much. Breathing, who could help it? Fucking, however, which had so recently been reintroduced to her repertoire of bodily functions, was not a part of those days. Fear was a part of them, though, for obvious reasons.

Had his wife returned? Had he meant it when he said it was over?

Men were evaporating like contrails in Linda's wake.

Speaking of wake, she should get rid of their boat. Palm Beach was reopening enough for her to be able to put it up for sale. She could add that to her list of activities, alongside breathing.

She called Michael multiple times. That was one of the things she'd been doing. Both on his cell and at the precinct. She alternated those calls with her calls to Argentina. Michael's cell—like the Alonsos' phone in Buenos Aires—was never picked up. Someone did answer at the police station, of course, but Linda hung up after asking for Michael Collins and being told he was not around. She did not leave messages anywhere.

If he was truly finished with her, why wasn't he calling her to come into the station to discuss what washed up from the sea?

She realized he might be sick. He had coughed repeatedly when she was with him last. When she had slept with him. He might have COVID-19. So far, she had no symptoms, but it might be a matter of time. She could at least get the boat on the market before she fell ill.

Speaking of bodily functions, she had to go to the store. While she was not eating much, she was eating something. And nothing was left. She no longer went to Publix, where the lines stretched out the door, and instead went to Amici Market, where she could get in and out more easily. Hopefully without running into anyone she knew. At least no one would recognize her masked self. But somewhere near the produce section, she ran into Devon. Linda resolved to scurry by with her head down, but Devon called out to her.

"Linda! How are you? Staying well?"

"Hi, Devon." She turned to face her. "Yep. All good for me. You?"

"Health-wise we're fine. My daughter is stir-crazy, though, and I am, too! I've temporarily closed my practice and I am so not used to the full-time mom thing. Plus, we haven't had our housekeeper. I'm in love with my Roomba!" Devon laughed. "Maybe we could get the kids together? Outside somewhere?"

"Um, maybe." Linda knew as soon as she said it that it was stupid of her not to tell Devon about her family's trip to Argentina.

"I'll call you then. How are your ribs?" Devon dropped her voice to a near-whisper to ask that question.

"Oh. Fine."

"Well, good. I'm glad. If you want another laser treatment when things are open again…"

"Sure. Thanks." Linda turned to resume her shopping.

"Oh!" Devon said in a way that meant Linda had to turn back to her. "Did you hear about Maeve's husband?"

"No." Linda tried to make her face—what little of it was showing—a blank slate. "What about her? I mean him."

"He's been admitted to Good Sam. He has the virus."

"I'm sorry to hear that." Just how completely sorry she was she could not share with Devon. "How is he? I mean, all of them? Their kids are boys, right?"

"Right. They have two boys. Well, they're all fine because they've been in Chicago. They've been there a while, since before all this started. It kind of freaked me out that he might die and his family hasn't even seen him for weeks. I mean, this is all so crazy!"

"He might die?" Linda asked.

"Well, I mean, once you get to the hospital, it's not good. I don't think he's on a ventilator, though. That's like the kiss of death."

Linda thought about kissing and nearly gagged. And yet, she saw the possibilities in this improbable turn of events.

36

A WRITER'S THOUGHTS

True confession: my love for my mother was entwined with so many threads of conflicting feelings that it was hard to untangle one from the other at any given moment. She frightened me. In fact, she terrorized me. She engaged in an unconscious game that would always be unwinnable by either of us.

The gaping wound of her childhood injury was so open and ugly I thought it would engulf me. And as an act of self-preservation, I endeavored to keep myself from falling into it. Like a person in fear of slipping off the edge of a cliff, I pushed against the edges of her personality and tried to hold onto my own. None of this was understood by me as a child, and none of it was entirely successful. My mother simply thought I was cold, which made her feel maligned and unappreciated. She did not have the ability to hold a mirror up to herself. All faults in our relationship, according to my mother, were mine.

Of course, I believed her.

But we have already established that my mother did not so much love me as she needed to keep a hold on me. Once again, she did not perceive this essential—and essentially damaging—fact. Our relationship was one of transactions. We exchanged with each other what the other demanded—at least, we did so on the surface.

My mother required a variety of performances from me, my father, my grandmother—really, anyone she had any kind of relationship with— that would assure her of her goodness. From the vantage point of years, it is easy to see that my mother did not believe in her own intrinsic worth. This core belief was constantly reinforced when her exigencies upon others would only serve to drive them away from her.

That said, as hard as I tried to establish boundaries between the two of us, I was not able to. My name, for example. I should have changed it once I was old enough. My mother had changed her own, going from Liz to Beth. But my mother's hold on me is still stronger than I care to admit. My father should have stopped my mother from giving me the name. He did not approve of it. But by the time of my birth—which was pretty early in their relationship—he had already abdicated his place in the family power structure and had his eye on the door and the open road beyond it. With my mother, it was always easier to give in. To rephrase that, it was nearly impossible not to.

It is not hard to guess what my name would be. All signs point in one direction. You may have thought I would go through this story with my name concealed, simply identifying myself as *the writer*, like the nameless heroine in *Rebecca*, whose rival's name is known but not her own. That I would tell you Linda's name but not mine. Noelle Huber's name but not mine. Nope. I'll give it to you now.

Noelle. My name is Noelle, in honor of my mother's raped and butchered best friend. How's that for complicated?

The story of what happened to Noelle Grace Huber was still widely known in the time and place I was born. My parents had not moved far from the old neighborhood in Pittsburgh, and the suburb they chose was populated by people who had come from the same part of the city. It had been a kind of group migration from Homewood-Brushton to Gibsonia.

Their neighbors—it would be an exaggeration to call them friends— must have been appalled when Beth called me Noelle. It could have been seen as a form of negligence to saddle one's child with the moniker of one's murdered friend. A form of bad taste. Even cruelty. At least a form of morbidly dwelling on something that was best left forgotten. At its core, a form of calling attention to herself. To *her* friendship with the dead girl. To *her* role in what happened that evening. To *her* own importance.

The fact of me—the living entity inhabiting the Noelle suit my mother had wrapped me in—was secondary.

Perhaps I am being harsh on my mother. She did things for me. She cooked. I remember her meatloaf with fondness and even make it, sometimes, myself. She made lemon meringue pie—my favorite—for my birthdays. Although, I have to admit I developed an aversion to it after an indulgent bout of binge/purge and have not touched it for years. She knitted sweaters for me to wear to school. Although she would not teach me to knit. Left-handedness, she claimed, made it impossible for me to learn. So yes, I was fed and clothed and housed. By all standards of this big, wide world, I was an extremely advantaged child.

My adult life has never been actually bad. Nothing catastrophic has happened to me. No significant losses have been endured. No painful betrayals or infidelities suffered. No. I have not experienced great emotional upheaval as an adult. I have not experienced great emotional anything. I have—as I think you understand by now—simply lived my life apart. Apart from others and not a part of others. This is not so bad at all.

37

THE WIFE

Chapter Twenty-One
Tuesday, May 19, 2020

Linda came home from Amici Market and stood in the garage, vigorously rubbing her groceries with Clorox wipes. She hesitated to put bleach on the fruit and carried those items inside to rinse in the sink instead. She realized her exposure to COVID from her encounters with Michael Collins far exceeded anything she might pick up in a market. She thought of her babies in Argentina and washed her hands until they burned. She did not want to die, and she did not intend to. She had a reason—two reasons—to live, and they were Gogo and Espie.

Despite the fact that she had just stocked the house with healthy food, Linda ate popcorn for dinner, washing it down with a glass of vodka. Or two. She watched the endless loop of the same news over and over on CNN as she absently twirled her wedding ring around and around her finger.

The daily press conferences on coronavirus had stopped weeks ago, but the news was nothing but. She did not take her ring off to look at the inscription winding around the band. She knew it by heart. She had engraved it there, after all, she and Miguel, when they married eight years before. Both of their rings bore the same sentiment—*siempre juntos*—along with their initials. His first and last. Her first and last. Of her maiden name, of course. *Always together.* That is what they intended to be. She shuddered at the thought that it might, in the end, prove to be truer than she had ever imagined.

They were married in the summer of 2012, at Sacred Heart in Shadyside. Her parents had moved out of Pittsburgh years before to the leafy suburbs beyond, where her father could be near to what was dear to him: golf. Oakmont Country Club was—is—one of the premier courses in the nation. And yet, when it was time for their little girl to marry, especially to a fancy South American, the family decided to go back to the center of things and held the ceremony at the majestic church downtown. The reception followed, of course, at the club, and Linda caught her father wistfully eyeing the links throughout the evening. Given half a chance, she suspected he would have gone outside to hit a few balls between courses. Maybe he did sneak out there after all. Who could have blamed him?

Miguel was intoxicating then. He had a way of telling Linda that no one would ever love her the way he did that was hypnotizing to her. For some reason inexplicable to her now, it both captivated and frightened her. She was scared not to be loved that way again, because being loved that way was like a drug. But drugs wore off.

And Miguel changed. His intensity went from feeling loving to feeling claustrophobic. His way of keeping tabs on Linda stopped feeling attentive and began to feel controlling. When did it happen? Was it all at once or was it a gradual transformation? And was the change in him or was it, in fact, something in her that could no longer tolerate the force of his personality upon her own?

She had always hated the old-fashionedness of her name. She had wished to be a Morgan or a Whitney or a Drew, like the other girls at school. Linda was an actress's name from black-and-white movies. But then Miguel came along and played with her name. Teased it and touched it and made Linda feel overwhelmingly that her name—that she—was the laser focus of his desire. That was part of the early magic of Miguel. He made Linda feel. That was it. Every feeling she had when she was with him was ramped up and blown into a heightened proportion. She, whose emotions had, frankly, always run a bit cool, was drawn to the feelingness of it all.

Like eating too much candy, however, it all started to make her feel sick. And maybe that was when he changed to a crueler version of himself. Maybe he saw Linda withdraw into herself and decided to draw her back out. By the time her mother was dying last year, their marriage was hanging by a thread. And that thread was really their children.

But the wedding had been lovely. She remembered their fathers' toasts, each man trying to overcome his trepidation that his child had married someone so far out of the family's cultural background that their union would be doomed. A wealthy Argentine family melded with a middle-class American one. *At least they were both Catholic* was a sentiment that was evident on the faces of everyone in the parental generation. At least they would not have to negotiate the religious upbringing of their offspring.

Miguel's toast stood out, though, in its purity and simplicity. Like the inscription on the band that she twisted around her finger now.

"Linda. *Mi linda novia.* I am so proud and happy to stand here and call you my bride. My beautiful bride. I pledge to you my life and my love. Forever. *Siempre juntos,*" he added as he held up his left hand and wiggled the finger with the ring that bore those words inside of it. "Just like it says here. I also pledge to your family, to your parents—Mr. and Mrs. Huber—that I will always take care of your little girl. Linda Huber belonged to you. Linda Alonso belongs to me."

Maybe it was a little creepy, after all. Even then.

38

A WRITER'S THOUGHTS

Surprised?

You thought I made her up. You thought I was sitting all by my lonesome in my crappy apartment with my old dog and my old body and my endless obsessions with food and murder and arcane statistics and just making stuff up.

I'm afraid not.

Linda Alonso is Matt Huber's daughter, born late in his life. What we used to call "a change of life" baby for Mr. and Mrs. Huber. She is the niece of the late Noelle Huber. She is not the product of my writer's imagination. She is a product of the loins of the man who raped and killed his sister. Those same loins. That same family.

I don't make anything up. What I do is, I *embellish*. You will come to see how I know what I know about Linda Alonso and about what she did. What I know for certain are the *facts*. What I have filled in is simply the *color*.

Here is a perfect example: How do I know exactly what Miguel Alonso said in his toast at his wedding to Linda Huber? Easy. I watched the wedding video on the Alonsos' computer. How did I have access to that computer? Hold your horses, you'll know soon enough.

On the other hand, how do I know that Linda's father was longing to leave the wedding reception and go outside and hit a few golf balls? Well, that would be embellishment. I don't actually *know* the man's thoughts. But from what I do know about him and his devotion to the game of golf, I can fill in that little detail. It allows us to say, "Oh, I like golf, too." Or, "I despise golf." No matter which, we've got an association with the man. Golf.

Among other things.

At first, of course, Linda did not know that I watched her, kept tabs on her life, her husband, her children. It wasn't a big deal in the early years. We lived in the same town. I knew her family history; I would even say it had something to do with me. At least it was of strong personal interest to me. So I observed. I found reasons to drive or bike down her street, reasons to notice her schedule—when she dropped off or picked up her children at school—reasons to be in her general vicinity.

I am sure you've done something like this yourself. Isn't there someone you pay a little extra attention to? You like the way she cuts her hair, so you start frequenting the same salon. You can't get over the new handbag she shows up with at lunch, so you buy one of your own. You are jealous of the vacation she takes so you organize to go there, too. And it is possible—probable—that this person is much less aware of your existence than you are of hers.

Enlarging the scope, isn't there some celebrity you follow? A movie star, a singer, a royal? Maybe you Google Taylor Swift or Meghan Markle, check out what they're wearing or where they're eating. Maybe you like Reese Witherspoon's book recommendations or Oprah's? I know you do. I am absolutely positive you do something in the vein of what I did with Linda Huber Alonso.

All I really did was pay attention to her.

The rest of it just unfolded before my eyes. Let's go back to last spring, a little more than a year ago, before there was even a hint of the pandemic. Before Linda's mother died. Before the metaphorical shit hit the metaphorical fan.

39

THE WIFE

Chapter Twenty-Two
Friday, March 15, 2019

The Ides of March dawned in 2019 much the same as every other day in March—really, the best month of all in Florida—warm and dewy, gearing up to sunny and hot. Linda wished she could tell you now, from the vantage point of hindsight, that there had been something notable about the day. A wind from a different direction. A lunar eclipse. A freak storm.

But there was nothing.

Nothing had been terribly wrong between Linda and Miguel that day. At least, nothing much worse than the general torpor their relationship had slumped into long before. Miguel was increasingly controlling and critical of Linda for an ever-widening sweep of items he found worthy of his attention. The mail. Bedtime. Toys left loose. Lint.

Yes, lint.

Miguel had taken it upon himself to check the dryer from time to time to make sure Linda kept it cleaned out. He had recently read about dryer fires and intended to position himself as the wall between that outcome and his family. Linda had tried to reassure him that she swiped the lint out of its little basket each and every time she used the dryer. But he felt that Manuela could not be trusted to do the same. That she might *say* she was doing it but not really do it. A sort of passive-aggressive employee/boss game that he pedantically explained to Linda, as though she could not understand it herself.

And then there was the Fabulosa, which was an ongoing source of argument. Linda wondered where he found the time to think about all of this crap, when he had a job he was supposed to be doing.

So—while these things were annoying, to be sure—nothing was out of the ordinary for them. They had had a normal dinner that night, put the children to bed in their normal way, and were getting ready to go to sleep themselves when an abnormal sound was heard.

A small sound. A sound that could have been misinterpreted as something going on outside their house that had nothing to do with them. A sound from the natural world: a night roamer, like a raccoon or a possum. But it was not a natural sound, and Linda was the first to hear it because Miguel was in the bathroom brushing his teeth.

Someone was knocking on their door.

"Miguel?" she called from the bed—where she had just settled in with a book—to the door of the bathroom which he had left ajar. "Did you hear that?"

"What?"

"I think someone's at the door."

"Now?"

"Listen." She motioned him over to her side. "Do you hear that?"

Miguel crossed the room with his toothbrush in hand. "Yeah," he said. "I hear it. I'll go."

He went, but he did not return.

Linda listened from the bed to the sound of the door opening. She heard muffled voices from that general vicinity, which went on for quite a while. Then she heard the front door close again. After a beat, the voices continued from the direction of the kitchen. Who could have come to the door in the dark that Miguel would have let into the house?

Linda rose and went to the bedroom door to hear better. She strained to understand what was being said, but all she could really identify was the fact that there were two male voices speaking: Miguel's and someone else's, each one low and rumbling, but a little distinct, one from the other. It didn't sound like English, but it was hard to tell. She got back in bed in an attempt to wait it out but found herself returning to the doorway more than once.

Forty-five minutes of this felt like hours. She was in the process of throwing on some clothes in order to join her husband and the visitor when Miguel appeared at the bedroom door. His face was ashen.

"What's wrong, Miguel? Who's here?"

"Stay here, Linda."

"Who's out there?"

"It's my brother. It's Diego."

"*Your*...?" Linda sat on the edge of the bed, working to comprehend what her husband had just said.

Miguel came over and sat next to her. Rarely had she seen him at such a loss for words.

"Shouldn't I...?" Linda began. "I don't know. Make coffee?"

"I did already. And he's eating what's left from dinner."

"Did you heat it up?"

"Yes."

"Okay." Linda stood. Then she sat again. "You're sure you don't want me to come out? Is he leaving, or...?"

"He will stay here."

"Here? Jesus, Miguel. We thought he was dead! I mean, where's he been for twenty years? How did he get here? Is he in some kind of trouble?"

"I need to discuss all of this with him, and it's better if it's just the two of us."

"I guess. Will we put him in the guest room?"

"Yes. Is it in order?"

"Yes...um, yes. It has sheets and towels."

Miguel got up from the bed with some effort, as though his body had taken on weight. He walked to the door to make his way back to the kitchen. To his recently un-dead brother, Diego.

"Wait," Linda called out before he left the room. Miguel turned to face her. "Did you know? I mean, that he wasn't dead?"

"No, I didn't know," Miguel said and, with the same heaviness, left the room.

Linda remained on the edge of the bed, considering what her husband had told her. Who was this brother? Why on earth would he spend more than two decades hiding out or whatever the hell it was he was doing when his entire family thought he was dead? And why was he here now?

At that thought, Linda jumped up and tiptoed to her children's room. She opened the door quietly and looked at them as the light from the hall spilled softly onto their small, sleeping forms. Gogo was named for this man, but she never expected he would actually meet him. That *she* would meet him.

Linda closed the door softly but firmly, pulling on the knob to make sure the latch had taken hold. It gave her an eerie feeling to think that Miguel might open the door to show this namesake brother their children while they slept. Or to think that he—the brother—might do it on his own.

There had to be something wrong with him to do what he did. What kind of person just vanishes into thin air and lets his parents think he is dead all this time? Their father died a broken man, believing he had out-lived his eldest son. None of it made any sense, and Linda was alarmed that her husband had invited this stranger to sleep in their home.

Wait.

How could Miguel even be sure this man *was* his brother? Linda had seen that movie, *The Return of Martin Guerre*. That woman's hus-band came home from however many years he'd been away at war and she wasn't even sure it was him! The village didn't think it was him. No one thought it was him. But the new man knew so many intimate sto-ries that only her husband could have known that everyone eventually accepted him as the guy. The wife was happy because the man who returned was nicer than her husband had ever been. But she knew he wasn't her husband. Her husband had been a creep. She liked this guy better, so she let it be.

What if this was something like that? What if this guy had spent time with the real Diego—what if he'd killed him—and that was why he knew whatever stories he was telling Miguel right now?

Stranger things had happened.

Linda crept silently down the hall to try to get a look at him from a distance. There was a spot at the end, just before the archway to the living room, where she could just see the kitchen table. If that was where they were sitting, she might be able to see him. Once in position, she peeked her head slowly around the corner. Miguel's back was to her as he spoke to the man who sat opposite.

The man had dark hair, no surprises there. It was long and kind of wild looking, which was also not a surprise. He'd been living God-knows-where, maybe a forest. His head was higher than Miguel's, so he must have been a little bit taller. He looked very thin, gaunt, which did not surprise her either. What had he been eating? Bananas? Nuts?

Miguel got up from his seat, gathered both of their coffee cups, and walked in the direction of the counter. She heard the hum of the Nespresso maker. The man sat alone, looking down at his hands. And then he looked up.

At Linda.

It was not a sharp movement, like someone who had been living on the lam who heard a sound and might have to spring into quick action. Escape. It was a slow raising of his head. An unrushed lifting of his eyes.

And he looked straight at Linda. And for the second time in her life, she was looking at the most beautiful man she had ever seen. Diego looked nearly identical to Miguel, which shot a hole in her Martin Guerre theory. There was no possible doubt they were brothers. Yet, even in his currently unkempt condition, Diego's features were more favored by the gods of beauty. They were arranged just a little bit differently: his nose and his brows more finely drawn, his lips more full.

And the color of his eyes was brighter than Miguel's. Brown, maybe, like her husband's. But there was something more animated about them. A touch of yellow, like a cat.

And as he looked straight at her without flinching, that vibration began in her midsection, that anxious feeling that the earth had shifted beneath her. Only it wasn't quite what she would later pretend to Devon, her chiropractor friend—that she'd been anxious because of something Miguel had done. It had nothing to do with Miguel. It had everything to do with his brother. The one who had, until today, been dead.

40

THE WIFE

Chapter Twenty-Three
Tuesday, April 16, 2019

After they made eye contact on the fifteenth of March, Linda and Diego avoided each other almost completely. At least they practiced as much avoidance as could be accomplished in a three-bedroom ranch house over the course of a month.

They did not speak the night Diego arrived. Linda had slipped back into bed quickly, before her husband saw her standing in the hallway. She stayed awake, though, and listened through the door much later, as Miguel led his brother down the hall to the guest room. Just as she had predicted, she heard Miguel open the door to the children's room and heard the men's muffled voices as they talked while they looked at her sleeping babies. Finally she heard the guest room door close and Miguel enter their own room.

She closed her eyes and pretended to be asleep.

The morning after Diego's appearance, Gogo—always a keen observer—was quick to ask why the spare bedroom door was shut when normally it was left wide open. Diego had not yet emerged from the room.

"We have a guest," his father answered. "And we're going to play a game. We're going to see who is the best at keeping secrets. Will it be Espie or Gogo? We aren't going to tell anyone about our secret guest. And if you want to win the contest, you have to be very, very good at keeping that secret."

Linda almost choked on her coffee.

"I'm best!" Espie cried out.

"No, you're not. You're just a baby," Gogo said.

Espie broke into a full wail and Linda jumped up to console her, ready to throw her coffee in Miguel's face. What kind of a thing was it to say to your children that they had some stealth visitor? And how on earth did he expect a toddler and a preschooler to hold onto that one? Honestly, if she didn't know he'd gone to a great college and was successful at his job, she would have said the man was an idiot.

"Daddy didn't really mean that," she scrambled for damage control. "Daddy just meant..." What the hell *did* Daddy mean? Why was his brother's arrival to be kept secret? What had his brother done? What were they getting involved in?

"C'mon." She changed tacks. "Let's take Gogo to school!"

Espie was not yet in preschool. She still spent her days at home with Linda, napping for two to three hours after lunch. Miguel went early to his office in West Palm Beach. Though he had left the Latin American division of Citibank for a boutique investment firm seven years ago—a move that had brought the Alonsos to Florida—his clients were still primarily South Americans. Many of them had second homes in Florida—glass-walled apartments in Miami or houses in Coral Gables, Coconut Grove, and Palm Beach. Miguel was diligent about getting out the door so he could read *Crain's Miami* and the *Wall Street Journal* on his iPad in the relative calm of his office, unaccompanied by the squeals of his children.

Diego never appeared before his brother left the house. Linda always had the kitchen cleaned up after breakfast, Gogo dropped off at school, and Espie engaged in an activity, like sitting on the family room floor doing puzzles, before Diego made his first cup of espresso. He never asked for help, but he always asked permission.

"May I?" he would ask before turning on the Nespresso machine.

"Would you like?" he would offer her a cup of coffee to go with his.

"It's okay?" He would point to a container of yogurt from the refrigerator.

"Yes, no, of course, please, you don't need to ask." Linda returned these responses to his half-formed queries.

At night, they all dined together. Diego was polite and helpful and funny with the children. He spoke to them only in Spanish and, for some reason, Espie and Gogo responded to him in kind when they had flatly refused to do so with their father. Maybe it felt like a game to them. In any case, they willingly used their own, very broken Spanish to talk with their uncle.

After dinner, he always smoked a pipe. Linda added tobacco to her shopping list when she'd seen him carrying the thing around. It was an odd affect, she considered, something perhaps left over from an earlier era, a time when he had abandoned the world and ceased to follow its progress. Had he smoked a pipe all those years on the lam in Bolivia or wherever he'd been?

Pipa, the children called him. *Pipa* for pipe. Soon, the house rang with calls for Pipa. *Pipa, juguemos! Pipa, leamos! Pipa! Por favor!* Linda and Miguel had been relegated to second and third place by the arrival of this dashing uncle. Linda was charmed by the children's enjoyment of him, and it was a relief to get a little respite from her normal routines.

Miguel was not so sure.

It soon became evident to Linda that there was something very complicated in the relationship of the brothers. At the most obvious level, the questions had still not been answered about Diego's twenty-plus year walkabout. Miguel never discussed any of it with Linda. When she would probe him in bed at night about what sort of information he was getting out of his brother, he was uncharacteristically quiet.

"Linda, he's been through a lot."

"Oh yeah? What?"

"I'll find out. He doesn't like to talk about it."

This was rather galling to Linda. Had *she* tried that excuse with Miguel to avoid answering any of his questions—*I don't want to talk about it*—she knew it wouldn't fly. What was known was that Diego's friend, Nico, the guy he took off with on his motorcycle trip in 1998 was, in fact, dead. And Nico's death had happened when both of the men were presumed to have died. How and where Nico died was still a mystery. How and why Diego survived but went underground, even more.

"Is he a drug dealer?"

"Linda!"

"Don't act so surprised, Miguel! What else would the guy be doing out there for *two decades*? Is he a terrorist? A member of the FARC?"

"Bolivia's not even next to Columbia."

"I don't care! You don't *know* he was in Bolivia. Your parents got a *postcard* from there. He was gone so long he could have walked to the moon and back after he sent that postcard, for all you know. He could have been anywhere! You really surprise me, Miguel, with your lack of curiosity about all this!"

"*Querida*," Miguel said. "Give me time."

41

A WRITER'S THOUGHTS

Michelle McNamara was part of the tribe. And membership in it had killed her.

This particular tribe is like most, if not all; we do not choose to be members. We are born—or made—a part of it. Our tribe consists of those of us who—for reasons of geographical proximity or genetic relationship—can't quite shake loose the grip the murder of someone close to us has had on us.

McNamara grew up in Oak Park, Illinois. Her seminal event—the exact moment she joined our tribe—came when she was fourteen years old and a girl was murdered in her neighborhood, not very far from her house. Like the murder of my mother's best friend, McNamara's neighbor's killing remains unsolved today. And *that* can be one of the sources of power for this particular hold: the fact that the murderer remains at large. McNamara described it well in her nonfiction book, *I'll Be Gone in the Dark*, which has also been turned into an HBO series by the same name:

If you commit murder and then vanish, what you leave behind isn't just pain but absence, a supreme blankness that triumphs over everything else. The unidentified murderer is always twisting a doorknob behind a door that never opens. But his power evaporates the moment we know him. We learn his banal secrets. We watch as he's led, shackled and sweaty, into a brightly lit courtroom as someone seated several feet higher peers down unsmiling, raps a gavel, and speaks, at long last, every syllable of his birth name.

Every syllable of his birth name. That is it. It is the thing that could free us all.

McNamara developed from the girl she was in Oak Park into one of our premiere *citizen detectives*. Remember that term? It was used disparagingly by the superintendent of the Pittsburgh police to describe the Pittsburghers who were running around trying to solve Noelle Huber's murder. But it is not used disparagingly anymore.

McNamara grew up to research and write about murders. Most specifically, she spent years trying to solve the multiple rapes and murders committed by one man whom she eventually dubbed *The Golden State Killer*. Her moniker stuck to the man who had been known at various times and at various locations around the state of California as the *Visalia Ransacker*, the *East Area Rapist* (EAR), the *Original Night Stalker* (ONS).

For years, no one knew that this perpetrator of at least fifty brutal rapes, more than a dozen grisly murders, and countless acts of breaking and entering and robbery was a single man. McNamara was influential in tying all the cases together. She worked closely with police forces all over the state. She collaborated with writers, bloggers, journalists, and other citizen detectives for years to find this one man. Sadly, she did not live to see her years of dogged work come to fruition.

McNamara correctly predicted that it would be advances in identifying DNA that would finally bag this fiend. She also correctly predicted that he was still alive, even though his spree of violence ended in 1986, decades before his capture. Many others had presumed him dead. But not McNamara. And then she died before finishing her book. She died before his capture. She died before every syllable of Joseph James DeAngelo's birth name could be spoken. In fact, DeAngelo was not even one of the suspects she and the others had so meticulously researched.

DeAngelo would not have been found if it were not for the bodily fluids he left behind—fluids that eventually allowed detectives to pinpoint him. DeAngelo might have gotten away with it. He may have thought he had. He had been careful. He probably stopped his activities when he did because he could see that it was becoming increasingly difficult to avoid detection. He was, for many years—years when he was perpetrating the most depraved sorts of crimes—also a police officer. He lived an ostensibly normal life. He had a wife. He had daughters. He had a granddaughter. He had a roast in the oven the day he was arrested.

Michelle McNamara worked and worried herself to death. She relied on a dangerous combination of Adderall, fentanyl, and Xanax to get her through her long days and longer nights. It did not work. Her body gave out and her book was finished by her editors and postscripted by her husband. But.

But.

McNamara had the final word. The epilogue of the book is hers. In her *Letter to an Old Man*, she writes:

> *One day soon, you'll hear a car pull up to your curb, an engine cut out. You'll hear footsteps coming up your front walk...*
>
> *The doorbell rings.*
>
> *No side gates are left open. You're long past leaping over a fence. Take one of your hyper, gulping breaths. Clench your teeth. Inch timidly toward the insistent bell.*
>
> *This is how it ends for you.*
>
> *"You'll be silent forever, and I'll be gone in the dark," you threatened a victim once.*
>
> *Open the door. Show us your face.*
>
> *Walk into the light.*

That is exactly what I want of Matthew Huber.

And Linda Alonso will help me get it.

42

THE WIFE

Chapter Twenty-Four
Wednesday, May 1, 2019

"*Querida*, give me time," Miguel had asked of Linda. As though time were hers to give.

In the end, though, time was not on Miguel's side. Time weighed more heavily on the side of his brother. Diego had been using time to his advantage since the day he disappeared from the land of the living two decades prior. He knew how to knead time like dough, to stretch it out long, to pat it back tight, to roll it up and store it away in a cupboard, to allow it to fester and grow fat with yeast. Time was Diego Alonso's friend and Diego Alonso knew it.

And all it really took was a little time for Diego to soften the hard edges around Linda. Edges, it might be argued, that were sharpened by his brother, Miguel. Whatever happened to Miguel in the fullness of time—whatever fate he suffered, deservedly or not—Miguel Alonso was not an innocent man.

But, then again, who was?

On the first of May in 2019, Diego had been holed up in the pretty, sea green room in the Alonso house on Reef Road for about six weeks. Holed up is probably too harsh a term for sleeping in your brother's guest room, playing with your brother's children, eating from your brother's table, and getting to know your brother's wife.

But holed up might actually qualify as the correct term since everyone was still keeping Diego's presence in their guest room a secret. Diego Alonso had been, after all, dead for twenty years. And this was not the moment he had chosen to unveil his living status to the world at large. Just to his brother and his brother's family. Manuela probably did not pose a risk of exposing them. Linda could not imagine the authorities tracking down Manuela to question her about an undocumented person living in the Alonso household.

The children were banned from telling anyone of their uncle's presence. This was not an easy feat for children of two and four. The Alonsos made it a game, inviting Gogo and Espie to play it.

In turn, they adored their uncle—their Pipa—who played with them much more than their own father had time to do. Yet, it had taken a little while after his appearance on Reef Road for the butterfly of Diego to emerge from his filthy chrysalis. For Diego Alonso had arrived at their house covered head to toe with vermin.

Linda was the one who had to go to the pharmacy to pick up treatments for head lice, scabies, and crabs. Diego came up with those words—which were not in anyone's normal vocabulary—with translation assistance from Miguel. How he had determined exactly which insects were keeping him company, Linda did not know. And she was not about to verify. The thought of how long he had been infested made her shudder.

Naturally, on her foray to sanitize her brother-in-law, Linda skipped Green's, the local pharmacy on the island, where she might run into her friends. Instead, she hit the CVS on Southern Boulevard in West Palm Beach. The likelihood of being recognized there while picking up a cornucopia of medications for human infestation by parasites was at least a little slimmer.

Fortunately, Diego had mostly stayed in his room in early days—the days of his de-bugging—so his situation did not affect her family. And once Linda had purchased the medications, Diego executed the operation himself. How he ran a nit comb through that mane of his she could not imagine. It was not until she saw him with a cleanly shaved head that she understood his methodology. She wondered if he had shaved his entire body. Other than for the scabies, it would have been as good a cure as any.

Linda furiously disinfected the kitchen and anywhere else she thought he had been, without mentioning any of it to Manuela. And she made Miguel swear he had not taken his brother into the children's room. She left a Hefty bag outside the guest room door. Knocking quietly, she announced, "Diego? Here's a bag. Maybe you could put your clothes in it?" When she saw the bag reappear, full to the top with who knows what—clothing and tufts of his hair?—she gingerly took hold of it with one hand and marched it directly to the curb. Thankfully, it was garbage pickup day and the bag didn't need to stay on their property for long.

Shortly after, Diego peeked his newly bald head out the door and emerged in a bathrobe. It was the nice guest robe she kept in there. She stared at it, wondering if she would need to throw it away.

"Linda?" he asked in his soft voice. Softer than his brother's. "Might you have some vestments for me?"

"Vestments? Um, sure." Linda quickly ran into her bedroom and scrounged up some items from Miguel. One of those Armani T-shirts he liked and a pair of black sweats. Boxers, too. "Here you go," she trilled as she emerged from the room.

"*Gracias.*" He took the items from her and smiled. She could see that his eyes were yellowish brown, just like she had thought. But they weren't like a cat's at all. They made her think of a wolf.

"You're welcome," she said, turning away.

"Linda. May I have shoes?"

"Oh. Of course."

"*Gracias,*" he said again, as she handed him a pair of espadrilles.

"Well. I hope it all fits," she said.

In the end, everything fit in width, but hung just a little bit short. Diego was three inches taller than his brother.

That was all weeks ago. Since then, Diego's hair had grown in enough to give him a military appearance. And he was starting to fill out. He still had that hungry animal look to him, but now he was somewhat less disturbing. But that was only Linda's perspective. The children had never had any hesitation with him.

The matter of Manuela was complicated. Diego's charms seemed to work on her, but Linda couldn't be sure. Sometimes, on Manuela's days at the house, she seemed happy to prepare a meal for him and laughed readily at his jokes. Other times, Linda caught Manuela peering at her brother-in-law with what she could only characterize as hostility.

43

A WRITER'S THOUGHTS

Allow me to step in and shed a little light, as Betty Grable would sing it, "Down Argentine Way."

The Alonso brothers were born two years apart: Diego in 1976, Miguel in 1978. Interesting times in the country of their birth. *May you live in interesting times* is the phrase we often use sardonically to describe periods of unrest, famine, pestilence, war—really any out-of-the-ordinary events that fall into unpleasant and life-threatening categories.

In Argentina in 1976, "interesting times" were kicked off when the government of Isabel Perón—widow of long-term leader, Juan Perón (who, in turn, had been widowed, himself, by his megawatt wife, Evita), was overthrown by a military junta. The United States may have been (most certainly was) involved. It was a period of multiple coups taking place all over South America, which were sponsored and supported by the US under the mission name of Operation Condor.

In Argentina, thirty thousand people disappeared between 1976 and 1983. In fact, the verb was turned into a noun after the magnitude of the campaign: those lost souls became known as "the disappeared." They came from particular subsets of Argentine citizenry—student radicals, teachers, union leaders—comprised of those deemed to have been a threat to the stability of the newly formed right-wing government. The Catholic Church was suspected of collusion.

Out of this wholesale abduction of human flesh, five hundred babies were believed to have been delivered in confinement. Some of those babies may have been in utero when their mothers were grabbed, hooded, and stuffed into cars to be driven to detention centers. Others may have been the result of sexual relations between captors and captives. Presumably forced.

For the *coup de grâce* (really more a coup of disgrace), after giving birth, these mothers were made to write letters to their families, telling their parents they had decided to flee the country, to find safe harbor outside the borders of Argentina, and would take their babies with them. And then the five hundred babies were believed to have been given to other families—friends, colleagues, members of the ruling elite—while their mothers were dropped into the ocean from the open doors of flying airplanes. Alive.

In time, the mothers of these mothers—those whose daughters had been hauled off in cars, robbed of their babies, and flung into the sea— began to protest. They wore white headscarves as a symbol of the diapers of the babies they never would hold. The *Plaza de Mayo* in Buenos Aires is where they began to speak out in 1977, taking the name of the *Asociación Madres de Plaza de Mayo*.

The military government viewed these women as subversives, turned against them, and some of their number were rounded up, never to be seen again. One of their founders and leaders—Azucena Villaflor de Vicenti—disappeared herself and was tortured and killed on a similar death flight to those that had rid them all of their respective children. The women were not cowed and they did not stop, even continuing during the 1978 World Cup, hosted by Argentina in Buenos Aires.

This period became known as the Dirty War. Modern genetic testing has solved some of its mysteries. Adults in their forties in Argentina— those who were adopted as babies in the late '70s and early '80s—are often subpoenaed to turn in their DNA test results. Some of them resist, but those mothers and grandmothers in headscarves are headstrong. The skeletons of that time are still washing up like driftwood in various places around Argentina—even around the world—some as far flung as Reef Road in Palm Beach, Florida.

Señora Alonso had never taken to her older son. He had arrived—wizened like an old man—after years of frustrated attempts to conceive a child. And she *had* conceived. Five times in ten years. But all of her babies had abandoned her body—long before they could survive in the world—as though they found her womb inhospitable. Her husband's family had long since written her off as barren.

Anyone would think the firstborn son of a woman who had tried for so long to have one would have been greeted as the second coming of the one who was born in a manger. But this baby, carried into the apartment by her husband's driver, did not look right. He did not smell right. Diego had not even bothered to bring the baby in himself. If he had expected her to welcome the child as her own, he might have tried harder to present him well. And he never even said where he had come from. As though babies were to be had on the streets. Which, she guessed, in those days, they were.

Diego was as good a name as any. She could hold her head up high in her husband's family, in her own, and among her lady friends. They had a son and a namesake for her husband, and an heir to the Alonso fortune.

But, try as she might have—and she *had* tried—she just could not stomach him. It began with the look of him. Who had ever heard of a skinny baby? Babies were meant to be plump and pink, to show off the prosperity of their families and the ample milk of their mothers. But not this one. He was wiry and wrinkled and slight. And then there was his smell: tangy, like a cabbage. It was a vegetable she never had cared for and perhaps this was the cause of her disfavor. But there was nothing sweet about him. She even tried putting sugar into his formula—away from the eyes of the nanny—to see if it would change his aroma. It did not.

The one good thing the eldest brought was an end to her own barrenness. Thirteen months after his appearance, she conceived again. And this time, she carried the child to term. Her son. The one who should have been named for her husband. The baby who arrived in the basket augured the arrival of the baby who came from her womb.

When Miguel was born, he was everything Esperanza had ever imagined a baby to be. Fat and smiling, redolent of yeasty bread. She could not stop holding him. She snuck into the nursery to feed him from her own breasts—despite her husband's warnings that she would ruin them. As if she cared about those appendages for any other purpose than to nourish this tiny life. She found reasons to send the baby nurse off on errands with the older boy, to steal time alone with the baby. This son. Her son.

The fact that the first one bore the name of her husband rankled. She never thought he deserved it. Had it been up to her—which, of course, it had not—she would have switched their names later, once her own precious son was born. The one she actually birthed. Not the one who came in a basket. That one—the two-year-old—would surely never remember what they had called him the first couple years of life. Anyway, who cared? It was perfectly all right to change a child's name. And her little one deserved the moniker. He was *hers*. But their names remained as given.

The years passed. The boys loved each other. Her husband preferred the elder. She loved only the younger. But she tolerated the older one and kept her thoughts to herself. At least, she meant to. Once the boys started to look alike, though, once the thought entered her mind that the first one was possibly her husband's child, a child conceived with someone else, one of those depraved women who disappeared during those terrible years, the task of being nice to the child became nearly impossible.

44

THE WIFE

Chapter Twenty-Five
Saturday, May 25, 2019

If you were among the snowbirds slow to accept the end of season in Florida, Memorial Day weekend was your signal. For those who were not year-rounders, it was the last hurrah. Palm Beach was now officially humid and hot. It was also rainier than it had been for the past six months.

And yet, there was something to be missed if one cleared out now, for this was the moment when the ocean became the calmest it would be all year, often resembling glass. A sea so becalmed was never the delight of sailors. For power boaters, on the other hand, this was what they lived for. They seized this moment to go to the Bahamas.

Miguel had left yesterday at five a.m., skippering his Boston Whaler with a couple of his workmates on board. All of them were experienced fishermen, and all of them carried the twinkle of the great Florida catch in their eyes: a tarpon, a sailfish, a swordfish, a shark. Anything was possible. In preparation, the boat had been stocked with copious quantities of beer and tequila, beverages guaranteed to fuel the blood lust of its passengers. Steaks, tortilla chips, and fiery hot salsas were the other three food groups included, covering protein, starch, and vegetables to every passenger's satisfaction.

Linda stayed behind with Gogo and Espie. And, of course, Miguel's brother, Diego. On Friday—yesterday—the day Miguel took off, Diego had been with them exactly ten weeks. Seventy days. Linda had heard—from her prenatal yoga teacher—that forty days was a mystical period of time, a span during which transformative things could unfold. Precisely what those things were, Linda did not know. But her yoga teacher was convinced of it, always likening the first trimester of a pregnancy to the voyage of Noah's ark or Moses crossing the desert. Linda didn't think her teacher had those time spans correct. And Diego had been with them for seventy days, not forty. But there was no denying that transformation was afoot.

By now, the children treated their Pipa as an extension of their parents. For them, these seventy days equaled forever. That was how long they acted as if they had known Diego. From that first day of his presence in their lives—March 15th—to now, Diego had carved out pieces of each of their hearts and inserted himself inside.

All except for Miguel, whose initial warmth toward this prodigal brother had begun to take a turn.

Manuela was not with them over the holiday weekend. Linda struggled to think what to do with this brother-in-law who was confined to the house. She struggled to understand what he did with his time, period, as the weeks of his confinement stretched on. But he seemed content to fill his days with reading and household help.

She couldn't very well leave him, though. It would have been bad manners to trot off without him to the beach or zoo. Even though his own brother had no such compunctions. The depths of their growing discord—these brothers—was palpable to Linda, though neither of them had offered an explanation to her.

Anyway, Espie and Gogo would not think of abandoning Pipa. So they ran through the usual activities that one runs through with small children. And, no matter how many items were on their list, none of them took very long. Diego pushed Espie on a swing, Gogo worked to pump his legs himself. They scooted their bikes as best they could on the backyard grass, avoiding the driveway in open view of the neighbors. They played in the pool with a beach ball and lay on the concrete to dry off. When the rain kept intermittently falling, they transferred themselves inside to read books, stack blocks, color with crayons, and squeeze a bunch of Play-Doh, mindful to keep Espie from eating it.

Linda went to Publix and—at Gogo's strict instructions—picked up the ingredients to cook Memorial Day dinner. He wanted his uncle to experience typical American cookout cuisine: hamburgers, corn on the cob, watermelon, potato salad, and brownies. Diego stayed with the children while she shopped, and he read to them while she cooked. When the meal was ready and they were all seated under the patio umbrella to escape the rain, Diego ate most graciously and made complimentary comments, although Linda couldn't tell if he actually liked it.

"What are you used to eating?" she asked, since, thus far, no one had shed any light on any aspect of his activities for the past twenty years.

"I am a simple man. I am happy with whatever is given to me."

It was a good dodge, Linda had to admit, very gracefully done. She would not push him to reveal more in front of the children, but she might after they went to bed.

Diego helped with the dishes and sat outside the bathroom door while Linda bathed the children. It seemed a little intimate, but Espie and Gogo had insisted.

"Pipa!" Espie cried when she was zipped into her footed pajamas. "Story!"

"Espie," Linda tried to dissuade her, "Pipa may be tired. Mommy can do it tonight."

"Pwease." Espie looked at Diego with her big, soulful eyes.

"*Por supuesto*," he answered. "*Me encantaria.*"

Espie silently handed him her favorite book. Of course it was *We're Going on a Bear Hunt*. Diego read it haltingly. The children were delighted with his hesitation over pronunciation. Gogo jumped in to help him and felt like a very big boy, indeed. They ended up reading the book six times in a row.

Afterward, when Linda and Diego had tucked the children in and kissed them both twice, Linda apologized. "I'm afraid they're taking advantage of you." She laughed. "You didn't need to read it so many times."

"It was a pleasure for me. They remind me so much of myself and Miguel at that age."

"Really?" She had a hard time imagining Miguel as sweet and innocent as her babies.

"Oh, yes. We made our nannies read books many times."

"Would you like a drink?" Linda asked. Maybe wine would loosen his tongue. If Miguel had succeeded in worming the truth out of his brother, he hadn't revealed any of it to her. This might be her chance to probe.

"I do not normally drink," he said.

Even better, she thought. "Try vodka," she said as she poured a double. "It's not like drinking at all."

"Linda..."

"What?"

"I do not drink."

"Fine. I'll have it," she snapped. She took the glass of Tito's and sat on the couch in the living room. "Sit down, at least. You do sit, don't you? Now that you don't have lice?"

Diego smiled at her, said nothing, and sat on a chair opposite. Linda took a big swig of vodka. Maybe she was the one who needed to loosen up.

"Okay, I'll just say it. Where have you been, Diego?" She took another sip as he sat there, stone-faced. "I mean, twenty years? Your parents thought you were dead. We all did."

Diego turned his head to face the window. There wasn't much to see; it was already dark out there. In profile, his resemblance to a wolf changed to that of a hawk. She considered, for a wild instant, the idea that he was some sort of Native American shape-shifter, inhabiting animal after animal as the spirit moved him. "What do you know of my family?" he finally asked, interrupting Linda's reverie.

"Um. I know your mother. I knew your father for a little bit. Miguel and I dated for a long time before we got married. Ten years. I met your father twice before he died."

"Why did you wait so long to marry?"

"Good question. Why did you wait so long to come alive again?"

Diego laughed. "Good question."

"If I tell you, will you tell me?" she tried.

"Linda, I will tell you. It is not a secret from you."

"It's not?" Maybe Miguel was lying.

"It is not. I left Buenos Aires after I had argued with my parents," he said. "With Señora Alonso."

"I know your mother's name." Linda laughed.

"I left after we had quarreled. My father was upset. He begged me not to go. But I could not stay."

"What did you fight about?"

"The story of my birth."

"Your…?"

"What do you know of Argentina? Our history? Our dirty war?"

"I…" and suddenly a lightbulb went off. "Oh my God. They're not your parents? You're one of those babies those women in the white scarves are trying to find?"

"She is not my mother," Diego answered. "But he was very much my father."

"No wonder she hates those women!" Linda blurted as the pieces reassembled in the puzzle that was her mother-in-law. "She's always saying things about how terrible they are. And the girls who gave birth to those babies. She hates them, too."

"One of those girls was my mother," he simply said. "And my father was my father."

"I thought those girls were already pregnant when they were abducted?"

"Not all of them. Some of them were forced to be with men. Men like my father."

"How do you know all this?"

"She told me."

"Oh, Diego. I'm so sorry."

"You see why I had to go. I did not wish to poison Miguel against them. He was such a sweet boy."

"I guess. But where did you go? And then why did you come here now? I mean, you were filthy when you got here so you can't have been in a very good place!"

"It was the journey here that made me so dirty. It was not dirty where I lived."

45

A WRITER'S THOUGHTS

It wasn't hard to meet Linda. Amici Market is small and—in the days before COVID—an amiable place where conversations could be started. I am not really an Amici Market kind of shopper—too expensive for me—but I frequent Green's Pharmacy next door. The luncheonette at Green's is my speed for dining out. They serve an enormous greasy breakfast for a very reasonable price. I can afford the cost in dollars, even if I begrudge the cost in calories. There are ways to deal with that, though, and I know them all.

I noticed Linda going into the market most mornings last spring. March of 2019. Around the time I would later learn that Diego Alonso had landed on her doorstep. She had one child in tow—the small one, the girl. I knew she had another and figured she had dropped that one off at nursery school before stopping to buy groceries.

I spent time considering how to do it. The simplicity of the plan I came up with surprised even me. I loitered in the produce section, waiting until she was near, and then I "fell" into a pile of oranges, which naturally rolled all over the floor. The child loved it and ran around picking them up. Linda stopped to help. We ended up laughing and chatting. I identified myself as a novelist, which seemed to get her interest. Turned out she knew who I was. She had even read a couple of my books. She was, dare I say it, a little starstruck.

I think it is important to point out that I looked good then. If I was not exactly on Linda's level of beauty, at least I was put together. My hair was regularly trimmed and my roots were not springing up gray the way they have done since all the salons have shut down.

Linda invited me over for coffee.

Well. She started to invite me, then checked herself. As though she remembered a reason I should not come to her house. It piqued my interest so I pushed a little. Not enough to be a weirdo, though.

"Reef Road?" I asked. "Oh wow, I love that part of Palm Beach! It makes me feel like I'm in California!" I was using too many superlatives and needed to tone it down a notch.

"Yeah," she said distractedly. "It's great. Um. I just remembered my house is being painted. We could meet at Starbucks on Worth. That might be better."

I stepped it back. "Sure. That could work. Tomorrow?"

"Oh, um. I can't tomorrow. Why don't you give me your cell phone number and I'll text you. Maybe next week or the following?"

"Here." I pulled out my phone. "Give me your number and I'll call you now. Then we'll have each other's contacts."

I was not surprised she never called. Or texted. Women like Linda led "busy lives." I waited two weeks, which seemed an elegant and non-creepy amount of time. Almost as if I had forgotten about her.

I had not forgotten her in the slightest.

Early in April of 2019, I texted. Much more casual than a phone call. *Hey Linda*, I typed, *it's Noelle. I'll be in your neighborhood tomorrow morning for a meeting. Coffee?*

I wanted to get a look at her house, beyond what I'd already seen from the street. And that one time I had walked around to the backyard. I'd just wanted to check it out. And I had made sure no one was home. No harm done.

She did not text me back for seven hours. I am not a young person, so I don't know the culture code of appropriate return texting time, but seven hours seemed too long to be considered polite. It sent a message that the person was not terribly interested in talking with you.

Sure, she finally replied, *painters just finished. Ten?*

Perfect, I typed back instantly. I didn't believe that she had been painting her house at all. It would be evident the next day, anyway, whether or not the house smelled of paint. But I wouldn't mention it. I didn't want to be antagonistic toward Linda. I wanted to be Linda's friend.

I showed up the following morning at one minute before ten. I had been waiting around the corner, not wanting to be early but not wanting to risk a mishap along the way that would make me late. I waited the final minute at the curb and approached the front door at ten a.m. on the dot. I had brought pastries from Blue Provence. Best croissants on the island.

She took her time getting to the door—nearly five minutes—which is a long time when you're waiting outside. She was flushed when she finally appeared and smiled broadly at me.

"Hi!" she said with too much excitement. "Nora! Come in!"

"Noelle."

"Right! Noelle! You know," she said as she motioned me past her at the door, "I had an aunt named Noelle."

"Really?" I could not believe we were already on this subject. "Huh. Funny small world. Had?"

"She died," Linda said, and before I could say anything else, she continued, "What kind of coffee do you like? I make a mean cappuccino."

"Cappuccino sounds great. I brought croissants!" I held up the bag like a trophy while I sniffed the air for the smell of house paint. There was none.

"Oh," she sounded disappointed. "I've already eaten."

Of course she would say that. She was exactly the type of woman who would have eaten bran flakes or a single boiled egg for breakfast. Five blueberries. She was not the type for a croissant.

"Well, here." I thrust the bag at her. "For the little one."

"Oh, thanks. You met my daughter at Amici, but I actually have two children."

"Really?"

"My little boy's in preschool. Espie—the one you met—will start this fall," Linda said as she handed me a frothy cappuccino and the sugar bowl. "My son's name is Diego, but we call him Gogo. That's the way Espie first pronounced it and it stuck."

I dropped two cubes of sugar into my coffee. If we weren't going to eat—and I could hardly eat if she didn't—I needed a little something. "Those are Spanish names?"

"My husband's from Argentina. Come, let's sit down." She motioned back toward the living room where the furniture was all very pristine and pale.

I was a little nervous to follow her there with my coffee and was suddenly glad not to be stuffing a croissant into my mouth. "Oh, wow," I said as I followed her. "How did you meet?"

"Well, I went to New York after college—like everyone—and met him in a bar!" She perched on a white upholstered armchair.

"Sounds romantic." I sat on the aqua sofa and took a sip. "You weren't kidding. This is a very good cappuccino."

"How did you start writing?" she asked me. "I mean, did you always write?"

"I was the typical lonely, only child and I guess it was a natural extension of that. Not so original." I took another sip of coffee. "Do you write?"

"Me? Ha!" she let out a whoop and then made a shushing motion. "Oops. Espie just went down for a nap. She doesn't normally nap in the mornings anymore, but she was off today. No. I don't write. Although I have plenty of stories I could tell."

"That's all it takes," I said. "All you need is a story."

46

THE WIFE

Chapter Twenty-Six
Saturday, May 25, 2019

"Okay." Linda got up to pour herself another shot of Tito's. "So it wasn't dirty where you lived. Any other clues you'd like to share?"

"I have said it is not a secret," Diego said as he lit his pipe and drew a few contemplative puffs before placing it in the ashtray Linda had left there. Then he extended his legs and lifted his arms above him. She was surprised by how relaxed he seemed, about to confess his twenty-year history on the lam and stretching himself like a house cat. "I was living in Mexico. In a beautiful village in the mountains. San Miguel de Allende."

"You're kidding." Linda plunked the vodka bottle on her glass-topped bar with too much force. She paused to make sure she hadn't broken it, then turned to face him. "Miguel and I honeymooned there. Eight years ago. You were right there?"

"It is ironic," Diego said.

"That's an understatement!"

"It is very beautiful, no?"

"Yes, it's beautiful. But why?"

"I left my family in haste, vowing never to speak to them again. What I learned from Señora Alonso made me sick. She had always hated me. I knew it. I did not know why until that day she told me everything. I could not stay."

"But the story of the motorcycle trip with Nico?"

"It was true. We were planning it already. Señora Alonso found me before I left. She waited until I had packed my bags. It was convenient for her. She did not wish me to return. In fact, it was she who suggested I disappear."

"*She* did?" Linda's mind was frantically re-ordering the Alonso universe as she had always understood it. "But what about your father?"

"Ah, yes. The patriarch."

"Miguel said he loved you very much."

"He may have loved me, but he did a very bad thing." Diego stood up and walked over to the window. "He was not the man I thought he was."

"Had you ever suspected any of it?" Linda was dying to pour herself more vodka but knew it would be one shot too many. It was evident that Diego was a high-minded man and she risked looking like a lush. A glass of water was what she needed. She started walking to the kitchen. "Would you like some water?"

"Yes, thank you," he said. "Did I suspect? Miguel and I both looked like our father, I even more so. Why would I suspect I was one of those stolen children?"

"I guess you wouldn't," Linda said as she came back and handed Diego a glass. Standing near him like this, she could feel the heat radiating off him. She quickly returned to the sofa. "But, wait, did your friend actually die?"

"Yes," Diego said as he stood up and began to pace from the window to the kitchen and back again. "Nico died in a road accident in Bolivia. It was very serious, but I survived. It was then that I saw my opportunity to carry out the suggestion she had placed in my mind."

"Your mother? I mean Miguel's?"

"Yes."

"Did you ever speak with your father?"

"Right after she told me, before I left with Nico, I went to see my father at his office. He did not lie. He said he had been waiting to tell me everything for years. He told me his wife had been unable to carry a child to term. When it all started—the Dirty War—his friend who was a general…"

Diego sat down on the chair closest to Linda's and leaned his head forward into his hands, rubbing his stubbly head. "This man was a friend to our family. My father told me that everyone knew of their problems. That they could not have a baby. They had been married nearly a decade and nothing. So, this man called my father one day early in 1976. He told him to wait in front of our apartment building. That he would be picked up.

"My father stood outside for two hours. He was ready to turn around, to go back inside, when a driver came to get him. He was asked to put on a blindfold. He was not serving in the military, my father, so he was not allowed to know where they were going. They came to a place that was not far. We—the world—later learned it was an old military base in the middle of the city of Buenos Aires where all of this happened. But my father did not know the place then.

"Inside, they went up some stairs. My father still had his eyes covered. He was taken to a room and the door was closed behind him. He never saw his friend. The general. He only saw the girl, who was tied to the bed. No one said anything but my father understood what he had to do. To that girl. To have a child. To have me."

Diego sat in silence, his eyes on the water glass he still held. Then he looked straight at Linda. "I am complicit," he said. "I exist. The girl who gave birth to me does not. She does not even exist in my mind. I never knew her name."

47

A WRITER'S THOUGHTS

I could tell from that first day at Linda's house that she was leading a complicated life. The exact nature of those complications took time to discover. She had mentioned the child who was napping at the time, and she intermittently rose from her chair to walk down the hall toward what I could only assume were the bedrooms. Even I, who have never had a child of my own, found it a little odd. Surely the child took a nap every day. Surely Linda did not pace the halls in this way every time the child did so.

Linda was jumpy and overly bright. She laughed too readily at certain things I said, which were not even terribly funny. She asked me to repeat other things more than once. She was not listening to me at all.

"What?" she asked, squinting her eyes in my direction, as if by bringing me into sharper focus, she might be better able to follow the thread of our faltering conversation.

"The Four Arts," I answered.

"What about it?"

"Have you gone to any of their *Florida Voices* talks? The series that features local writers? That's where I'm speaking next."

"Um…" At this she hopped up once again when a noise came from the same hallway. It was a bump, as though someone dropped something.

Or maybe the kid had climbed out of the crib and fallen? Who knew. Off she dashed.

While she was gone, I got up and wandered around the room. The colors made me feel like I was inside a fish tank. On a glass-topped side table, there was a framed photo of what was obviously her family. Linda was in it, of course, in a shoulder-squeezing embrace administered by a man who was dark and very handsome. He didn't look to be much taller than she was. And the two kids: one a boy and dressed accordingly, and one quite clearly a little girl—the one sleeping down the hallway now (or crashing around her bedroom).

Linda reappeared before I could study the photograph further.

"I need to go," she said in a breathy rush. "You need to go."

"Oh, okay," I replied. "I'm sorry if I stayed too long."

"No, it's not that. It's just kind of a crazy time and I forgot I had an appointment."

"Sure. No problem. Well…" I moved to the door and turned around when I'd opened it slightly. I added a humble brag, "I can get you a ticket to my book talk, even though they say it's sold out. And thanks for the coffee and conversation. My life is a bit lonely sometimes."

I probably should not have said that. She may have felt sympathy, but she might just as easily have felt creeped out by my middle-aged-loner vibe. I saw her cringe, just a little.

"Well," she said to cap off our visit. "We'll have to do this again."

I knew she did not mean it. Even so, I came back three days later. This time, I did not call or text first. This time, I brought her a vegetable smoothie from Celis Produce. She obviously did not eat croissants and she appeared to be the type of woman who drank green drinks. I hoped this offering would soften the blow of my unannounced arrival. I also hoped to get a look at whatever it was that was going on down the back hall, which I was quite certain had nothing to do with a child.

I very consciously rapped on the door three times in quick succession. Conveying, I thought, a cheerful sound that would signal to the inhabitants of the house that a friend was paying a call. Firm and confident. Not tentative like a neighbor. Not hostile like the FBI. When she opened the door, her expression was even more flustered than it had been the other day.

"Nora!" she said as she stepped outside, blocking me with her body.

"Hi." This time I didn't bother to correct her. If she was so distracted she couldn't even remember I had the same name as her murdered aunt, it could only work to my advantage. I held up two plastic cups of the viscous concoctions. "I brought you breakfast!"

"Did we...?" she trailed off and gazed over her shoulder and in through the window, where a man could be seen moving quickly in the direction of that mysterious hallway. Her husband? Then she whipped her head back to me. "I'm sorry, did we have a plan to meet?"

"You asked me to come back today," I lied. I figured she was so spacey the other day she wouldn't remember what she said to me when I was leaving.

"I did?" She narrowed her eyes and her tone became sharp. "I don't remember saying that."

A door closed from inside the house.

"I'm sorry. If this is a bad time, I can go." I started to turn toward street and noticed the plastic cups I was still holding. "Oh, here. This is for you."

Her face softened as she took one. "Thank you. I'm sorry. I just can't see you today."

"No problem." I smiled an overly wide smile. One that I knew always made me look ridiculous. "I actually couldn't stay anyway."

With that, I turned and practically skipped down her front path, intending to demonstrate how very insouciant I could be.

48

THE WIFE

Chapter Twenty-Seven
Sunday, May 26, 2019

Diego's expression of his sense of complicity in a crime that was none of his doing struck a very deep chord in Linda. She held a similar secret closed up inside of her. She knew that her aunt had been murdered as a child. And she knew that her father had been questioned multiple times for the very same murder. She knew that many of the people who had known her family back then—decades before her own birth—considered her father a killer.

Her aunt had been called Noelle. The same name as that writer she had struck up a conversation with at the store. A writer she had always admired. A writer she had wanted to get to know. And now, a writer who was turning out to be kind of weird, a little bit stalkerish, and someone who was giving her the creeps.

The sins of the father came home to roost, and Linda and Diego shared eerily similar backstories. Not, perhaps, in exact detail, but certainly in overarching theme. Diego's father did a bad thing. He raped a young woman who bore him a son. Did he know that the woman was

later flung from a plane—while still very much alive, even if sedated—
into the ocean below her? Did sedation work when you were hurtling
through the air to your imminent death? Did one wake up while tumbling down? Or on impact with the ice-cold water, which inevitably
took on the consistency of a stone wall due to the speed with which you
crashed into it?

Oddly, after this one conversation, Linda knew more about Diego's
father than she knew about her own. Her father was still alive in
Pennsylvania. He was old and senile now, but—even when he was clear-
headed—she had never been able to extract a thread of information from
him about what had happened to his sister. He simply would not speak of
it. Linda had learned what little she knew in the usual way that children
learn such things.

From the cruel mouths of other children.

She was playing with her cousin, Vincent, in the backyard one day,
when Linda was nine and Vincent was ten. They were arguing about
something she could no longer recall. She must have said or done something particularly annoying because Vincent suddenly blurted out, "Your
father's a murderer and you don't even know it!"

Linda reeled from the sting of that outrageous remark and shot back
the only obvious response: "He is not!"

"Is too."

"Is not!"

Vincent grabbed her arm at that point and gave her an Indian burn
that was the worst he'd ever administered. "Admit it," he said. "Your dad's
a killer! Everybody knows it!"

"*Mom*!" Linda screamed at the top of her lungs. The pain in her arm
was at least helping to focus her mind away from the hateful words of
her cousin.

Obviously reluctant to tangle with Linda's mother—his own mother's older sister and cut from the same tough cloth—Vincent promptly
let go of her arm and trudged off toward his house. "Ask your mom," he
called over his shoulder. "Go ahead!"

When the last of him disappeared around the corner of the house next door, Linda looked down at her red and stinging flesh. Only when Vincent could no longer see her did the tears spring up in her eyes. She ran into her own house to find her mother. "Mom!" she called out. "Mom! Mom!"

Her mother was no help at all. Linda had expected her to confirm that Vincent was a mealymouthed toad and had made the whole thing up. Instead, her mother had sat her down in the living room. That is when Linda knew it had to be true. Her family never sat in the living room unless tragedies of epic scope were unfolding. The last time she had been invited into the living room was when her parents had told her their dog had died.

"Linda," her mother began. "Sometimes bad things happen and nobody knows why. And when people don't understand why those things happen, they look around for someone to blame. Your father had a sister he loved very much. She died in a terrible way. Someone broke into their house and murdered her when she was only twelve years old and..."

"Twelve?" Linda was so alarmed by hearing that number she could not help interrupting her mother.

"It was terrible." Her mother repeated with finality, as though Linda would even dream of disputing the terribleness of it. "She was killed by a monster. But you know your father. And your father is not a monster."

Those two facts were undeniably true. Linda knew her father. And she knew him to not be a monster. Her father was kind. He was funny. He walked Linda to school. Sometimes, he even took her out for ice cream, just the two of them. What she knew of her father did not jibe with what her cousin Vincent had said.

"But," Linda began, "why did Vincent say that?"

Her mother's face pinched. "Look, my sister is my sister, but she has no business spreading such lies about my family. I intend to give her a piece of my mind!"

"Oh, Mommy, don't say I said so!" Linda was terrified her aunt would be displeased with her for ratting her out. Although it was Vincent who'd actually done it. But why would her aunt say such things about her own sister's husband?

Linda left the conversation with her mother more disturbed than she had been on entering it. The intervening years between that day and this had done nothing to put her mind at rest. There were no mementos, scrapbooks, clipped newspaper articles in boxes—really nothing—that she could find in her childhood home that referenced her Aunt Noelle and the cruel fate that had befallen her. And she had looked for them. She combed the house over, even into her adulthood. There wasn't even an acknowledgment that his sister—her aunt—had existed.

Years later, she was able to find things on the internet. And none of it looked good for her father. She had no way of reconciling the man she knew with the one she read about. And, after all, he was never even formally charged. He must have been innocent and it must have been exactly what her mother said, an attempt to put the terrifying murder of a child into an easily quantifiable box that eliminated any possible threat to anyone else.

Earlier this evening, hearing Diego's confirmation of his father's crime and his own sense of self-blame for it, she felt she was in the presence of a soulmate. The first she had ever met. After all, the fellowship to which she and Diego belonged was a small one.

It had happened so naturally. He kissed her or she kissed him, but who really cared? They kissed each other and they could not stop. They tenderly peeled off the layers of each other's clothes as they gingerly peeled back the wrapping of their darkest secrets. Linda knew one thing for sure—even if she would never know if her father had killed his own sister—that this was what she had been waiting for her entire life.

And that she would do anything to keep it.

49

A WRITER'S THOUGHTS

By June of 2019, I considered Linda a friend. I can honestly say she was coming to rely on me and—dare I add—to trust me. Which turned out to be one of her biggest mistakes in a very long string of them.

She liked those green drinks I brought her. They were a bit dear for my budget, but I went without in other ways. As the weeks progressed, she sometimes texted me to pick up items at the market on my way to her house. You know, since I didn't have a baby to haul into a car seat, it would be easier for me than it would be for her. In all fairness to Linda, she would offer to pay me for these items. And, also in the spirit of fairness, she never asked for much. Milk (always organic, grass-fed, if possible), carrots, maybe some yogurt for the baby. I never took her money. I was trying to establish a bond and it just seemed wise to render myself useful.

I am not saying that Linda was self-centered. She was a busy woman with two children, a difficult (I was coming to learn) husband, and something strange going on in her house that took me a while to pry out of her. Pry is too harsh a word. I was never forceful with Linda. She told me of her own free will. Because she liked me, I believe. I liked her, too, but her amped-up energy level continued unabated and was, frankly, irritating to be around. I suspected she was on Adderall.

By the middle of June, I had been friendly with Linda for a few months. This was the time period when she was flying on a regular basis to Pittsburgh to be with her dying mother. We had not yet spoken openly about her family or the murder of her aunt and my namesake, Noelle. I had not yet told her anything about my connection to her family.

Linda did not spontaneously confess to me about Diego. First, I saw him. And she saw me see him. And I could see it unnerved her. And then I could see it was a relief. She had to have been lonely in her secret. And now she got to tell someone. I—by virtue of proximity—got to be that someone.

I came by one morning a little earlier than usual, around 8:15 or so. I figured, since school had closed for the summer, she would be home with both children and in need of a little relief. Linda had not yet trusted me to help her out with the children. She probably assumed I didn't know anything about kids, and she would not have been wrong. In any case, I walked up the front path and saw Linda perfectly framed, in the big picture window, in the embrace of what I thought was her husband. Odd that he would be home. I could have set my watch by his departure for his office in West Palm Beach at 7:45 each morning. But there he was.

I hesitated and considered turning around and going home. This was awkward in the extreme and I did not want to annoy Linda. The plastic cups I was carrying must have flashed in the sunlight, or some other motion on my behalf caught her attention, for Linda turned to look straight at me. As did her husband.

Funny. I had looked at that family photo more than once and I could have sworn her husband wasn't much taller than Linda. But maybe it was an illusion of how or where they were standing for the picture. Here, in person, he stood a good head taller. But that was not all. His hair was so short as to look like a military brush cut. His features were more angular than I remembered in that photo. He could have lost weight. Cut his hair. But there was something else. The face I was looking at was finely featured, the eyes were piercing, the look—the mien—was different from the man in the photo. And, in an instant, it came to me. This man was not her husband.

Linda and the man moved as one. He darted back down the hall-way—shedding a brilliant beam of light on why Linda had been so fixated on that hall every time I visited—and she walked toward the door, obviously about to open it for me.

"Noelle!" Her voice went up in an exclamation point, but she was not smiling. "Did we have an appointment?"

"Um. No. I..."

"You can't just come to my house, Noelle. You just can't do it like that. Unlike you, I happen to have a life."

It was the first cruel thing she had said to me.

"I know that," I said as quickly as I could to keep myself from crying. I fumbled for what I could say to repair the breach I had just made in our friendship.

Just then, a bunch of those crazy, squawking parrots—the ones that usually live down near The Breakers, the ones said to have descended from a couple of caged pets set free by Hurricane Andrew—flapped over us in their jagged, chaotic flight. Linda and I both looked up at the screeching noise and stayed looking as the shadows passed over us.

"Linda, I..." I went back to trying to right the course of this ship.

"Oh, Noelle," she blurted as she started to cry. "I've made such a mess of everything!"

50

THE WIFE

Chapter Twenty-Eight
Wednesday, July 24, 2019

Linda's mother left her body—cutting whatever chains had shackled her to her daughter and her husband, the sister he may have killed, and the secrets she might have harbored for him—most fittingly on the Fourth of July.

Independence Day.

Linda had been lost in a blind fugue of lovemaking with her husband's brother at the moment it happened, twisted up in sweaty sheets in the middle of the afternoon, sunlight peeking through waving palm fronds in the dappled way of a disco strobe, illuminating sections of Diego's body, then her own, in short, staccato bursts. She was fucking her brother-in-law while her mother died, while her children were fobbed off to the neighbor's pool, while her husband was fishing for the great elusive marlin in the Gulf Stream off the coast of Florida.

She had meant to be there for her mother. She had taken all those flights to and from Pittsburgh in the preceding months, stayed at that dreary hotel more nights than she cared to count, sat by her mother's bedside fluffing pillows, reading aloud, holding the bendable plastic straw to her mother's parched mouth, and smacking the buzzer for advance doses of painkiller to lessen her mother's agony. But Linda was not there at the crucial moment. The lure of illicit love had turned her away from her responsibilities and into the worst kind of selfish person. Or maybe she had always been that. She had choked at the finish line. She had left her mother to depart this world exactly as she had entered it.

Alone.

Still, not as bad a departure as that of her father's sister. Noelle had left her life in the company of someone, but the question remained just exactly who that someone might have been. Linda had assiduously worked to avoid any image of the aunt she hadn't known. Until recently. Until that writer of the same name had adhered herself to Linda. But now, in the sordid afterglow of her abdication of daughterly (let's add wifely and motherly) duties, Linda found herself contemplating what little she knew of Noelle Huber's grisly murder.

She was shocked by how much there was to be known about it. A quick stroll down Google Lane paid off in troves of newspaper articles, opinions, and weird secondhand books, like a potboiler called *Terror in Our Cities*. Linda found herself stunned by the number of people who were interested in what had happened in her very own family when she had kept her mind so firmly closed against it. It gave her that creepy feeling that people were talking about her behind her back, watching her without her knowing it.

She knew her father had been a suspect. But she knew it in the way it had been packaged and delivered to her by her parents. She did not know of the wild speculation on behalf of the press and the citizen detectives who hounded him. She did not know what her father had gone through. And she did not know if he deserved to have gone through it.

Here she was, nearly forty, and she had exercised minimal curiosity about any of it. Obviously, a psychiatrist would have had a field day with her. Obviously she was in denial. Who wouldn't be? Her father had not only been accused of savagely murdering his sister but of having had an ongoing sexual relationship with her in the lead-up to it. And all of it when his sister was only twelve years old.

The man she read about here was a monster, even if he was still a teenager himself at the time. The man she read about was not the man who raised her. How could she be related to such a man? And then she thought about her own recent activities with her husband's brother, the uncle of her children.

Linda slammed her laptop shut. What could she do about any of this now? What did it have to do with her? Clearly her mother had not believed her father had done it, or how could she have married him? And stayed with him? Linda was born in 1980, thirty-two years after the death of her aunt. Her father had been fifty-one at the time of her birth, her mother fifteen years his junior. It seemed like a vast age difference when Linda was little. People sometimes took her father to be her grandfather. Age differences like that were common now; people took second and third spouses as greedily as another helping of dessert. And Linda, well, she might still be married to her first husband, but she certainly wasn't restraining herself.

Could her father have committed this act in some sort of bout of temporary insanity? Was that really even a thing? Could he have been the brother who killed his sister and then gone on to be the daddy who walked his daughter to school? Maybe he walked Linda to school, mindful of what kind of perverts were out there, precisely because he *was* one. Her head spun. She had been home from Pittsburgh—the funeral, the burial, the paperwork, and a string of empty days with her father, who she didn't even think recognized her—for forty-eight hours.

Miguel and Diego had stayed with the children in Linda's absence, dividing chores like a married couple. Miguel went to work each day and did the grocery shopping. Diego took care of Gogo and Espie at home. Fortunately, preschool was closed for the summer, so drop-offs and pickups did not need to be navigated. Despite the fact that they couldn't go to the beach or on a walk or any outdoor activity outside of their secluded backyard, the children had been in heaven with their Pipa. Linda had the sense that they'd hardly missed her.

DEBORAH GOODRICH ROYCE

Linda considered this added layer of secrets and lies they were all carrying. Diego was still living under cover. No one was to know of his presence in their house. Manuela would not tell anyone. At least not anyone in a position of authority.

That writer, Noelle, was another story. Linda was sorry she had ever struck up a conversation with her at the market. She was strangely intense. When she looked at Linda—and she looked at her a lot—it felt like a scanner was probing her innermost organs. She also came to the house way too much. She had even seen Diego.

And that, of course, had led to the biggest risk of all. Linda, after bursting into tears, had allowed Noelle to drag the entire story out of her. Linda had poured out every detail of her affair with Diego over that damned green juice the woman carried around with her. She must have owned stock in the company the way she was always foisting it off on Linda.

What did Noelle want from her? Because it was no longer possible to ignore the fact that she wanted something very badly, indeed. Linda had gone from finding her kooky to finding her weird, to finding her a little bit frightening. Maybe a lot frightening. But after the foolishness of spilling her secret, Linda was not comfortable severing ties. Keep your friends close, your enemies closer. Which one was Noelle? And when would she tell Linda what she was after? The wait was excruciating. And it added to the edge-of-madness feeling that dogged those summer days.

51

A WRITER'S THOUGHTS

My mother spent the entirety of her life—certainly every day of my childhood—vigilant to exploitation from whatever corner it might strike at her. She constructed a castle wall and manned the parapets, eyeing the horizon for invaders. These took the form of any and everyone who interacted with her. People looked at her wrong, spoke to her wrong, were just plain wrong in their dealings with her. The adult, Beth, was not able to err on the side of charity, to grant anyone the benefit of the doubt. Since, I suppose, it hadn't been granted to the child, Liz.

She was especially sensitive to perceived slights and applied her wariness both in protection *of* and, from time to time, *against* me. I was sometimes seen as her angel—her defense against an unsafe world—but just as frequently, I was called a traitor, an ingrate with no loyalty to her mother. Fealty was a standard that loomed large for her. And it was a standard unachievable by me, no matter how hard I tried.

Once, on an earlier foray to the aforementioned cousins, the ones who lived in McCandless, the ones who had the pony, the ones from whom we eventually became estranged, my mom actually slapped my cousin Becky. Slapped her. In an era when parents routinely chastised other people's children, they certainly did not slap them. That was a step too far. My mother, as usual, took it.

We were in the kitchen, the women drinking coffee, the children having a snack. Ring Dings were on offer. Becky was the oldest, so she was in charge of distribution. She did this in a backward way, serving herself first, her brother second, and me—their guest—last. But it was what she did when she came to me that really got my mother's goat. Actually, it was probably my reaction to Becky's act that enraged my mother.

"One for me," Becky intoned, placing an unwrapped Ring Ding onto a napkin on the table in front of her. It was an old birthday party napkin sprigged with balloons in garish primary colors, with a stain from what looked to have been an earlier-enjoyed chocolate cake. My aunt was a proponent of reuse, though not for ecological reasons. My uncle was just cheap.

"One for you," she continued. This one went to Joe, atop his slightly ripped old napkin.

And then Becky took a good, long look at me. "You," she said, picking up a knife and brandishing it in the air like a weapon, "are fat. You should only eat half."

Down came the knife on the Ring Ding, squirting out cream on the table. She hadn't even placed it on a napkin—dirty or not—and was cutting it right on the wood. And up came my tears. I tried very hard not to cry. I did not want to embarrass myself in front of Becky and Joe. I knew I was a chubby child. And I knew that Becky was right. But still, it hurt.

So caught up was I in my own emotions that I did not see it coming. I heard Becky's gasp before I could even process the visual of my mother's hand connecting with her face. And that made it all the more mortifying. Not only was I fat—a cousin no one liked yet had to entertain with their precious Ring Dings and ponies and bicycles—but now I was so lame that my mother had to defend me by physically assaulting my cousin.

My aunt Darlene plunked down her coffee mug so hard it sent coffee sloshing on the Ring Ding Becky had been slicing on the table. The mess of the cream of the cake mixed with the coffee, all of which oozed in a trail toward where I was sitting, was the final straw that broke all of our backs that day.

"Get out!" Darlene hissed at my mother, very close to her face. "I've had just about enough of this shit. More than enough! Take your crazy ass out of my kitchen and out of my house!"

Becky's cheek was flaming red. Slop was creeping toward my lap. My mother was hyperventilating. I had never heard my aunt swear. And this was the moment I wet my pants.

I don't remember leaving their house. I don't remember the car ride home. I don't remember anything else of that day except the deep shame of being one with my mother in the eyes of our family. We—she and I— were irreparably broken, flawed, unable to crack the code of how to be normal people who visited others and sat at their tables without incident.

It was no better outside of family. My mother applied her ruler to any child who might pass through my orbit as a transitional friend. Her snide remarks about a kid who'd caught my fancy forced the two of us into hostile roles. I had to assume the position of defending the other person to my mother, even if I had not yet had the time or maturity to work out on my own whether or not that person was defensible. My mother was the adult, she was the better arguer, and she—it took me years to realize— wanted me to be isolated more than I actually wanted to have friends. It was an unwinnable proposition, and it only grew worse as I got older. All my friends remained transitional.

Borderline personality disorder was the official diagnosis that was eventually given to my mother and it always garnered sympathy from the diagnosing psychiatrist. "That must have been hard for you," they would say. "It is not easy to be the child of a borderline." Borderlines are famously difficult, and I accepted their kind words as my due.

I should probably fine-tune what I just said. My mother never saw a psychiatrist in her life. She found the idea absurd. So she was never actually diagnosed to her face. I, on the other hand, have seen several. And they were the ones who diagnosed my mother with this particular malady. Right after they diagnosed me with the same.

There seem to be two strong paths toward becoming a borderline. One is childhood trauma. With the seminal event of Noelle Huber's murder, my mother had that box checked in spades. Another is familial relationship with a person who has BPD. So I am pretty well covered, myself. It is not entirely clear if my mother gave it to me through her genes—the fronto-limbic network of neurons plays a central role—or through her very presence in my life. Was it that, simply by being her daughter, I was exposed to a wealth of childhood trauma, myself?

The National Institute of Mental Health cites childhood exposure to unstable, invalidating relationships, hostile conflicts, abuse, abandonment, and adversity as predictive of development of BPD. And life with Mama—plus abandonment by Papa, I should add—was all of the above. But, in the end, this is just chicken and egg. She had it. I have it. Does it really matter which came first? I would say it does not. What matters more than the problems you have is how you manage those problems. My mother did not manage hers well. I try to do better.

Linda unloaded everything about her affair with Diego. In one long, teary confessional, she laid out her predicament for me to see. She took me down a backstory lane—in an effort, no doubt, to justify her actions—and detailed her growing estrangement from her husband. Much of this was predicated on his controlling nature. Miguel kept the proverbial keys to their kingdom very much in his own back pocket. She told me he did not trust her to manage any aspect of their lives without his involvement. Annoying, for sure. Grounds for adultery, I don't presume to know, never having been married.

She moved next to detailing the arrival of Diego in their house. His sweetness, his beautiful face, his pipe smoking, the way the children adored him. She made it clear there was tension between the brothers. She told me much more than she should have—although which of these things should she have told me?—about Diego's history. His father's rape of his birth mother; the stealing of him, her baby; the murder of that mother; Diego's twenty-year disappearance; and his arrival on her doorstep that spring. All of it.

Finally, she moved on to the soap opera of their passionate love for each other, she and Diego, not she and Miguel. Why people who are in the throes of a love affair think the intimate details of their ardor are of interest to other people is a fact that has always eluded me. I don't really care that someone feels butterflies in her stomach while looking into the eyes of someone else. Who does? But I listened to Linda attentively, absorbing every last detail of their romance, knowing all of it could be useful to me at a later date.

I did not immediately reveal to Linda my connection to her family of origin. In fact, I struggled to find the right time to drop that truth bomb. At first, we were getting to know one another. At that point—the honeymoon phase of our friendship—it would have been too soon to mention. Then, her mother died in July. It was pretty clear that it would have been a cruel moment to saddle her with my baggage. And then, well, summer drifted into autumn—if such a word can be applied to Florida—and it started to feel like I had been keeping the secret for too long, and the revelation of it would land with a thud.

I finally did tell her. I am not so divorced from good sense that I couldn't see it was unhealthy to keep it hidden. It all came out in December, in the lead-up to Christmas. It is obvious now that this was a bad time. Linda was stressed out with Christmas cards and Christmas shopping, Christmas cookies and Christmas dinner, screwing her lover and screwing over her husband. It was a lot for one woman to handle.

We met at Hive in West Palm Beach. Linda intended to wrap up some final purchases and I intended to tell her the truth. We moved on to the outdoor picnic tables at Cholo Soy. The eating of tacos while baring my soul seemed like a bad combination, doomed to failure before it had even begun, but Linda wanted to go there. My attempts to steer us to a quieter spot went unheard. So, there we were, in the blazing sun, holding tacos in our hands and talking. Well, I was holding a taco and talking. Linda was busy texting.

"There's something I need to tell you," I began. Linda had not touched her food and looked up at me from her phone as if she was surprised by my presence. She did this a lot.

"Okay, sure. What's up?" she said and finally took a bite.

"Well, you know how my name is Noelle?"

"Um, yes." Her phone pinged. "Hang on a sec."

I waited. Just as I gave up on her finishing in any timely manner and took a large bite myself, she set the device on the table and turned her attention to me. I swallowed some water and resumed, "I wasn't just named that randomly. I don't know quite how to say it, but I was actually named for your aunt." At that, I led what I hoped would be the table in a little round of laughter. Linda did not join in the merriment.

"You *what?*" she said.

"Yeah, I know it's weird. But my mom actually grew up with your aunt. They were friends." I took another big drink of water to hydrate my burning throat. None of this was going as I had planned.

Linda became as still as I had ever seen her. Her hand fluttering, hair flipping, skittering persona came to a crashing halt. She just stopped. Had I not seen it with my very own eyes, I would have told you it wasn't possible. And she also became very ashen. Her face turned white. Combined with her stillness, she gave the impression of a statue.

"I just, well. I know I should have mentioned it sooner," I blurted, grabbing my water and draining it. "There just wasn't the moment and I…"

Linda interrupted me with something I hadn't quite heard.

"I'm sorry?" I asked. "What?"

"You fucking stalker," she said as she rose from the picnic table. She almost fell as she scrambled over the bench. She righted herself and turned back to face me before she fled. "Stay away," she practically spat, pointing a finger at my face. "Stay away or I'll call the cops."

But, you know, I really didn't think she would.

52

THE WIFE

Chapter Twenty-Nine
Tuesday, December 24, 2019

I t was the night before Christmas. The tree had been up for a couple of weeks and, despite the Florida heat and humidity, was actually a real tree. It was an increasingly dead and desiccated tree as time passed, however, necessitating daily runs of the dust buster to pick up the needles that dropped off in sticky clumps. Linda couldn't wait to chuck it to the curb as soon as she could without upsetting the children. It would not survive in her living room much past New Year's Day if she could help it.

Today, two weeks into the tree's tenure in their living room, an enormous black spider emerged from its canopy and moved rapidly across the white area rug in the direction of the kitchen. All at once, it stopped in it its eight-legged tracks and made a quick jog to the left, toward Linda and Espie. Mother and daughter, who were sitting on the floor placing gifts on the needlepoint tree skirt, screamed and jumped up on the sofa, dropping their boxes in the process. The thud of the packages got the spider's attention. Again, it paused, considered, then resumed its original path.

Their screams drew Miguel, Diego, and Gogo from whatever corners of the house they'd been in. Diego was the first to act, stepping on the thing on the tile of the kitchen floor. It made Linda think of the forest in which she had imagined him living, before she had learned he was actually in an artist colony in Mexico. It was a quick and savage act—the killing of that spider—one she would have associated more with her husband than his brother.

Linda stared at Diego—they all did—each nursing whatever private thoughts they had about the killing of spiders that were practically as large as hummingbirds. At least Diego hadn't smashed it on Linda's white rug, which would have been impossible to clean. Diego seemed not to notice the attention of the room and grabbed some paper towels to clean up the mess.

For Linda, even worse than the sighting of the spider and its subsequent slaughter was the awareness that the thing had been living in their midst without making its presence known. The symbolism was not lost on her. She was pretty sure it wasn't lost on anyone else either, children included. Even if their awareness was subconscious.

Everyone was in a correspondingly strange mood the rest of the day. The children were wired as though they were on a sugar high, even though Linda had not fed them anything chemically sweetened. They talked too loudly, laughed too much, and jostled each other to the point of tears on more than one occasion. The rarity was that even Gogo had cried once today—when Espie knocked down his meticulously constructed dragon castle—when it was normally only Espie who reached that level of frustration.

It made Linda think of an expression her old college friend, Maddie Cox, always used. "Tuesday's gonna be bad," Maddie would say to signal that something or someone was about to go off the rails. It had come from seeing some movie—Linda didn't know which—that starred Tuesday Weld. Two women seated next to Maddie in the multiplex had had trouble keeping quiet. The phrase they used, whenever they suspected the character was about to misbehave, "Tuesday's gonna be bad," rattled around in Linda's head today, though today was no worse than most days of late with Miguel.

Nine months since the arrival of his brother, Miguel seemed to wallow in a pervasive state of disgruntlement. He was snappish with Espie and Gogo, even more critical of Linda than usual, and barely spoke to Diego. She couldn't blame him for that. She knew it was due to his family's excessive attachment to his brother: overt on behalf of his children, covert on behalf of his wife.

Linda and Diego tried to hide the true nature of their relationship, but, she knew too well, this only resulted in a stilted, Kabuki-like avoidance of each other. They never made eye contact in the presence of Miguel, which could not have made their affair more obvious than if they had French kissed each other at breakfast. Their politeness and reserve and the way they kept to different sides of a room telegraphed their guilt most vividly. But she did not know how to play it any differently.

Things were definitely coming to a head.

Tonight, after they had gone to early Mass at St. Edwards with the children—a mass that Diego avoided like he avoided all outings; after they had opened one "Mommy and Daddy present" for each child, before the onslaught of Santa presents to follow the next day; after they had read *The Night Before Christmas* three times and tucked two exhausted but bug-eyed children into bed; after they heard all rustling and chatter settle down behind the door of the children's room; and while Linda was in the midst of putting Santa's gifts around the tree; Miguel turned to Diego.

"So, my bro..." Miguel struck a tinny note of jocularity as he poured himself a tumbler of Tito's. "We're coming into a new year. Twenty-twenty. What's your plan?"

Linda was surprised he asked this in her presence. Normally, Miguel siloed his conversations with his brother away from his wife. He kept his queries about Diego's time "away," as they now were calling it, private and unknown to her. And she certainly was not discussing anything said between her and Diego with Miguel.

She kept her head down as she sat on the floor, mindful of another spider. She placed Gogo's gifts on one side of the tree and Espie's on the other. She was still waiting for one last Amazon delivery, a set of walkie-talkies that Gogo had added to his Santa list last minute. There was a chance it wouldn't make it for Christmas.

"My plan, my bro," Diego parroted that term, which sounded sweetly deferential coming out of him (or maybe it was sarcastic, Linda couldn't tell which), "is to start a new life here. As soon as I can."

Miguel sat on a chair and set his glass on the coffee table—also made of glass—with a cringeworthy clink. "What exactly is it that's holding you back?"

Linda rose to go out to the garage to retrieve another bag of gifts, hidden on the top shelf of a cabinet. Her stomach was flopping around and she needed to put some space between herself and the men. In the garage, she opened the big Gladiator metal cabinet, pulled a ladder close to it, climbed up, and grabbed the bag. Then she reversed the process, put the ladder back, and closed the cabinet doors.

Casting about for another reason to stay away from the living room and whatever confrontation might be unfolding there, she set the bag down and exited the side door of the garage—avoiding the loud noise of the big automatic door—to check the mailbox for Gogo's last gift.

As Linda slipped around the side of the garage and was about to walk down the driveway to the mailbox, she saw her. Noelle. Standing under a tree on the opposite side of the street and looking at Linda's house.

Linda stopped in her tracks. Noelle did not turn her head in Linda's direction. Evidently she hadn't seen her. Linda hugged the wall of the garage, deeper in shadow, and watched Noelle watching her house. At one point, she saw Noelle lean forward, as if she were straining to hear what was being said between Miguel and Diego inside.

Linda felt sick to her stomach. She had called Noelle a stalker right to her face when they had that blowup three weeks ago at the taco place. But the reality of the word—the magnitude of danger Noelle represented to Linda—finally sank in. Noelle *was* a stalker. And she was stalking Linda. Maybe Linda's family. Maybe even Linda's children.

Before Linda could question her motives, before she could think twice and avoid all she was about to unleash, a white rage overtook her and she ran at Noelle. As she ran, the panoply of the neighborhood's Christmas lights blurred into prisms of vivid color—a perfect approximation of an ocular migraine—in Linda's peripheral vision.

As she sprinted from the side of the garage and over the lawn, then sidewalk, then street, Linda saw the older woman turn, a stunned look on her face, her mouth hanging slightly open. Then she watched as Noelle's head snapped to the left, looking for her car or her bicycle or her fucking broomstick, whatever the hell mode of transportation she'd used to get here tonight.

Linda saw Noelle's shoulders lift in fear and then sag in resignation as Linda closed in on her. And Linda watched herself, as if from above, grab the creepy old writer by her creepy old shirt and shake her. Like a mop or a rug or she didn't know what. She just shook her.

"What do you want from me?" Linda uttered in a loud, whispering hiss. "*What?*"

"*Stop!*" Noelle cried out. "You're hurting me!"

"You're hurting *me!*" Linda retorted like a child, her fury still boiling from some nether region far below her stomach.

At the same time, Linda became aware of Noelle's head wobbling back and forth, her glasses sliding askew down her nose to dangle off one ear, swinging in counterpoint with her head. She realized, all at once, that she *was* hurting Noelle. Maybe seriously. This realization redoubled her ire and she pushed Noelle away from her.

Noelle landed on her bottom on the Andersons' grass with a whoosh of air from her lungs. The fact that all of this was playing out—that Linda was actually assaulting someone—on the lawn of her friends and neighbors on Christmas Eve, shamed her. Spent, Linda slumped down to sit on the wet grass next to Noelle.

"What do you *want* from me?" Linda's voice was hoarse from her exertions. She felt herself ready to sob, to descend into a crying jag right in the middle of Reef Road as the Andersons' blow-up/light-up Santa bobbed in the breeze behind them. "You need to leave me alone. I'm begging you!"

"But Linda," Noelle said, snot running out of her nose, mascara dripping. "I'm here to help you."

"I don't even know what you're talking about. I don't need help."

"I think you know what I mean. I think you know you need help."

Linda used her hands to hoist herself up from the grass, then she wiped them on the front of her pants. She started across the street, looking in her living room window, her own white Christmas lights tightly strung in a clean, straight line above it in a strident bid for order. She could see, from here, Diego sitting in a chair. It looked like he was reading. Miguel must have been in the kitchen. It made her shudder to think of this woman peering into her window—her life—in the way Linda was doing now. It felt obscene.

"Leave me alone," she said, without turning her head to look at Noelle.

Yet, even as she said it, she felt a seed being planted.

53

A WRITER'S THOUGHTS

Is it okay for a writer to be sly? To wink at the reader a little? Is it all right to allow oneself a little fun along the arduous path of plotting and pacing and character-building a book? Charlie Kaufman does it in film. Think about *Being John Malkovich* or *Adaptation* or *Synecdoche, New York*. Wes Anderson does it too, albeit in a different way. Think of every movie he has ever made. The novelist, John Fowles, does it, certainly in his postmodern masterpiece, *The French Lieutenant's Woman*. But, as Hitchcock said, "That, sir, is no MacGuffin." *And you, madame*, I might add on your behalf, *are no Charlie Kaufman or Wes Anderson*. And no John Fowles, either.

Yes, I was shaken up by Linda on the night of Christmas Eve. Metaphorically, literally, the works. But, in the end, I think that evening was the key to her breakthrough. Linda's unseemly outburst with me that night helped her to see that the path she was on was untenable. And I was the gateway to a different path. At least I was the gateway for Linda to begin to consider that she would be able to forge her own path. She didn't need Miguel. She didn't need Diego, either, but that would take longer for her to see. That one might require some subtle encouragement on my part. Her children, well, sure, she needed them. I would not dream of coming between a mother and her children.

Naturally, I didn't bother Linda on Christmas Day. I allowed her to have the day in the bosom of her family. Such as it was. Cordelia and I had our own plans for the holiday. We took a long walk—as long as Cordie could manage—and came home to watch festive holiday fare. I am partial to *Miracle on 34th Street*, but I can muster up enthusiasm for *It's a Wonderful Life* every third or fourth year.

I make it a point to not write on Christmas, to allow myself that day of leisure. So I cooked up a large steak and shared it with Cordelia. I ate a pumpkin pie by myself, accompanied by a can of Reddi-wip. And then I threw it all up.

I stayed away through New Year's Eve, too. That night, I walked alone to the seawall along the lake to watch the fireworks that the Coconuts put on every year. I never bring Cordelia for this. Dogs and fireworks are not a good mix. The Coconuts—a group of men, originally bachelors but later inclusive of married men—get together once a year to throw a blow-out New Year's Eve party at the Flagler Museum. They do this to return the invitations of all the society hostesses who have had them for dinner in the preceding year. It is all very correct in an old-fashioned sort of way, revolving the way it does around social obligations. Over time, the pièce de résistance of their bash became the pyrotechnics display shot from a barge on the lake, accompanied by a rousing musical soundtrack. While I was certainly never on the guest list for their party, I—like the rest of the regular folk—have been able to watch it all from the Lake Trail. It's enough to make a girl feel included.

Sort of.

But that night—in what would turn out to be my first inkling that the year 2020 was dawning differently from years prior—no fireworks erupted at midnight. I waited for a while, perched on someone's seawall. As I waited, I noticed there were fewer people waiting alongside me than usual. Eventually, two by two, the others rose to leave. I wondered what was going on. Had there been some sort of announcement I hadn't seen, canceling the fireworks? I shrugged it off and made my way home, away from the dark water and along the dark streets of Palm Beach.

After that, I still kept my distance from Linda. Well, sort of. I did go to her house on a nightly basis, I just never let her know I did it. I wanted to prove to Linda that I was not the terrible person she thought I was. She had called me a stalker, which I found a tad arrogant. How did she know what I did with my time? How dared she assume from the few hours she spent with me that I gave her excessive thought when I was away from her? I waited until February 12, a date that—how could I realize at the time?—would be one month before the world would shut down. It was a Wednesday, the middle of the week, in the middle of the month. Not such a dreary month in Florida as it had been in Pittsburgh. In fact, February is one of the nicest months down here. You might even get to wear a sweater.

And I had a sweater on that morning, a pretty Kelly-green cardigan. It was a crisp (by Florida standards) day. I rode my bike up County Road, stopping to remove the sweater as I passed the Palm Beach Country Club because I had, by then, become overheated. It is right there, when you round the bend, that the ocean opens up in front of you. It is there that you see the surf rolling and the sky stretching wide in all directions, clouds banking down to the horizon in shades of pink and purple and orange.

Florida is the land of big skies. Back in Pittsburgh, the hills creep up and obscure the larger view. In Florida, the flatness allows the sky to spread in a one-hundred-eighty-degree arc all around you. Especially when you are facing the water. So, there I stopped, took off my sweater, and stuffed it into the basket on the handlebars. I also paused to take in the big container ships far out to sea. I love that juxtaposition of the exotic, foreign world passing by while we are here living our minuscule lives. Some—like mine—more minuscule than others.

I listened to the seagulls and the rolling surf. I felt myself lift up for a moment, out of my own confines, and knew—in a way that I do not often know—that I was exactly where I was meant to be and doing what I was meant to be doing. On my way to Linda's house about to help Linda.

For I had seen in the window that night. Christmas Eve. I had watched them all there, sitting near the tree, a perfect little family group exchanging gifts and laughing. Linda, her daughter Espie, her brother-in-law Diego. All of these people I recognized. The little boy was there, too; Gogo, Linda had called him. I hadn't ever seen him because he was always at school when I visited. And there was one more person I had not seen who was among their party that night. Miguel. Linda's husband. And the doppelgänger of his brother, Diego.

That night, there under the stars—before Linda came out and so rudely interrupted me—I began to see clearly a way to help my friend. A way to help my mother resolve the past she never could put to bed. And, perhaps, a way to finally help myself break free from the whole sorry lot of them.

54

THE WIFE

Chapter Thirty
Wednesday, February 12, 2020

"Gogo, let's go!" Linda called to her son in an effort to light a fire under him. She was sure he was in his room reading a book and not brushing his teeth for school. He had recently started reading more fluidly on his own and his joy gave Linda an equal—if not greater—pleasure. But now was not the time for a book. Now was the time to get in the car. Linda turned to Espie, who was dogging her heels this morning, following her from room to room as she tidied up the breakfast table and started a load of whites in the washing machine. "Espie, honey, what's wrong? Why are you following Mommy?"

"It's just..." Espie faltered and picked at the hem of her sunshine yellow dress.

Linda always loved seeing Espie in this dress, which would only too soon be too small for her. Her little ones were growing up. Linda knelt down to her daughter and straightened her matching yellow ribbons, slipping, as usual, from her fine, dark hair. "What is it, sweetie?"

"Monkey doesn't want to go to school." Espie finally said.

"He doesn't?" Linda set aside her own sense of hurry and sat on the floor of the laundry room, pulling Espie onto her lap. "Why not? Doesn't Monkey feel good?"

"He feels bad."

"Hmmm. How come?" Linda asked, pressing her cheek to Espie's forehead, her tried and true way of diagnosing a fever. Linda's method always irritated Miguel, who felt a thermometer was a more reliable gauge. "You're not warm, Espie. Do you think Monkey's sick?"

"He's not sick," Espie answered. "He's sad."

"Oh honey! Why is Monkey sad?"

"Because Monkey likes Pipa."

Linda laughed and held her daughter close, breathing in her clean, powdery smell. "That's not sad. Pipa likes Monkey, too. And Pipa likes you very much, Espie. He loves you."

At that, Espie started to cry and pressed her face into her mother's chest. As much as Linda never wanted either of her children to cry, it was so deliciously sweet to be the consolation object for another little human. Her own little humans.

"Sweetie, Pipa does love you," Linda insisted.

"But..." Espie struggled for breath now that she was in full sob. Her voice came out in ragged gulps. "Daddy is making Pipa go away!" she wailed.

If Miguel had been here right now, instead of off at his office as he always was starting at the crack of dawn these days, Linda would probably have smacked him. How dare he let his feelings for his brother come out in front of their children? Wasn't he supposed to be one of the adults in this scenario? Okay, admittedly, Linda and Diego were not exactly behaving in a mature fashion, themselves. But at least they kept their affair hidden from the children.

"C'mon honey," Linda said. She gave Espie an extra hug, straightened her ribbons one more time, and worked to haul them both up from the laundry room floor. "I heard that Miss Course has a special treat for you today at school."

"Really?" Espie asked. "What?"

"Mom," Gogo interrupted from the doorway. "I've been waiting in the living room for you. I was looking out the window. There's a lady there."

"What?" Linda felt panic rising up with the coffee she had just consumed, which threatened to leave her body by way of her mouth. She hadn't seen that writer for almost two months and thought (prayed!) she had disappeared. Linda worked to sound calm for the sake of the kids. "Okay, Gogo, come on. Let's all go to school."

She took her children by the hands and marched to the garage. If Noelle was outside, Linda would not have to talk to her. She could just load everyone in the car and drive right on by. Ha! Maybe she could run her over. With Linda's luck, Noelle wouldn't die. She would just pop back up like a Whac-A-Mole toy.

What did she want from her? Linda reflected on this question once again as she helped Gogo into his seatbelt. He could climb up onto his booster himself, but he still needed Linda to fasten the buckle. Noelle wouldn't even answer Linda that night—to Linda's embarrassment, it had actually been Christmas Eve—when she shook her until her teeth rattled. All she would say was that stupid thing: *I can help you, Linda.*

Linda walked around the car and hoisted Espie up into her car seat.

"Ow, Mama," Espie said as Linda grazed her head on the ceiling of the car.

"Sorry, love. Duck your head a little. You're getting so big." Linda's hands trembled, making her fumble with Espie's straps and fasteners. Why did they make these car seats so difficult?

Finally, a full sweat building up from her exertions, Linda plopped herself in the driver's seat, started the car, put on her own seatbelt, and pressed the garage door clicker. She had backed in yesterday, so it would be easy to just drive straight out of the driveway.

"Moooooommm!" Gogo yelled from the back seat. "Espie's touching me with her smelly feet!"

Linda swiveled her head around to look at them before the garage door finished opening. "Stop touching your brother, Espie. Okay, honey? Keep your toes to yourself."

The motor that opened the door of the garage stopped humming, signaling that the door was fully open. The children did not answer Linda. They were staring straight ahead with a weird expression on their faces. Like they had seen a ghost.

Feeling nauseous, Linda slowly turned her head to face forward. And there stood Noelle in Linda's driveway. Fully blocking Linda's exit from the garage unless Linda did, in fact, run her over.

What the hell was going on here?

"Just a second," Linda said over her shoulder to her kids, as she undid her seatbelt and opened the door.

"Mommy! I'm scared!" cried Espie.

"You're a baby," Gogo dismissed his little sister.

"Gogo. Espie." Linda looked straight at them and spoke softly. Intently. "I need you both to be very good right now. Quiet. Okay?"

The children grasped her seriousness and said not one more word.

Linda got out and stood for a moment with her hand on the car. She wracked her brain as to the whereabouts of Diego. He had gone back to his room to shower. When was that? Fifteen minutes ago? Surely he would be out by now. Should she talk to Noelle? Should she go into the house and get Diego? Her brain was spinning.

Noelle stood still, too, with a simpering smile on her face.

Linda moved toward her before Noelle could get anywhere near the children. "Noelle," she said. Just that word. The woman's name. How dare this woman be named for her dead relative. What the bloody hell was that supposed to mean? Had she made it up? Was she crazy?

"Linda," Noelle started, "I didn't want to bother you, but..."

"Then don't! Don't bother me, Noelle! Go away!" Linda felt herself rising to a shout and she realized her kids might hear her. She dropped the register of her voice to add, "I've asked you what you want from me. You haven't answered."

"Well. I thought it was clear. I want to heal the past. For both of us."

"My past doesn't need healing. And you certainly wouldn't be the one to heal it if it did."

"Linda, can we talk? Just talk. I have an idea—a creative solution, if you will—to help you sort out the difficulty you're having." Here she paused and gave Linda an even more overblown look than she'd been giving her thus far, "I mean with your husband and his brother."

"Jesus!" Linda spat out. "Do you see my children sitting there? Do you?"

"Yes, Linda, I do. And I don't want to cause problems. I can wait for you to return."

Linda shook her head at this impossible—and crazy—woman. She looked back at her children. She looked at her watch. They were horribly late. She had probably missed the damned bridge, too, which would make them even later.

"Fine!" Linda said and had the overwhelming sensation of falling. And backward at that. Off a mile-high cliff. "Wait here. I'll be back in half an hour."

"Thank you, Linda," Noelle said to her, like the Devil to Dr. Faustus. "You won't regret it."

But Linda feared she would.

55

A WRITER'S THOUGHTS

Linda is making me wait. It is a passive-aggressive technique that, quite frankly, is not so passive. I bide my time in the blazing heat on her porch, which, facing south as it does, absorbs the full wrath of the sun. Florida is heating up, as am I.

She returns, finally, with no children. With no packages. With not even the ruse of a CVS bag to justify her tardiness. She is late because she wants to be late and she is letting me know it. She has probably been sitting around the corner texting from the comfort of her air-conditioned car. Linda has left me baking in the sun like a lizard because she wants to demonstrate the balance of power in our relationship.

When she finally turns into the driveway, I still foolishly expect her to park the car and rush over. There's no fool like an old fool, as the saying goes, and Linda does not hurry to me. She pauses in her car while she opens the automatic garage door. I hear its mechanism turning. She then pulls forward, disappearing from my view, and I hear the same mechanism again. It takes another five minutes for her to appear at the front door, opening it from inside.

"Come in," she says.

I am relieved I won't have to remain outdoors since I am close to the point of fainting. But it isn't kindness on her part that welcomes me into her home. Linda has a cruel streak. I picture her roasting me under a microscope, like a bug she's trapped on a sunny sidewalk. No, she only asks me in to avoid doing business in public. Period.

She motions me into the room but she does not take a seat. Awkwardly, I stand as well. Once again, I think I might pass out. "What do you want?" she says.

"Well, like I said, I want to help you."

"Cut the crap. Come to the point and then go."

"You don't have to be this way, Linda."

"Oh really, Noelle?" She pronounces my name with distaste. Can't say I blame her for that. "How would you suggest I behave with the person who trapped me in a grocery store with a bunch of rolling oranges? The person who stands outside my windows watching my family on Christmas Eve? The person who probably has been following me for years? You want me to offer you tea? Or some of that green juice you're always carting around?"

"Don't exaggerate, Linda. I haven't been following you for years."

"How would I know that? Huh? From the example of your stellar behavior since I met you?"

"Look," I begin.

"No, *you* look. You look right at my face and listen. I have tried to ask you to leave us alone. I have tried to warn you. I am really serious now. Leave. My. Family. Alone!"

"Don't threaten me, Linda. I want to help you."

"I don't need help!" she practically screams.

"But I want something in return," I forge on, ignoring her outburst.

"What could you possibly want from me? I have absolutely nothing that might interest you."

Linda is a bitch. She is a judgmental bitch. She is cruel and insulting and has a sharp tongue on her, as my mother would have said. Speaking of which. "I want to meet your father," I say. "I want to go to Pittsburgh with you and meet him."

Linda blinks at me like she has lint in her eye. Her mouth makes a little "O" and I wonder who's the foolish one here. And then she rears her head back and laughs. A deep belly laugh comes out of her, causing her to walk in a circle, bending over at the waist, holding her stomach, and occasionally rubbing her eyes. It is an overly theatrical performance and, frankly, she is starting to piss me off.

It is then that I decide to sit on one of her white, white chairs. Her Freudian chairs. I just walk over and plop my sweaty carcass down, and none too gracefully at that. This gets her to leave off the laughing jag and rub her eyes once more. For effect, I'm sure, but I can see I am gaining the upper hand.

"Feeling calmer?" I calmly ask.

She doesn't answer but she takes the chair opposite me, sitting quietly. I wonder where that brother-in-law is with all the hysterics going on in the living room. Maybe he sleeps in the day like a bat.

"We each have something the other wants," I say. "I have a way for you to extract yourself from your current—very sticky—situation. No one will get hurt. But it is a way out that will enable you to start over again in comfort. And you have access to your father. And that is something I am finally ready for. To meet him. To put my demons to rest."

Linda snorts at the word *demons*.

"You have a fair share of your own," I say. "I wouldn't act so uppity if I were you."

"Well," Linda retorts like a schoolgirl, "you're not me."

I stare at her, clamping my lips over my teeth. Like this, the power ever so slightly shifts.

"What do you have in mind?" she asks.

"It's a pretty simple plan. It will yield a lot of money. And it isn't even illegal. Well," I correct, since I don't want to be an out-and-out liar, "it isn't illegal until you leave town and don't give the money back."

56

THE WIFE

Chapter Thirty-One
Friday, March 13, 2020

De trop. Linda thought about that French expression. It conveyed exactly what Miguel had become to her in recent...recent what? Months? Years? How long had it been since she'd felt that longing for him that had consumed her until it simply didn't? What did it matter when it had happened, really? He had become excess baggage to her. To their children, too, if she were to be honest. After all, even at the best of times, Miguel was focused on Miguel. He wasn't like other dads of their generation who diapered, bottled, and pushed their babies on swings, just like their wives. Miguel, citing his Latin heritage, remained aloof, swooping in and out for a bedtime story or a peck on the cheek. He was like a 1950s television dad. Decorative, distant, and—to use that phrase again—*de trop*.

Diego was a better Miguel. He excelled at all of Miguel's roles in their little family. He was a better husband. A better lover. A better father. Where Miguel was simply sullen, Diego was tender and sad. There was a melancholy about him that was irresistible. In close proximity, Linda felt the ache of him oozing beyond his borders and crossing hers. But, in spite of that—or because of it—he had taken over her being and there was no room left anywhere for her husband.

Maybe it was because she finally learned what had happened to him in Mexico. Diego had kept that secret buttoned up inside himself for nearly a year after he came to them. And he had been traveling to get to them for a year before that. Two full years had passed between the time the *terrible thing* had happened to him and the moment he was finally able to tell of it. And it was a terrible thing, the most terrible that Linda could imagine happening to anyone.

He had been married, Diego, to a woman named Luna. Moon, it meant, and they had spoken, as lovers do in the early days of courtship, of their moons and planets orbiting each other through the end of time. He disclosed this to Linda without a tear in his eye. Dry-eyed and dry-voiced it came out, after they had made love on the sea green sheets of his room. But the end of time, he said, had not been meant for them. Or the end of time came sooner for them than they expected. But the hard thing was—and it was harder than anything he thought a human being could endure—was that the end of time came for Luna and their little girl, Gabriela—had he told her the name meant messenger of God?— before it came for him. He was cursed to carry on beyond the end of time without them, leaving him circling their phantom orbs, like limbs that are felt but not present.

He told Linda, still with dry eye, how he had had a shop in that pretty little town of San Miguel de Allende. The very place she and Miguel had honeymooned, not knowing that Diego and Luna and Gabriela were there, somewhere behind the door of a boutique they had not entered. A tiny store selling art and artifacts to Americans and other tourists. Why had they not crossed that threshold, she wondered, before the sound of Diego's voice called her back to him. He told her how he had recreated himself there in that town beyond his wildest hopes. How he had reached for the stars and attained the moon with Luna and the heavens with the addition of Gabriela.

Then he told Linda the bad part, the truly terrible part. He cleared his throat and rose in his nakedness to cover himself with a blanket. He stood looking out the window. He could not face her for this. Like Adam after tasting the apple, he had become ashamed. He waited a long time, focused on that window. In the time he waited, Linda sat up and covered herself, as well. She sensed he could no more abide her nakedness than he could his own.

Finally, he spoke.

There, he said, in that little town where life with Luna and Gabriela had been so perfect, where he felt he had so much more than he ever deserved, he came to know just how correct that perception had been. How undeserving he truly was. That there was a price to pay for all of it. Just like in the myths of yore, an ogre had appeared—a demon from a fairy tale—to force Diego to pay, specifically, a portion of his shop's income to a local mob. Small-time thugs really, not even an important gang. Not one of the cartels you read about in the paper. They were a bunch of nobodies and he did not take them seriously. He was proud. He was unafraid. He refused to pay. He was stupid enough to not be humble.

But they humbled him.

One day, a sunny day that began with laughter and kisses, his wife and daughter were taken by that mob as Luna walked Gabriela to school. And they were killed. But not before they suffered untold tortures that Diego was never to know. Would not know and, consequently, would never stop knowing. What he did know for certain, six weeks after they had disappeared, was that his little girl's finger appeared one morning in a brown paper bag on the stoop of his shop. What he did not know was what message God was sending him.

He stared at that finger for days. He recognized the small chip of pink nail polish that was all that remained from the salon game his wife had played with Gabriela. Had it only been two weeks before they were taken? He could no longer piece together the components of time. Were they still alive, his wife and daughter? Would a ransom note follow the bag with the finger?

And then Diego received the photographs which put to rest his questions. At least those questions as to what had befallen his family. He burned the pictures in a bowl that he'd had in the shop, made by a local artisan to sell to the gringo tourists. It was over for him. He could not envision a future without his wife and daughter. It was then that he began his wandering trail that eventually led him to Linda's doorstep.

All of this Diego recounted to Linda with nary a tear, in a voice that was clear and crisp. To Linda, it was like he was reading a book. Or reciting a script from memory. Trauma, she realized, could make a person go to such a strange place. But she could help him, she felt, heal him, love him, save him. She could not bring back his Luna or his Gabriela. She could not wipe out the memory of the finger found in a bag. A bag that had been used in a prior purpose to carry tortilla chips. A bag that was greasy and salty and dusted with crumbs that clung to his little girl's finger.

It was the bag he brought with him when he left that town. He did not go to the cemetery to inter what was left of his child. He did not call the police. He did not lock up his shop and fasten the chain. He walked out the front door to fall in with a street full of shoppers, leaving that door gaping wide. He moved down the cobblestone street with the bag in a box that he'd taken from the window display. A pretty, carved wooden box in which he would bury this tiny piece of his daughter somewhere. Just not there.

He walked out of the town and kept walking. He did not go in the direction of Guanajuato, though it might have been a logical destination. It was there, he said to Linda, where the mummified bodies of ordinary people were displayed in a bizarre museum, that he could have buried his relic. Frozen where they fell, those bodies, they were twisted in strange positions, with hardly any clothes remaining, but all with their stockings on. No. He would not take the box that held the bag with his daughter's remains there. He would not leave what was left of his family anywhere near where they had been killed.

He would go north, instead. After all, it was the direction he'd been heading since that day so long before when he'd left Buenos Aires on the back of a motorcycle with his best friend, Nico. He would go find his brother. He knew Miguel lived in the US. In the American state of Florida. Not in Miami, the place of which he had heard. But some other place. Palm Beach. He had learned all this on the internet. He knew it was risky. But what in his life had not been? And he just kept walking, like all the other migrants. He, scion of a prominent Argentine family, the last (that he knew of, for he did not yet know of Gogo) Diego Alonso in a long and (so they said) illustrious line of Diego Alonsos, would cross the border on foot. Would hop the wall or dig the trench or traverse the desert like the fugitive he actually was.

The journey took him a year and most of it he did not remember.

The day Diego told Linda this story—Friday the 13th of March, 2020, nearly a year after he'd first arrived at her door—would turn out to be the last day of school for Gogo and Espie. The last day that anyone went anywhere. The last window that Diego and Linda would have to themselves, alone in the house. A vise was closing around them, sealing them all in the little house on Reef Road.

57

THE WIFE

Chapter Thirty-Two
Friday, March 20, 2020

Miami had now locked itself down completely, as had the entire country of Argentina. Other cities and countries were following suit, like dominos knocked over by an unseen giant. It was becoming clear to Linda—to everyone—that this was only the beginning.

Linda considered Noelle's request. Could she—would she—offer up her father like a sacrificial lamb on the altar of Noelle's desires? Could she do it as a daughter, whatever her father had done, even if he had killed his sister, this author's namesake? Could she even do it in the most practical sense, since air travel had ground to a halt? She was saved from having to make that decision by unforeseen events in the external world. Noelle could hardly blame Linda for the quarantine lockdown, now, could she?

It occurred to Linda, in her reflections—and she had extra time for reflection these days, like everyone else in the world—that if she took Noelle to meet her father, she could use it as an opportunity to find out, once and for all, what really happened to her dead child-aunt. Noelle was going for that very reason and she and Linda could make a party of it and gang up on her dad for the shakedown. Maybe the sheer force of the two of them would get him to tell what, to Linda's knowledge anyway, he never had told anyone.

With a pang of remorse, she chastised herself for thinking such a thing about her father. He had only ever been kind and loving to her. But everything was growing increasingly relative in her head. The relativity of her father's pretty good fatherhood weighed against the fact that he may also have been a murderer was a tough one to sort out. How could she reconcile the person she knew with the person he may have been outside of her awareness? And the fact remained that he'd never been convicted. She didn't think he'd even been formally charged and tried.

These thoughts had eddied around her brain like the tide she stared at on her illicit beach walks. And there they swirled still, along with her endless flashes of insight and counter-insight as to what she should pre-cisely do about her marital conundrum. Relativity described her entire life right now. There was no clear sense of right and wrong and every little playing card component of decision was resting on another equally flimsy playing card.

It was ridiculous to think her father would talk to Noelle. His brain left his body a little bit more each day. He hardly had anything to say at all. And why he would speak to a total stranger about his alleged murder of his sister was beyond Linda's ability to fathom. She had known her father for forty years and he had never discussed the incident in any soul-baring way with her.

Once again, she reflected on the monomaniacal quality to Noelle. The woman was bizarrely obsessed with whatever happened all those years ago in Linda's family. It wasn't even her own family! Yes, she had some tale of her mother being Noelle Huber's best friend. But really? Her *mother* hadn't been murdered. Her mother had survived and gone on to get married and give birth to her. Although that couldn't have been a happy outcome for any mother, in Linda's view.

It also crossed Linda's mind that the lunatic writer might want to kill her dad as a revenge murder for her namesake. How would she do it? Pillow over the face? Bullet to the back of the head? Garotte? Linda reeled herself back from these thoughts. She was surprising herself—and not in a good way—daily. She was so fixated on getting away from Miguel and being with Diego that she was entertaining the possibility of playing fast and loose with her father's life. If Noelle's plan worked—and it seemed pretty simple and risk-free—Linda could at least get out of her marriage with some money to start over. Diego had no money at all, but he would be helpful in the art of self-reinvention. He had the requisite experience.

It all came down to money. *Cherchez la femme* it was said, but Linda did not think so. Find the money was more to the point. It could only be an influx of money that would enable her to walk away from Miguel. Linda and Miguel were always strapped. Over the entire life of their marriage, Miguel had spent money freely, indulging himself with boats and cars and even jewelry for his wife. Linda saw the baubles he gave her as treats that were dispensed to satisfy his own ego more than they were for her pleasure. Miguel liked to be that kind of guy, the one whose wife wore Verdura.

Linda had begun the execution of the plan. She had applied for the home equity loan. She had forged Miguel's signature. She had signed his name so many times before—with his permission—that it hardly felt like a transgression at all. All of this was so minor in the annals of wrongdoing that it did not count for much. It was such a dumb little non-crime—it was not illegal to borrow money against your own house—that Linda was surprised it took Noelle, a thriller writer, to come up with it. This was certainly no *Double Indemnity* insurance scheme. She would borrow the money. She would walk away. And she would keep that money for herself, Diego, and the children. Not particularly honorable, no, but not a major crime.

Especially now when the world had so many real problems. What difference would it make that one Palm Beach wife made off with a couple million bucks in the arms of her lover? That would just fall under the category of getting what she deserved. No one would get hurt in any meaningful way. The plan was in motion and there were only a few more steps to carry it out to completion. At the end, Linda hoped to never see Noelle again.

But, as Robert Burns once said, "The best laid plans of mice and men go often awry." Or something like that.

No one was meant to get hurt. No one.

58

A WRITER'S THOUGHTS

I visit Linda's house regularly, but I still don't let her know it. Why should I? She has been incredibly rude to me, which I have tolerated with, I think, rather remarkable grace. She has insulted me verbally, more than once, and has even physically assaulted me that time on Christmas Eve. There is a deep vein of violence that runs through the Huber clan, that much is abundantly clear. Linda has proven herself to be a chip off the old block, if you can forgive a writer one tired cliché.

Lest anyone think I have nothing to do, I would like to disabuse that person of that particular notion. I am under a deadline for my latest novel, which was accepted last year as a pitch. Right about when I met Noelle that day in Amici Market. I am not a fast writer. I get to a draft in a year and then it all depends. My editor died last year. Old age. He was a bit of an *éminence grise* even when he took me on thirty years ago. Still, it is a loss. I miss him.

There is someone new who has taken his place. A girl. Well, I am supposed to say a young woman, but, really, she is a girl. Ten years out of college. Nowadays, those years don't even count. Young people spend their twenties in the way we once spent our teens. Actually, that is not true at all. They are more immature in their twenties than we ever were in our teens. We had jobs and did our own homework and got ourselves into colleges, with minimal parental involvement. We got in where we got in and our parents could not have cared less. At least mine paid no attention when I got myself into Pitt.

My new editor, Brandy is her name, went to Rollins. She says she went there for the weather. It is an astonishing concept to me, choosing a school based on weather. Not to sound like the old fogeys who regaled us with stories of walking to school in the snow, but no one ever thought to ask us what sort of weather we wanted to study by.

When Brandy was promoted to editor, when I was told that they were computer dating us (based on what algorithm, I don't know), I had a moment of panic. It occurred to me that she might not be interested in working with me. Why should she be, after all? She wasn't even born when I published my first book. I was halfway expecting her to ask me if I could do my next thriller as a graphic novel. In the end, she liked my idea. She sent me off to write it, with the cursory response, "Cool beans."

Cool beans, indeed. Cool-as-a-cucumber beans.

So now I write. I will give Linda some time. I have asked her for what I want. It is best to give her space and let her come to the right conclusions. And it is best that I meet my deadline. For Brandy. For me. For all of us.

59

THE WIFE

Chapter Thirty-Three
Friday, April 17, 2020

"Linda," Miguel called to her from his throne-like perch on the living room sofa. As he read, he swirled his glass of Tito's to some internal rhythm, the ice tinkling in a way that had her ready to scream. She was cleaning up after dinner while Diego was putting the children to bed. Increasingly it was their Pipa who Gogo and Espie wanted to read to them and tuck them in, leaving Miguel and even Linda out of the bedtime ritual. Miguel set the glass down hard and continued, "Diego is leaving next week. I've told him he has to go. Enough is enough."

Linda stopped scrubbing the pan in her hands, setting the Brillo pad on the edge of the sink. This was all happening too soon. The coronavirus shutdown had hampered everything, especially her plans to leave Miguel. The loan for two million dollars had been theoretically approved a month ago. Actually getting the money, however, was delayed. Her contact at the bank was working from home now, like everyone else. Which meant that everything had to be done by email. Which posed the pesky problem of potential discovery by Miguel.

Linda checked her own inbox compulsively, but she also checked her husband's. That banker might just as easily email Miguel as he would email Linda. Linda had Miguel's password. He was too cocksure to ever worry about her looking at his emails. In fact, he had always relied on Linda as a backup to his secretary at work. He liked to have her scan his emails to make sure he didn't miss anything. Which she was compulsively doing. But the banker had gone radio silent.

"Why don't you give Diego a little more time, Miguel? Don't you think it's kind of a challenging time to reinvent himself? I mean, where's the guy going to go in the middle of a pandemic?"

"I don't really care," he said as he slammed his book shut. "And neither should you, my darling wife."

"Well, I mean, I don't *care*. It's just basic human decency. We've taken him in and we've housed him for a year. It doesn't make much difference to keep him here a little longer, does it?"

"It does to me. And I'm starting to think it does to you, too." Miguel stood up and walked toward Linda at the sink. She tried not to look at him doing it, but the anticipation of what might come next made her shudder. When Miguel reached her, he placed both hands on her waist from behind. Another twitch of revulsion erupted at his touch. Linda felt Miguel stiffen in reaction.

"That tickles," she said, trying to make light. "You know how ticklish I am."

"Leave that," he said, pulling her away from the sink, forcibly turning her around to kiss her. He came at her with his mouth open and she had the ridiculous thought for a half second that he was going to lick her face. She instinctively jerked her head backward and saw Miguel's eyes harden.

"Stop." She pushed him, laughing awkwardly as she did it, trying to make it all look playful. "You know how you hate for me to leave dishes in the sink."

"I don't give a shit about the fucking dishes, Linda." He grabbed her arm hard and pulled her toward the bedroom.

"Stop it, Miguel. I mean it."

"You mean it?" he panted as he dragged her through the living room, nearly toppling a glass end table in their path. "You fucking mean it?"

"You're drunk. Let me go." Linda made her voice as authoritarian as she could while still struggling against his bruising grip on her arm. "Now!"

"Or what? Or you'll cry to my brother?" He turned to give her a cold stare. "Jesus Christ, Linda, my own brother! How could you?"

"I don't know what you're talking about but you're going to wake the children."

"What, now you're mother of the year?"

Linda slapped him. She had not intended to but she did. And, just as suddenly, he hit her back, so hard across the face she cried out from the pain or the shock, she wasn't sure which. Her mind was skittering like leaves on the ground as she tried to formulate a plan of action when she saw Miguel unbuttoning his trousers.

"No!" Linda cried out. Was Diego still with Gogo and Espie? She turned to run back to the kitchen while Miguel was busy with his pants.

Not fast enough. He grabbed her by the hair, which—when she pulled against him—pitched her forward onto her hands and knees on the hard marble floor. Then he was on her, yanking up her skirt, ripping off her panties, and mounting her from behind with a ferocity that tore through her. It felt like she was being stabbed.

There was no more use in struggle. The shorter route to the end of this would be to suffer through it. Linda surrendered to him and stuffed a fist in her mouth to muffle her moans. *Please don't let the children wake up*, was all she could think. *Please don't let the children see this.* For that reason alone, the sake of her children's last remaining illusions about who their parents really were, Linda would endure this rape. There was no other word for what her husband was doing to her.

And then he stopped, sooner than she had dared hope, collapsing upon her with his full weight. And it was only then that Linda allowed herself to cry, her cheek sliding a little as her tears hit the marble beneath her. Miguel didn't even have the decency to lift his weight and it occurred to her that he had fallen asleep. He must have hit the Tito's harder than usual.

"Get off me!" she said. "Please?"

Still, he did not move. Linda mustered the energy to push herself up with her hands and roll herself out from under him, shoving him to the side. What an animal he had become. She scrambled to her feet, pulling her skirt down and wiping her wet face with her hands. And then she saw the blood. Her hands were covered in it. Had Miguel actually cut her? She had no recollection of it. Linda could not identify the source of it. She turned to walk down the hall to get a look at herself in the bathroom mirror. It was then that she saw Diego crouched in a corner of the room.

"Diego?" Linda looked from him to her husband, inert on the floor, and the source of the blood became apparent. It was coming from Miguel's head, specifically a wide-open gash on the back of it.

Linda stared at Diego, who remained on his haunches against the wall, like an animal who had accidentally entered their house. The feral quality she had originally observed in him, but forgotten for so long, had returned. "Diego, what did you do?"

Diego did not respond.

Linda cast her eyes around the room and saw the Steuben glass olive bowl tossed aside on the floor—the one that had been a wedding present from her parents—with a telltale streak of blood on it.

"We need to call an ambulance," she said as she moved to take Miguel's pulse. "He needs to go to the hospital."

Linda pressed one wrist and then the other, frantically trying to locate that familiar throb of a living being. "Diego, help me! I can't find a pulse." She rolled Miguel onto his back and lowered her ear to his chest to listen for a heartbeat. She worked to find the pulse on his neck. "Diego," Linda begged. "Please, I need your help."

But Diego just crouched in the corner with his wild animal eyes staring at his supine brother.

"Pipa?" Linda saw her little girl, her tiny Espie, standing in the doorway in her footed pajamas, clutching her monkey to her chest. She must have heard the commotion and climbed out of her new toddler bed to investigate. And here she was in the wreckage. But she was looking at

Diego, not at Linda and not at her father, stretched out on the floor. "I heard a noise," Espie said to Diego. "Can you read to me again?"

And it was this, finally, this child, Linda and Miguel's daughter who possibly reminded Diego of his own little girl—his Gabriela—who brought Diego to his senses.

"Yes, *querida*, I'll read to you," he said as he rose slowly from the floor and walked over to Espie. She reached up her arms to him, in a gesture of complete trust, and Diego picked her up. Linda watched Espie lay her head on Diego's shoulder and close her eyes, secure that she was safe in his arms. She did not appear to have looked into the room where the carnage had unfolded. She did not appear to have seen her mother. And she did not appear to have seen Miguel.

Linda stood for a moment with the thought of the relativity of good. The relativity of evil. Then she dropped back down to her knees and threw up on the floor, narrowly missing the body of her husband, who was most assuredly dead.

Diego had killed him. Diego, who was in the bedroom with her children now. Diego, who was possibly not at all who Linda had thought he was. What in God's name was she to do? How would this all look? It would look intentional, that's how. After Linda had applied to borrow that money, it would look like she had planned to kill her husband.

How would she get out of this?

Linda scrambled to her feet and made her way to the kitchen. She grabbed a paper towel and used it to turn on the faucet, trying not to get blood on any surface. She turned the water on hot and washed her hands just like they were telling everyone to do to avoid falling ill with COVID. There, with her husband dead on the floor in a growing pool of blood, she intoned the happy birthday song twice through, as she scrubbed and scrubbed her hands. Just like the lady in the play whose name she would not mention. When she was finished, she turned off the kitchen and living room lights. She did not want to risk the chance that anyone might be able to see anything through her front window.

"Linda?" Diego had entered the room so silently that Linda jumped. "I am sorry. I did not intent to hurt him. I only intended to stop him."

"Espie?" she asked.

"She is asleep."

"Good. Diego, listen. We need to start cleaning up. The blood and all. Don't use cloth. Use paper. We have to get rid of it."

He remained mute, staring at the body of his brother.

"Okay, Diego?" she prodded. "Are you listening? We have to clean up."

"What then?" he asked, turning his eyes to her—those eyes that had that distinctly lupine sheen to them again.

"I don't know. I need to think. Let's clean," Linda said. "Cleaning helps me think."

Linda circled around Miguel's body, where the blood stain was expanding. One small mercy, he'd been killed on the marble floor, and not on the white area rug. She'd never get the blood out of that.

"Are your hands clean?" she asked Diego. "Go wash them quick. Then help me roll this rug back before anything touches it."

Anything. Like someone had overturned a plate of food that might stain her white carpet. Anything could only be blood. Or maybe brains. Or her own vomit. Blood and brains and vomit on the rug. Linda nearly retched again but controlled it.

Linda briefly considered removing her clothing to leave fewer sources of discovery. But, what did it really matter? Miguel had raped her in this outfit. He had bled out on it. She'd have to burn or boil it or dump it at the bottom of the sea. She may as well leave it on now.

Hurrying into the kitchen, she returned with paper towels, a huge bottle of Fabulosa, and some hefty bags, one of which she handed to Diego to enclose Miguel's leaking head. The bile rose up in her stomach for the third time, but she forced herself to continue.

60

A WRITER'S THOUGHTS

My new isolation is not so very different from my old isolation. And yet there is an amplified feeling about it, as though aloneness was only ever an informal condition in the past, transient even, but now has become immutable. In this state, I return again and again to those old newspaper images of Noelle. And in them I see Linda.

Now that I know Linda, I can't miss the resemblance between aunt and niece. The general configuration of eyes to nose to mouth, the shape of the jawline, and—most particularly—the smile. Although Linda has not bestowed many of her own smiles upon me of late, I have seen enough of them to perceive the similarities.

And in that odd way of time when it becomes historic, when it moves out of the tangible day-to-day of our existence and becomes abstract, Noelle Grace Huber could be the daughter of Linda Huber Alonso, for such are the ages of each party with which I am most familiar: Linda as a woman and Noelle forever as a girl. I lean in a little closer, squinting at Noelle's face and wonder, not for the first time, if it remained intact after her brutalization, or if it was as damaged as the rest of her body on that December night.

I push the papers and the photographs away from me and get up. Sleep will not come tonight. I glance at Cordie, stretched out on her old, ratty dog bed on the floor. Should I rouse her for a walk? No. Let her dream her dreams. I will take a bike ride. No one is out now. No one is ever out. I will have the town to myself.

61

THE WIFE

Chapter Thirty-Four
Friday, April 17, 2020

They dragged the body—encased in multiple Hefty bags—across a path of more Hefty bags laid out on the floor, all the way to the garage. There did not seem to be a more logical place for the holding of a human corpse while one figured out what to do with it. Linda collapsed next to it in pure exhaustion. Suddenly, the adrenaline that had coursed through her veins abandoned her and she was unable to take the next step.

Diego left her there. He did not reach out a hand to comfort the widow of the brother he'd slain. He went back into the house. She did not know where. Maybe he was heading to bed. It had been a long night, after all. Linda struggled to her feet and reentered the house.

Diego was nowhere to be seen.

She slipped down the hall, stopping at the closed door of her children's room. She listened without opening, saying a silent prayer that they had slept—and would continue to sleep—through this nightmare. She continued on to Diego's room and found the door ajar. From the hallway, she could see no light within.

For the second time tonight, she felt a pang of uncertainty about him, a niggling thread of doubt about the man for whom she had been willing to blow up her life. A man who had entered her life only a year before with wild eyes and a wild beard and bugs crawling all over him and had still managed to seduce and—was it possible?—brainwash her.

What if he was not who he had led her to believe? He was Miguel's brother, obviously, there was no mistaking that. But the story of the wife and the daughter and the finger in the chip bag? And the town with the mummies in the socks and the crossing of the desert for a year? Could any of it possibly be true?

Or did he make it all up? Diego freely admitted that he trolled the internet. Maybe he'd seen their wedding announcement in the *New York Times* that mentioned their honeymoon in San Miguel and he'd spun his wild tale from there. Her mind took to spinning at that. Miguel had not warmed to his brother from the moment he'd crossed their threshold. Didn't trust him in a way he would never explain to Linda. He obviously knew something about him that she did not.

Linda realized that Diego had been an exceedingly unreliable brother for fully two decades prior to his surprise arrival. But she had come to forget all that, had believed his stories, and fallen under his spell in much the same way as had her children. Does a leopard change his spots? Could Miguel have been right? Could Linda possibly have bet on the wrong brother? Could there have been a darker side to Diego that she was too blind to see? After all, he'd just murdered his own brother right there in the living room.

A sickening dread overtook her and she slumped to the floor of the hallway.

As she pressed her forehead to her knees to combat a swimming dizziness, Linda became aware of the sound of running water. And just as suddenly as misgivings had consumed her, they departed. Diego was taking a shower after cleaning up the scene of the…never mind that. It was a sensible thing to do. It would explain the eerie emptiness of the house. Before she could question herself, she walked through the guest room and into the bathroom beyond it.

"Diego?" This room was also dark. She could barely see him through the glass door of the shower, but a shadowy figure was in there.

"Linda?" he said as he poked out his head. "Would you like to come in and shower here?"

What an odd question. What an odd concept, showering with your lover after murdering your husband. Well. She had not murdered anyone. But she had cleaned up the scene of the crime. Aiding and abetting was what that was. Accessory to the fact. Maybe manslaughter. She was in deep. She might as well get clean before moving on to the next steps.

62

A WRITER'S THOUGHTS

turn my bike onto Reef Road, glad for the light of the moon. It is only a waning crescent now, but it provides enough illumination for me to see where I am going in the dark. Streetlights pop up occasionally and the sky is filled with stars peeking behind wisps of clouds. The sliver of moon comes and goes, as the clouds make their way in front of it. These clouds never disappear this time of year in Florida. The air is thick with water, which condenses and slips across the sky like silhouettes in a stereopticon.

I stow my bike in the bushes across the street from Linda's—the place I often hide it—and crouch down. It is very dark inside her house. Darker than usual. Normally, when I come here to watch at night, no matter how late the hour, the interior of her house has a glow about it. On my daytime visits, when she has deigned to let me in, I have noticed nightlights plugged into outlets scattered along the baseboards. Why is it so dark tonight?

And then I see a light moving. A flashlight. Is someone robbing her house? Or is Linda using it? Untwisting myself from my crouching position, I sit on the ground to settle in for a while and see what develops here. Something is definitely out of order inside the Alonso household.

63

THE WIFE

Chapter Thirty-Five
Friday, April 17, 2020

"We need to get rid of the body," Linda said to Diego when they emerged from the shower. "Tonight. Now."

"How will we do that?" asked Diego. "We are in the middle of Palm Beach."

"I'm thinking…" she said as she moved out of the room to get some clothes. Her soiled clothes she had left on the floor of the shower. She would come back for them later.

"We have a boat," she said when she reentered the room, feeling the beginnings of hope. "We keep it at the club. A couple blocks away."

"Do they have security cameras?" Diego asked.

"I have no idea. Maybe," said Linda, her spirits deflating. "Probably."

"Can we move around them and not be detected?"

"With a body? In the middle of the night?" It all seemed completely hopeless. The folly of even considering such a thing overwhelmed Linda with the blackness of the future she faced.

"Wait," she said. "Our friends. They're out of town. They have a boat and a dock. It's next to the club but the cameras shouldn't reach it."

"Can you operate their boat?" he asked.

"It's the same as ours."

"And you can gain access?" Diego asked. "Would you need a key?"

"It's probably hidden on board," said Linda. "I have a good idea where to look. It's worth a try."

"And then what?" asked Diego.

"We take him out to the Gulf Stream and dump him overboard," Linda answered. "The current moves so fast that his body will be in Nantucket within a few days. Maybe a week. And the decomposition—helped along by sharks, we can only hope—will be very advanced."

She looked at him in the dim light, hoping for some sign of solidarity. A visual cue that they were in this together. He said nothing and, worse, did nothing to make her feel his support.

"In fact," she went on, "we can hope the body totally bypasses Nantucket Island and just keeps moving into the North Atlantic."

Still he did not respond. Almost worse than the fact that he was a cold-blooded killer was his silence. Linda had never felt so alone in her life.

"We have to do it," she said.

"And then what do we do?" asked Diego. At least he finally said something.

"We come back here and work on getting you and the children on a flight. To Argentina."

"I do not have a passport," he said. "I have lived out of sight for many years."

"But your brother has one. And you look just like him."

"I don't know, Linda."

"You don't *know*? What don't you know? You killed your brother and you're going to have to act fast to make sure we both don't rot in jail the rest of our lives!"

"It won't work," he said.

"It will!" she said, feeling her confidence return. "You'll travel to Buenos Aires on the next available flight with the two children. You'll travel as their father, with his passport. You look enough like him and you'll be wearing a mask—which works to your advantage—that I think you'll navigate passport control at the Miami Airport very easily. The children love you. They'll go readily with you. And they call you Pipa! If anyone hears that, it'll sound as if they're saying Papa. And then…" she paused because she'd found herself speed-talking. "And then I'll follow you later. Once I get that money. Once this virus is over and I can get on a plane to Argentina."

A silence fell over them. A moment of mental readjustment was in order for each of them to face reality as it was now configured.

"Can you do this?" Linda finally asked Diego.

"Yes," he answered. He did not ask Linda the same question.

64

A WRITER'S THOUGHTS

I am asleep when a noise wakes me. It is a bumping and squeaking noise. Which would technically make it two noises. I hear one thing bump and another thing squeak. The same thing?

I shift position and shiver, remembering I am sitting on the wet grass across from Linda's house. I squint my eyes in the general direction of the sound, which seems to be coming from her driveway. The sliver of moon is farther down the western sky now and the clouds have thickened, making it difficult to distinguish what I am seeing. Because I am definitely seeing something. Something that looks to be rather large and in motion. It is moving down Linda's driveway toward the road, but it is not a car.

I hunker down farther, trying to make myself as small as possible and trying to be quiet as I do. The object, as it nears the street, reveals itself to be composed of multiple parts. Two people are moving something between them. One is in front of it. One is in back. The object between them appears to move smoothly. It must be on wheels. A wheelbarrow?

"Shit." I distinctly hear someone say it in a loud whisper. Linda. I am certain it is Linda.

The object has taken a lurch to the left, which is, I am sure, what prompted her profanity. She obviously is having some difficulty keeping the object aright, which implies that there is some weight to it.

I don't know what makes me do it. Maybe I shouldn't, but something takes hold of me and I stand up and loudly clear my throat.

"Linda?" I call out in a similarly forced whisper to the one she just used for her expletive.

The two people and the object they are moving stop dead. All motion and sound cease. As though they think they can make themselves disappear to better hide whatever it is they are up to. For it is more than evident that they are up to something extremely nefarious indeed in the middle of this night.

"Noelle?" she eventually says. "What in the living hell?"

I walk over to her and the person I can now identify as her brother-in-law. He stares at me with an inscrutable expression. I don't know if it is the dark or his face, but he doesn't look human, and I feel a chill clamp the back of my neck. I turn to Linda, who looks frantic and afraid. I look down at the object between them. It is a child's wagon, a red Radio Flyer. There is something in it that is large and lumpy. A Hefty bag? The two of them are dressed entirely in black: shoes, pants, shirts, baseball caps.

Realization comes slowly. They cannot have done what it occurs to me they have done. But it appears that they did do it. My horror yields to another feeling as I sense a golden opportunity to advance our friendship. Our system of mutual support. Dependency, if you will.

"Do you need help, Linda?" I address my question to her. I don't wish to deal with this man. My relationship is with Linda. If I am going to get involved in whatever it is that is going on, it is going to be with her. For her. And for me.

I wait.

"Yes," Linda says at the same time that her companion says, "No."

"Diego, we need her. We need help." Linda says and then turns to me, "Just come into the house for a minute. We can't talk out here."

She starts to make a turn with the handle of the Radio Flyer and Diego stoops down to push the back end, falling in line with her request.

252

They move the thing to the side of the garage and we all troop in through the door. We do not move any farther and stop in the garage to converse there. Linda clicks on a flashlight.

"What happened?" I ask.

"Miguel hit his head," Linda answers. "He's dead."

She looks at Diego and he looks at her. No one looks at me. The ridiculousness of the lie she is so blithely telling is laughable.

"Linda," I say. "If you want my help, you have to tell me the truth."

"There's no time, Noelle!" She sounds desperate. "There's no time to tell the whole thing. Miguel is dead. We have to get rid of his body. We have a way, and it would be very helpful if you would stay here in case my children wake up in the night."

"You want me to babysit?"

"They're sleeping. They won't wake up. But, if they do, it would really help me a lot to have you in the house."

"Where are you going?"

"Out."

"Come on, Linda." I look from her to him, who keeps his eyes studiously averted, staring at the garage floor.

"We're going out on a boat. To the Gulf Stream. To dump this..." She motions to the wall, on the other side of which waits the wagon.

"Husband." I provide the correct word.

65

THE WIFE

Chapter Thirty-Six
Saturday, April 18, 2020

In the wee hours of Saturday morning, Linda and her lover dragged her husband's bagged and battered body through the neighborhood, balanced on a child's wagon. Their destination was a boat privately docked on the lake just to the north of the club. Linda did not know what they would do if a police car passed them, but they encountered no one along the way. The desolation of the night matched the desolation of the day in the pandemic world and they had the streets to themselves. Other than their encounter with Noelle.

They followed the road from the house on Reef Road until they came to the bike path skirting the edge of the club. They made their way along that path, avoiding lights and cameras, until they came to the water. There was the Wilsons' dock, crowned with the objective of their trip, the Wilsons' Boston Whaler, shifting and creaking in the dark water under the nearly vanished moon.

The tide was low, making the chore of maneuvering Miguel's dead weight at least a little easier. Bringing the wagon to the edge of the dock,

Linda was able to hold it still while Diego rolled his brother's body off, allowing the body to drop two feet onto the deck where it landed with a dull thud. Linda worried they might have torn the bags, thus leaking blood and bodily fluids onto the Wilsons' boat. Close examination once they came aboard revealed that the plastic had held.

Linda moved to the console and began opening cabinets and drawers. Nothing. She went back to the seats, lifted the cushions, and pulled up panels to search compartments below. Still no key. For some stupid reason she hadn't considered the possibility that the Wilsons would not have left the key aboard. Everyone left their key aboard. Boats were not stolen in Palm Beach.

She did not have her cell phone with her because she had been worried about someone later tracing her movements. But she had that flashlight. Should she use it? Best not. She had no idea who was in any of the nearby houses or who might be patrolling the grounds of the club.

"Linda…?"

"Shh, I'm looking for the key!"

She went back to the console to reopen everything she had already opened. This time she stuck her hand farther in, feeling the bottoms, the sides, even the tops of drawers, cabinets, and compartments. She did the same under the seats. There, finally, she found it. Not on a floaty fob, rolling at the bottom of a drawer. But carefully fitted to a magnet at the top of an under-seat compartment. Those clever Wilsons.

"I have it," she whispered. Diego's uselessness was irritating her on a night when she could really use his help. A night, in fact, that was his doing. He had caused this and now he was sitting on the boat doing nothing.

Linda inserted the key and, mercifully, the engines turned over. "Diego, I need you. You have to get back on the dock and untie the lines. Can you do that?"

"Yes," he said as he hopped up to the dock.

"Throw the rope on the boat once you've untied it," she said. "Untie the front first."

"Okay." Diego moved across the dark dock, stumbling once on the wagon.

"Bring the wagon aboard," she said. "We don't want to leave it here in case someone comes by. We don't know how long this will take."

He pushed the wagon over the edge of the dock. It landed on some part of Miguel before it rolled to a corner of the boat's deck. Then Diego untied the ropes, tossed them aboard, and hopped back down. Linda struggled for a few minutes with the shift throttle control, found her forward gear, turned the wheel, and powered slowly away from the dock.

It was a very dark night. Lights on either side of the lake reflected somewhat back to her. She did not know if this Boston Whaler had any lights or where she would even find them. She had never driven their own boat at night. But she didn't wish to call attention to their activities, so she made her way as best she could. It was a short distance up to the cut. She squinted to see the channel markers and relied on them to navigate.

"Diego?" Linda said as she turned to enter the cut. "It's going to get rough in a second. Make sure everything is secure."

"Okay."

And, just like that, the waters of the lake met the waters of the ocean and the boat started to rock and roll.

256

66

A WRITER'S THOUGHTS

Their shadows moving down Reef Road with the loaded wagon is the last I see of Diego and Linda for the rest of the night. Linda did not take her cell phone with her, and I presume Diego does not have one. Linda has given me a job in addition to being present for the children. She has asked me to book their airline tickets. Before leaving, she retrieves her family's passports from a safe—Argentine passports, I notice—and logs on to the computer in Miguel's office. She opens up both of their email accounts, so I can begin the process of finding the flight to Buenos Aires. Diego will be traveling as Miguel, so any research on "Miguel's" travels should only be traceable to Miguel. His computer anyway.

American and Delta seem to be the best bets. Direct, nonstop flights. Leaving tomorrow night. Actually, I check my watch and realize it is after midnight. So, tonight then. Saturday, April 18. American leaves later— 8:45 p.m.—which would give them more time to do whatever else they need to do to get this show on the road. Or to keep it on the road that they—should I say we—have chosen already—each one of us. On the other hand, delaying can only cause trouble. It would be best to keep moving forward to limit chances of getting caught.

I walk out to the living room and search for signs of what happened there only a few hours before. I do not turn on the light. I think back to when I was looking into Linda's window from my vantage point across the street. She had kept the lights off then, too. From what I can tell in the semi-dark, they have done a good job of cleaning up. Of *redding* up this house, as my mother, old Pittsburgher that she was, would have said. From the proper English phrase "to make ready," I presume.

As a writer, I have always loved those colloquialisms that have persisted in different regions of our country. Particularly in the mountainous regions—and Pittsburgh is part of the Appalachian chain—where people were isolated linguistically in their own separate hollows. The old Pittsburgh accent to me—and I am not an expert—seems to follow a trail from east to west and has identifiable links to those of Baltimore, Philadelphia, even Washington, DC. The *ow* or *ou* sounds are often streamlined into a simple *ah*. Downtown becomes *dahntahn*, house becomes *haas*, mouse becomes *maas*. This is very similar to the Washingtonian pronunciation of shower, which comes out as *shahr*. So *yinz* better not forget who you are in the world, even if your accent is disappearing due to the ubiquity of television. I will miss the final departure of the usage of *yinz*. It is such a lovely pluralization of you—for you ones—as sensible and tidy as *y'all*.

I make my way back to the office to do a little rooting on Miguel's computer. I don't know if that expression is unique to Pittsburgh, but it's meaning is self-evident. I scroll through photos, including many of Linda's parents. I watch Linda and Miguel's wedding video and pay special attention to Miguel's speech. I read a slew of emails and find Linda's to the mortgage broker about the home equity loan. Nothing new here. Nothing that changes my understanding of the Alonsos or the Hubers before them. Well, maybe the wedding footage of Linda's father, Matt. I search his old face for traces of the young man—the killer—he used to be.

I roam around the house, opening medicine cabinets, drawers, closets. I know which door belongs to the children's room and I am quiet when I pass it. And I eat. I go into the kitchen and look for something that will make this time pass less anxiously. Linda does not keep much in the way of junk food—the chosen solace of the bulimic—in this house.

I discover a box of something called Cheddar Bunnies and am able to polish it off. They are definitely not as good as Cheez-Its but are along the same lines.

At about five a.m., when Linda and Diego have not yet reappeared, I can no longer keep my eyes open. When I close them, I envision Cordelia, alone in my apartment. She will wake soon and look for me. Because she is old, she will wet on the floor. I did not train her with pads when she was young, the ones that small dog owners in New York City apartments are adept at using to avoid walks in the middle of the night. By the time Cordie was old enough to need something like that, she wasn't interested in using them. Oh well. I can clean it up when I get home. I left her with water and a bowl of dried food, so that won't be an issue in the short term. And thus my mind drifts until it mercifully shuts off.

67

THE WIFE

Chapter Thirty-Seven
Saturday, April 18, 2020

The chop of incoming waves—the same waves pounding Reef Road beach just to the south of them when they emerged from the cut—slammed the Boston Whaler, causing Miguel's plastic-encased body to jump and the Radio Flyer wagon to fly. Linda heard it bang into something. Maybe Diego's knees. "Oof," she heard him say as he engaged in a struggle to secure the inanimate objects.

"Maybe flip the wagon over?" Linda shouted back at him. "So it doesn't roll!" The wind was blowing and, combined with the roar of the engines, she did not know if he could hear her.

There was another minute or so of scuffle, then all was quiet from the stern. Linda cast her eyes back to see what Diego was doing. It looked like he was sitting on the deck, between the body and the wagon, a hand atop each. Fine. She would drive in silence. She needed some time to think. Everything had happened so fast tonight she hadn't been able to process any of it.

Was it even tonight that Miguel had raped her? Had they gone from that act of violence to Miguel's death to the cleanup to Noelle's arrival all in one night? Like a child, she found herself wishing, for one brief moment, that she would wake from a dream. That she would find herself in her bed at home with Miguel—yes, Miguel—sleeping next to her, their children across the hall. No pandemic. No shutdown. No Noelle. No Diego. None of it. Linda wished to be rid of it all and she squeezed her eyes shut for a second to make it go away.

Nose down went the Boston Whaler again, followed by a jolting thud. Linda's eyes popped open as Diego, Miguel, and the wagon hit the seats in front of them.

"Diego," Linda shouted, "you need to find a way to hold on!"

"I am trying, Linda!"

Out they went, into the wide Atlantic, heading into open water, on their way to the Gulf Stream. Where the hell was it? Would she know it when she found it? Linda felt very alone and very small, a speck in the ocean, while her children slept at home in the care of that crazy writer. The world had turned upside down and she did not know how to right it. Every step she took, she saw, was making everything irretrievably worse. It was like she had drunk a reverse magic potion, a cursed potion, that had set her on a trajectory for disaster.

Once they got away from the beach surf, the water became incredibly calm. The tiny glimmer of remaining moon, a glow from the lights on the shoreline, and maybe a bit of phosphorescence enabled her to see. She felt rudderless and adrift.

"Diego?"

"Yes, Linda."

She wanted him to talk to her. To stand by her side and put his hand atop hers on the wheel and say something comforting. To tell her a story or tell her he loved her or tell her that everything would be okay. But he did none of those things. She was in a boat on the ocean at night with the man who had just killed her husband. A man she would send to a foreign country with her children. A man she did not know.

She must be totally insane.

Not even fifteen minutes into open water, they hit it. The Gulf Stream. Linda felt a slight tug of the boat to the left, to the north, to Nantucket. To the icebergs. "Diego," she called back, throttling down their speed. She nosed the Boston Whaler to the south to counter the Gulf Stream's flow. "Now, Diego! Throw him overboard now."

"In the bags?" Diego shouted.

"What?" Linda whipped her head around, straining to hear him, to see him, to get a grasp of what he was asking. She was also trying to keep the boat under control—something that was not in her natural skill set. "What did you say?"

"Do you want me to throw him in the bags or out of the bags?"

This time she heard him. She found his question—his entire being—increasingly, annoyingly, unhelpful. Did he think she was an expert on body disposal? He had more experience with that sort of thing, considering the Mexican gang and the severed finger. Once again, Linda wondered if any of it was true.

"I don't know, Diego!" she hollered. "If you take him out of the bags on the deck of this boat, we'll never be able to clean it up. Maybe you open them over the edge and kind of toss it all that way. Open but not empty."

Linda kept the Boston Whaler's throttle just above an idle to give herself a little headway while Diego figured out his part of the job. She heard more rustling and thumping and then an enormous groan, followed by the distinctive plop of a man overboard. Dead man overboard, but still.

And then a different object hit the water and for a chilling instant Linda wondered if Diego had jumped in. Had decided to throw in his fate with the brother he had abandoned and finally killed. To unite himself fraternally, once and for all, and leave Linda—no blood relation to him—alone to deal with the consequences. But then she saw the red wagon floating along to her left, resembling a raft atop the swells. Would it stay that way and make its way to the shoreline? Just as she was scrambling to think of a way to grab hold of the wagon, one end of it lifted up—like the sinking of the Titanic—and the whole of it slid down under the surface of the sea.

Wildly, she wondered if she could just keep going to countries unknown. To start anew and pretend none of this had happened. But, of course, her children were in Palm Beach and she was out here with Diego. And also, of course, the pandemic was everywhere. There was nowhere at all to go.

68

A WRITER'S THOUGHTS

"Noelle."

"Noelle..." the second time someone says my name, it is accompanied by a shaking of my shoulder. I open my eyes to Linda, still dressed in her burglar black. She is no longer wearing the hat, and her hair—her entire person—is disheveled. I look around to see Diego, three feet behind her. He's a mess as well.

"It's finished," she says, which is about the most ridiculously optimistic thing anyone could say right about now. How she imagines this sordid episode might be drawn to a close at this juncture I cannot imagine. "Did you find a flight?"

"Um, yes," I say as I straighten up from the office chair I am slumped in. "I think Delta is better because it's earlier. I think it's best for him," I point at Diego, "to get out of town as fast as he can."

"Diego?" she says. "What do you think?"

"What time does it depart?" he asks.

"Four p.m.," I say.

"And any other flights?" Diego asks.

"Yes, United goes later. Eight forty-five."

"We may need that time," says Linda.

"It's a risk to take it," I say.

"Why don't we all go?" asks Diego.

"You can't all go," I say.

"Why?" he asks.

"The money," Linda and I answer in unison.

There is a long pause while the magnitude of this particular problem—among their many problems—sinks in. This adventure they are on—misadventure you could surely call it—will be much more difficult if they don't secure that money.

Linda breaks the silence. "And travel to Argentina is banned to all but Argentine nationals right now. I can't get on that plane."

69

THE WIFE

Chapter Thirty-Eight
Thursday, April 30, 2020

A week passed.

By the time the following Sunday rolled around, Linda had not spoken to anyone for the entire tense duration of it. Not to Diego, who was presumably ensconced in his mother's apartment in Buenos Aires. Not to her children, who were with him. Not to Noelle, with whom she had agreed not to call or text or communicate in any way until that day.

They had set a meeting time and place: two p.m. on the beach at Reef Road. They figured it would be sparsely populated due to the town's closure of all beaches. Maybe one or two fellow trespassers would make their way around the yellow tape, but not many. They had agreed to arrive without vehicles in order to minimize attention to themselves. This was, of course, easier for Linda than Noelle. Linda could walk. Noelle would come by bicycle and stash it in the bushes.

But their meeting never happened.

Linda arrived early and sat in the tall grasses to watch a storm that was gathering. She hoped Noelle might come early, too, so they could get out of this weather as soon as possible. The rainstorm looked like it was going to be a big one. Not that she minded getting wet, but a chill had set in and the wind was whipping fiercely. There was no one on the beach— no other idiots who would brave a day like this. Linda was happy to be alone, to get this meeting over with, to check in with Noelle and make sure she hadn't lost her nerve or her commitment to keep the events of last week to herself. Linda was resolved to say something nice, to keep Noelle calm and malleable.

As she waited, she berated herself for sending her children off without their comfort objects. It was her fault. But it was also the fault of Noelle. Noelle was the one who had pushed them to take the earlier flight and it hadn't given her enough time to prepare. By the time Linda had packed a few items of clothing and snacks, and sorted the children out in their car seats, she had simply forgotten Gogo's blankie and Espie's monkey. The children were so excited by the prospect of the adventure with Pipa that they had forgotten, as well. Linda's status in the pantheon of bad mothers was fixed. On top of all her sins, and they were too numerous to mention, this one pained her the most.

It was then that she looked up and saw him. The only other idiot on the beach. She did not recognize him from a distance, but she knew as he approached exactly who he was. The guy from the airport. The guy from the preschool. She couldn't very well avoid him, sitting as she was in his path. Noelle might arrive any minute, but when this guy offered Linda a ride home, she decided it was wise to accept it. The fact that this Michael Collins turned out to be a cop could be taken as a blessing or a curse. Linda had no idea which it was, but she had to throw her lot in one direction or another. She chose to explore the possibility that he might have some use to her now.

As she turned to leave the beach with him, Linda saw Noelle struggling to shove her bike into the sea grape bushes. Noelle looked up as Linda and the man were passing. When the two women made eye contact, Linda cut her eyes over at Michael Collins. Noelle followed her unspoken direction and furtively looked at him as well. Then she just as quickly turned to busy herself with the bicycle. Well, she was a thriller writer. She should enjoy all of this intrigue.

Linda was probably providing the first really thrilling moments of Noelle's actual life, as opposed to her made-up life in books. Michael did not appear to see Noelle or the look that passed between them. Although, who could say? He was a cop, after all. Maybe he saw and did not let on.

Once she was home and the storm had broken full force, Linda did not know what to do about Noelle or their failed rendezvous. For the time being, she decided not to do anything.

The following days fanned out in a blur. Linda felt invaded by the creeping sensation that her house was not clean. That it was, in fact, a hotbed of evidence that would point authorities to the truth of what had happened to Miguel. The day after meeting Michael Collins, she began her cleaning assault on the house. With the use of bleaches, solvents, and even the dreaded Fabulosa, Linda was determined to scrub the property of any vestiges of her husband.

And then Michael Collins appeared again. Yesterday, in fact. Right in the doorway of the garage. A door she had left open to keep herself from succumbing to fumes from the cocktail of cleansers she was steeped in. And did Linda send him away? Shoo him off? Use the pandemic as an excuse for not inviting the man into her house? No, Linda did not. Instead, she got cocky and asked him in for coffee. Which led to the moving of the dresser. Which led to the discovery of the Bolivian coin. Which led, in a way that Linda could not fully explain, to her seduction of him in the guest room in order to…what? Draw attention away from the coin? Win him over to her side? Blind him to the facts that were swirling around him and hypnotize him with her sexual prowess? Ridiculous, of course. Laughable, yes. A big, colossal joke.

And yet she did it. A slut, she'd once read, was a woman with the morals of a man. Maybe so. Michael Collins, however, was no slouch in the immorality department. He had held his own alongside Linda.

But, of course, men operated on the level of purely physical stimuli. At least she hoped so. She was counting on it. She just needed to delay Michael Collins long enough to resolve the situation with the money—to get the money into her actual hands is what she really meant—and get on the first plane to Argentina. Once the skies opened. Once she was allowed to travel. Once the pandemic was under control and she was no longer trapped in this house and life could resume. Not life as normal for her. The die had been definitively cast and life as it once was would no longer be an option. But a new normal was within her reach, a new life with Diego and the children out of the country and safe from the dogs she could already feel snapping at her heels.

Of course, the truth was, this new normal was, for the moment, entirely beyond Linda's reach. She did not, in fact, have access to the two million dollars, even though the loan had been approved. She did not, in fact, have the ability to hop on a plane. She had not, in fact, even spoken to Diego since the moment he and the children walked out the door. Okay, so fine. None of it was real. Yet. But it was all so tantalizingly close she could taste it. And if everything went according to plan, she would touch it. Grasp it. Own it.

Of course, if she were seeing clearly, she would have recognized that nothing, as of yet, had gone even remotely close to plan.

Linda repeatedly called the apartment in Buenos Aires. The fact that no one picked up the phone there only served to further scramble her already scrambled sense of equilibrium. That had not been the deal she'd worked out with Diego. He had said he would answer the phone. He had said he would make sure to stand by at predictable hours (hell, any hour for that matter) when Linda might try to ring him. But, no matter what hour she called, the phone just rang and rang. Diego was not playing by the rules they had established together. Once again, the niggling suspicion that she'd made a grievous error in trusting him pecked at her, like a little bird that had gotten caught in her hair.

Linda also repeatedly dialed the mortgage broker. No one picked up at that office, either. Linda was aware that the broker would be working from home. The whole world was working from home. But she did not have his house phone number or cell and there were no referral numbers on the outgoing message of the firm. It did not seem wise to email him. That would leave a trail that would be hard to explain. It had been explainable that the Alonsos might borrow money for home improve-ment while Miguel was present in the household, when their family was intact and whole. But the idea that she would continue to pursue that money after Miguel had absconded with their children to a foreign coun-try would be harder to justify. The fact that the pandemic would delay fulfillment of the loan had not been foreseeable in Linda's planning.

And then there was Noelle. Linda did not know what to do about her. Maybe she had made a mistake leaving the beach on Sunday in the company of Michael Collins. At any rate, she had done it and was now left with a puzzle as to how to reach Noelle. She couldn't call or text her. She might be able to go to her apartment at night. In fact, that would probably be her best bet and she had better do it soon.

Linda questioned why she ever thought she could welcome the wild card that Noelle represented into her own highly sensitive situation. What incentive would Noelle have to protect Linda's secrets? The only answer to that was that Noelle still wanted to meet Linda's father. Linda could dangle that carrot a bit longer, as long as it was necessary.

Linda teetered on the brink of despair. The timing of all of this could not have been worse. The whole operation was feeling ever more like a bungled military sortie when, with hindsight, it was clear that the general should have aborted the mission long ago. But this pandemic was real. Miguel's death was real. Diego and the children's departure to Argentina was real. And none of it was in Linda's control.

How was she to put the brakes on any of it now? How was she to manage its forward trajectory. How was she to control the uncontrollable around her?

70

A WRITER'S THOUGHTS

I saw Linda and the man at the beach. Of course I did. I met her eye and followed the trail of the meaningful glance she cast in his direction. Who was he? She sure picked up men as easily as I picked up a doughnut. I suspected this one must have a role in our current situation, of which I was uninformed.

Could he be her mortgage broker? The person who had promised her the two million dollars but hadn't delivered it yet? Was he a colleague of Miguel? Could someone from the office have called Linda to ask some questions about her husband? I did not know, but I was determined to find out.

The utter deliciousness of circumstances was revealed to me when I was able to reach a friend who had helped me in the past with research. He ran a check on the man's license plate number I had so carefully memorized and what should turn up, but a cop! Yes, what to my wondering eyes should appear but a person who might prove to be of some as-yet unknown value.

Of course I stalked him. Her. Them. For it was abundantly clear that they were becoming a them. I watched them from my chosen perch in the neighborhood. A house that was kitty-corner to Linda's had been under construction for over a year and the pandemic had shuttered the proceedings to a grinding halt. Since no one ever visited it, I could be guaranteed a secure and private vantage point from which to watch the comings and goings of Michael Collins.

And—to put not too fine a point on it—the comings and goings of the two of them inside the four walls of Linda's house. She should really have invested in some curtains. Her living room window had offered me an opportunity to become acquainted with her rhythms of life for a long time now. Since we met last year. Truth be told, since before we met. She and her family paraded around inside that house as though they were alone on a desert island. It wasn't until the night Diego killed Miguel that Linda used a modicum of sense and kept the lights off indoors so that the cleanup could be carried out unobserved by the neighborhood.

This utter lack of paranoia that some people had—that Linda had— was attractive to me. It was something I did not possess. It made them seem innocent and somehow protected for it. I, on the other hand, was not at all innocent. I looked around every corner for the forces of harm closing in on me. And it had always been my undoing. But Linda's open trust of the world would prove to be hers.

I consider the possibilities.

Will I take Linda down? If I choose to go in that direction, it will not be easy for me. Like the father who beats his child with the disclaimer that it hurts him more than it hurts her, it would give me pain to harm Linda. I have grown fond of her in spite of her mistreatment of me. I can honestly say that I never had Linda's downfall in mind when I first pursued her. I did—I do—admire her. The story she's created is a thing of beauty. The handsome husband. The two adorable children. The clubby Palm Beach life of swimming and boating and barbecues. I am not precisely jealous of what she has. Or had until recent events. By the time Linda entered my sphere of awareness, I had long since given up any hope of that kind of normalcy in my own life.

I am a Writer with a capital W. My life—my time share, my mental share, my heart share—is dedicated to the pursuit of, the execution of, the written word. I also have Cordie. So I do not *need*. I am not actively in a state of *lack*. Or at least I am not aware of that state.

You know about my mother. You know about Noelle Huber. You know about the murder and my childhood and all of it. There is no need to rehash any of it.

Destiny is always that unquantifiable combination of the things that happen and what we do with those things. I have had success as a writer. That is because I work hard, you could say. But plenty of writers work hard and never manage to sell word one. It is not just the working hard that makes success happen, though success rarely happens without it. You could find examples of young Hollywood stars who fall into success by happenstance. Sure. Sometimes it happens. But almost always, success requires grindingly hard work over a sustained period of time. It requires Malcolm Gladwell's ten thousand hours before anyone can even begin to hope for the level of seeming effortlessness that takes a person to the next level.

But then, on top of all that effort, there is a fair amount of pixie dust required to bring any endeavor to a satisfying conclusion. And none of us can control pixie dust. Not a single one of us. We can only optimize our chances to place ourselves in its path. And that is its own level of work. Getting oneself under the gaze of the agent or the editor or the publisher or the social media feeding-frenzy crowd that will catapult a person into a position of having something called a *platform* is work. And it is that platform from which a writer can finally hope to write words that the world will read. But, even then, more pixie dust is required.

Conversely, many negative threads need to come together to get a person murdered. Bad events may seem to happen easily, but I assure you they do not. Noelle Grace Huber may not have been killed at all if many dark stars had not aligned on the night of December 10, 1948. So many things had to have happened. Her parents had to have gone bowling. She had to have been turned down by not one, but two friends when she invited them to be with her. She had to have opened the door. Or it had to have been her brother who came home with a key and let himself in. We could go on but there is no need. It is clear that all these elements had to converge on that one night to lead to the death of that one child. You could blame the murderer for his evil intent, or you could look at him as a creature of opportunity. Whoever killed Noelle Grace Huber that night may not have come to the house intending to do so. But then, as the saying goes, one thing led to another…

So me.

So Linda.

So the occurrences of the spring of 2020 in the town of Palm Beach when so many events had to conspire to lead us to one dead husband and one lover/brother displaced to another country and one cop/lover who appeared from the sea, like Aphrodite from the clamshell.

I am sitting on Reef Road beach on a sunny Saturday in May, the same beach where I saw Linda meet Michael Collins just a few short weeks ago. The same beach where I currently see two rambunctious teenage surfer boys come to a crashing halt to examine something they find in the sand. The same beach where these same boys somberly pass me, carrying the thing in a bag. A blue, plastic *New York Times* bag. I wonder if the boys even know what kind of a bag it is. I wonder if their parents take a newspaper at home.

And what I really wonder is whether they have seen me see them. They do not look at me. I am an older woman who garners no looks at all. It is an asset, this mantle of invisibility. How do the young people say it? Ah, yes. They would say it is my superpower. Age and the inconspicuousness it wraps me in have empowered me to act with increasing boldness.

71

THE WIFE

Chapter Thirty-Nine
Wednesday, May 20, 2020

Linda should have taken the ring. How could she have been so colossally stupid as to have left Miguel's engraved wedding band on Miguel's dead finger? Ugh. Fucking ugh was all she could say now. But what she could do was—she hoped—more effective than what she could say. She could seduce Michael and hope that...

What?

What could she really hope for? That Michael Collins—seasoned professional detective in full stride of his career, happily married man, and father of two beautiful boys—would succumb to Linda's Mata Hari wiles and ignore a man's severed hand, thereby throwing away the entire life he had obviously so carefully constructed? Even Linda, who in her fever-brained state had ignited a keg of dynamite under her own life, knew that most people would not do it. That Michael would not do it.

And then the virus.

Devon told her yesterday that Michael was in the hospital with a bad case of it. But he was young and vital and strong. Surely he would recover.

Yet it was becoming increasingly clear that a bad case of COVID-19 was not necessarily like a bad case of the flu. This bug was deviant and shape-shifting. Much like herself, she would have to admit. She read about odd side effects like kidney failure or cognitive impairment or blood clots that led to amputations. What kind of virus was that?

The exasperating inability for Linda to hop on a plane to Argentina coupled with her inability to reach Diego by phone heightened the mad-house feel. The chain-link fence that was surrounding her every action was about to make her scream. That was why she got in Miguel's fancy car. That was why she drove over to Good Samaritan Hospital in West Palm Beach. That was why she argued with the guard outside the hospital doors that she *needed* to get inside, *needed* to see Michael Collins, *needed* to right the rails of this runaway train. Naturally, it did not work. Good Sam was as impenetrable as a fortress and this guard was hip to trouble-makers like Linda.

And that was why Linda made her next move and drove over to Noelle's apartment. She was fraying at the seams and she needed to talk to someone about it. She had not seen Noelle for weeks. There wasn't really any reason to have seen her. Nothing had changed. Not one single aspect of Linda's progress toward a conclusion of her mission had moved for-ward at all. The best course of action may have been to exercise patience. But the appearance of the hand and the disappearance of Michael were two things too many for Linda to take.

Noelle did not appear to be home. At least she did not answer her door. Linda knocked and rang and made an attempt to lean over the exterior hall railing to peer into a window. But the curtains were drawn and the place was silent. Didn't she have a dog? Shouldn't the dog have barked? Linda gave one more round of battery on the flimsy door, which was enough to cause all the dogs on the block to bark. It was also enough to cause the door of the neighboring apartment to squeak open a crack so its occupant could peer out at the unhinged Linda.

"Hey!" Linda yelled at whoever it was who was skulking in the shadow of that door. "Do you know the lady who lives here? Is she home?"

The door squeaked open a bit more and the face of a child was revealed. A little girl about the age of Espie. A little girl with dark hair and dark eyes, and the similarity to Espie made Linda gasp and reach both arms toward the terrified child. Linda's lurch in her direction caused the girl to wail the word *Mama!* and slam the door in Linda's face.

On top of every other epithet that could be dumped on Linda's head, *menace to small children* could be added. Linda gave Noelle's door a final kick and stomped down the stairs in defeat.

Linda was alone. There was no denying it anymore. Miguel was dead. So was her mother. Her father was no longer her father, lost as he was in the cloud of his brain. Diego, Espie, and Gogo were last seen by her—touched by her—more than a month ago. The tenuous ties she may have had to either Noelle-the-writer or Michael-the-cop were illusory.

Linda could see it now, even if she had not been able to see it before. The people with whom she had entangled her life over the course of the past wild and reckless year—Diego, Noelle, Michael—should have come with alarm bells and warning signals that they were not safe for her to touch.

The writer had always been scary to Linda, but she had ignored her better judgement and forged ahead anyway. Diego had not scared her, though it was evident he should have. She had felt for him a tenderness of affection that was the closest she'd ever come to what she felt for her children. Michael Collins, being a cop, had frightened her. But he had excited her, as well. And she had underestimated him. She had underestimated all of them.

Linda *should have known.*

This was a common enough expression in the everyday world, but in legalese it took on more significance. In the world of law, whether you knew or should have known something had a different meaning than in normal life. Certain phrases prompted obligation under the law. *Should have known* fell under this rule, as it implied that there was an owed duty of care from one individual or entity to another.

For example, if you did not shovel your sidewalk and a dangerous coating of ice built up and your neighbor fell on that ice and ended up in the hospital and you tried to claim you did not know about the ice, it could naturally be put forth that you *should have*. The snow fell, the temperatures were cold, and then warmed, and then froze again. Assuming you were a *compos mentis* adult. Assuming you had seen in your life that water froze at thirty-two degrees Fahrenheit. And assuming you were the person in charge of maintaining the house and its grounds. Even if you had not walked out the front door to examine the sidewalk that day, you should, in fact, have known.

Linda should have known that her decisions and actions over the course of the past year would come to no good. She should have.

72

A WRITER'S THOUGHTS

I have had enough of Linda. Who does she think she is? Doesn't she see that she has always needed me more than I need her? She has mismanaged every single aspect of her life. Wifehood. Motherhood. Friendship. Even her illicit affairs, for crying out loud.

I was at home when she knocked on my door yesterday, but I did not answer it. I sat as quietly as I could inside my apartment while she pummeled the wood like a battering ram. The absolute entitlement she must feel to show up at my place and pound on my door like a narc staging a drug raid is galling. Cordie did not hear a thing. She is utterly deaf. The rest of the dogs in the neighborhood started barking, however.

I do not wish to see Linda. I do not wish to speak with her just yet. I have not decided what I will do with the information I have, but I am betting her cop friend would like to know what I know. I am betting those boys I saw on the beach took that severed hand to the precinct. I am betting the hand had something to do with Linda's murdered husband. Could it be a different hand from a different murder victim in our area? Sure. I guess. If murders are happening at a breakneck pace around here. But even I, who am conditioned to expect the unexpected, would be surprised if anyone else was murdered on Reef Road recently.

I have called Good Samaritan Hospital. I have spoken to a nurse I know, someone who'd helped me with some research for a book, and someone for whom I have returned the favor. She sounded exhausted, poor thing. This coronavirus is taking a terrible toll on our doctors and nurses. She couldn't take my call, but she did call me back. And she was kind enough to inform me that one Michael Collins had, in fact, been a patient. And that the same Michael Collins had, in fact, been released to go home in the care of his wife just today. The wife that Linda told me was in Chicago has evidently returned to Florida. And she—that wife—has Linda's lover at home with her now.

It is not difficult to find their house. I have the address from the license plate check I ran with my friend in town hall. It is in West Palm Beach, so I will go by car instead of bicycle. They—Mr. and Mrs. Michael Collins—have chosen to live in a newly gentrifying area called SoSo, which stands for "South of Southern Boulevard." Theirs is a mixed street, some houses looking sadly in need of repair. Closer to the water, however, where I find the house number I am looking for, the block perks up and looks more manicured and mowed.

Michael Collins and his wife live in a pretty Spanish colonial that must have been built in the 1920s. It is single story and looks more Mission style than the high baroque Spanish of Addison Mizner. There is an austerity to it, and it makes me think about who this man might be, whether he or his wife chose the house, and how it fits into what I will find when I ring his doorbell. A dog barks wildly from inside when I do so; the kind of whooping bark that can only belong to a beagle.

It is the wife who answers, beagle at her side. Naturally. Her husband is recovering from COVID-19, so would not be up and about. She wears a mask, as do I. From what I can see, she is very pretty. The map of Ireland is on her face, as my mother would have said, meaning she is a redhead with freckles. Her eyes are green. I wonder for a moment why her husband would have cheated on her. She is a nice-looking woman. They have children and a dog. What was he looking for that he could not find at home? That Linda Alonso could give him? I do not pretend to understand men.

"Hello?" she says with a tentative uptilt at the end of it, letting me know she has no clue why I am here at her door.

"Hi." It's as good a place as any to begin. "Do you have a moment to talk?"

"I'm sorry," she says. "Do I know you?"

"It's about your husband," I say. I've been writing long enough to know there is not a married woman alive who can resist such catnip, and Mrs. Collins is no exception. I add the clincher, "Something you should know."

She casts a glance over her shoulder at her children, who are watching TV in the living room. Some sort of Sesame Street-style educational program where letters of the alphabet are singing and dancing.

"Timmy?" she calls to them. "Sean?"

Neither one of them so much as looks up from his television-induced stupor. The wife, I know her name is Maeve, looks back at me with what I can see is both trepidation—I am about to tell her something she does not wish to hear—and disgust—it is I who will tell her this thing and she is not inclined to like me. Ever.

Then she closes the door in my face. "Just a minute," she says as she does it.

I wait. I turn around and look at the neighborhood. It is nicer than my block on the island of Palm Beach proper. But it is nowhere near as nice as most Palm Beach streets. I hear the door open behind me and turn back to my charge. Maeve Collins steps out, without her dog, and shuts the door behind her, giving the doorknob a little jiggle to confirm that it is unlocked. That she will be able to escape me, the deliverer of bad news, on a moment's notice.

"My husband has been sick," she says. "You're exposing yourself to this virus."

"Well, I won't stay long," I reply, as though the brevity of the action I am about to take will lessen its impact. On her, since I am about to destroy her husband's career and their marriage. On me, since I am standing at the threshold of a quarantined household.

"What is it you want?" she asks, in a not-very-polite tone.

"You've been away, am I right?"

"Why do I think you already know that?"

Instead of answering her, I pose a question in return, "Do you know what your husband has been doing in your absence?"

Maeve Collins's eyes grow narrow, and she takes the full measure of me. "Are you suggesting he has been doing something with *you*?"

The way she says it is unkind. *You*. As though I am not worth her time. The cruelty of woman-to-woman surprises me, and all for a worthless man. But I will disabuse her of that particular notion.

"Mrs. Collins. May I call you Maeve?"

She sighs and says, "Fine."

"Maeve. First, let me ask you how your husband is doing."

"Can you just say what you came here to say?"

"No need to be unpleasant." I smile when I say it, but, of course, she can't see the lower half of my face. "But fine. I'll get right to it. In your absence, your husband has gotten involved with a friend of mine. Linda Alonso is her name. She lives on the north end of Palm Beach. Reef Road. I think you may know her from your children's school?"

Maeve Collins goes increasingly white as I deliver that little spiel. Her freckles stand out in higher relief, almost as if they are raising up from the rest of her face. She reaches back to grab hold of the doorknob. I think for a moment she will just leave me there on the porch with this secret half delivered. But she doesn't move. "How do you know this?" she finally asks.

"Like I said, Linda is a friend of mine."

"Some friend," she snorts.

I ignore that crack. She is stressed out from the news, and it is expected that she would be snappish. "Mrs. Alonso. Linda. My friend has also done something…" How to put it? "Something that could bring her to the attention of law enforcement. I'm afraid your husband may be concealing evidence to protect her."

There is no going back now.

73

THE WIFE

Chapter Forty
Tuesday, May 26, 2020

Linda stared at the morning news reports as she drank her fourth cup of coffee of the day. Both were habits she had developed only since the departure of all other living members of her household. One habit—fixing her attention on doomsday news broadcasts and flipping from one network to the next—left her feeling frazzled and afraid. The other habit—filling her gullet with too much caffeine—ratcheted up that frazzle and left her in a constant need to pee.

Today's news was worse than other days of late, if that could be believed. A man was choked to death yesterday by a cop in Minneapolis and the country was erupting in protest. As horrible as what happened to that man—George Floyd—was, Linda knew the whole world was half mad by now and it would not take much to push any one of them over the edge. Or all of them. George Floyd's murder was a match on some extremely dry kindling. They—her fellow Americans—were the kindling. She—Linda—was about as dried up and desiccated and ready to spontaneously combust as any piece of kindling that ever existed. Even in spite of all that coffee.

She took a moment to call her father. He managed to pick up the phone but did not seem entirely clear on who Linda was. In a primal way, she was desperately in need of parenting.

"Dad?" she said.

He was silent to the point where Linda wondered if he had heard or comprehended her words. "Noelle?" he finally squeaked out.

"No, Dad, it's me. Linda."

Silence.

"Dad, I've done something. It's bad."

He said nothing. Linda could hear what sounded like a sigh. Was he crying? Did he even hear her?

"Dad?" she asked again.

Again silence. Linda listened to his breathing for a long while. If she had not been listening so intently, she may have missed what he said next, so quietly did the words come out. "I have, too," her father said.

"Oh, Dad," she said as she broke down crying herself. "What's wrong with us?"

It was all so messed up. All of it. The life of her father, her own life, the lost life of her child-aunt, the lost life of her husband, the loss of her children. Maybe they were all some train wreck of a Greek tragedy where no one could have avoided his fate as it was decreed by the Oracle of...what? The Oracle of Pittsburgh. The Oracle of Brushton. The oracle that must have visited her grandparents or the long-dead Noelle to warn them that brother would lay hand to sister in lust and violence and their clan would forever be cursed to walk this earth in the shadow of it.

She did not complete her thought. She did not tell her father what she had done. What could she say to him to make him understand—to make herself understand—any of it? If her father was, indeed, a man who had seduced and murdered his young sister, what did Linda understand of human nature at all? Nothing is what. She hung up the phone.

Then she picked it up again to dial the apartment in Buenos Aires. She could no longer pretend it was a quirk of timing that each and every time she telephoned the place no one answered. She could no longer pretend she knew anything about Diego at all. The man to whom she had handed her children like sacrificial lambs. She could no longer pretend she believed they were actually in the Alonso apartment in Buenos Aires. Where they were, she did not pretend to know.

When the doorbell rang, Linda could not say she was fully surprised. Surprise held no sway over her now. She had entered into a universe—created that universe—where anything could happen. Anyone could end up dead on a sunny and average day in the beautiful town of Palm Beach. Just like anyone could end up dead on a snowy and Christmassy day not long after the big war had ended, on an average street in Pittsburgh.

People were always worried about the big things. The plane crashes. The cancer. They weren't worried about being murdered by their brothers at home. They weren't worried about the doorbell that rang, signaling that their brothers had come for them. Matt, in the case of Noelle, coming to the kitchen door on a December night, interrupting her while she baked a cake. Diego, in the case of Miguel, coming to the front door on a March night, interrupting a life Miguel had created in his brother's long absence. Neither one of them, Linda would have guessed, could imagine what was waiting for them the moment they answered that door to find their brothers' faces smiling back at them.

Linda got up from the stool in the kitchen. She straightened her top, an old T-shirt she'd slept in, and shook a leg of her yoga pants to loosen where it clung to her calf. She touched her hair, unbrushed yet today, and slapped her cheeks twice hard. Thus prepared, as prepared as she could hope to be at this juncture, she moved through her pristine house to answer the door. Because she moved so slowly, the doorbell rang again just as she was turning the knob. It was loud and shrill in her ears at such close range.

The sun hit her full in the eyes, facing south as she was in the open doorway. The person who stood before her was backlit, a halo forming around his head and shoulders, making him look large and apocalyptic. Michael.

"Mrs. Alonso," a voice said, but it was not the voice of Michael. "I'm Detective Sanchez, Homicide Division."

Linda considered the name, Sanchez, and the sugar cubes that Michael Collins loved. "Are you Cuban?" she asked Detective Sanchez.

"Excuse me?" he said. "I'm American. And we'd like you to come with us. We have some questions we'd like to ask you."

Linda considered the *we*. When he said this—Detective Sanchez— he shifted his weight just a little bit to the left, turning his shoulder as he did. Like this, Linda could see him better. He, too, was a good-looking man. Darker than Michael Collins. He was wearing a suit, his tie slightly loosened at the neck in a nod to the sweltering weather. It was late May in Florida, almost summer. It was not suit-and-tie weather.

Linda could also see beyond him now, and she scanned the curb for Michael. Maybe he did not wish to come to the door. Maybe he did not wish to speak with her. Instead, she saw two uniformed officers who stood in front of a squad car at the curb. An actual police car with lights and sirens, though neither was operating at the moment. It was nice of Detective Sanchez, she reflected, to have asked them to stand at the curb. To have asked them to come quietly, without their lights and sirens blazing. To have tried in some small way to preserve her dignity in front of the neighbors.

Linda looked beyond the cops to the house of the Andersons across the street. It looked manicured and shiny and blank. No signs of life there. If Sarah Anderson was looking out the window now at the downfall of Linda Alonso, Linda could not see her. But the sun was on Linda, making visibility at that distance obscure.

Linda cast her eyes up and down the street, glimpsing the construction site of the old Carter property, where Mr. and Mrs. Carter—the couple who'd originally built that house when they fled the north in the '60s—had died within a week of each other. She did not know the people who'd bought, demolished, and begun construction there, but no one came around now. It had been abandoned, much like Linda herself, when this pandemic had set in around them.

Because of this, Linda had not anticipated the presence of someone standing quite still on the dirt in front of the property, the dirt that used to be grass. The figure was so still, in fact, that Linda considered it might be a newly installed statue. But why would they have put in a statue when construction of their house seemed to have been suspended? When what had once been lawn in front of it was now a blowing patch of dry earth? She squinted her eyes to bring whatever it was into focus.

And then it became clear.

It was Noelle. Not Noelle her aunt, returned in ghostly form to complete the Greek tragedy cycle that was coming to a close for their family. It was Noelle the writer. The woman who had entered her life at Amici Market not much more than a year before. The woman who had, she could now see, made it her mission to destroy Linda's life in the way she said her own had been destroyed by the actions of Linda's father.

"Mrs. Alonso?" Sanchez spoke. "Is there anything you'd like to bring? A purse?"

Linda tore her eyes from Noelle to look at the detective. Was this all about the ring? The hand that had washed up on the beach? Or had Noelle talked to him? Told him all she knew?

"Mrs. Alonso?" he spoke again.

"Yes. Okay." There was nothing for it now but surrender. "Let me get my things."

Linda turned to go into the house, crossed the white rug of the living room, walked down the hall, and stopped at her children's door. It was closed, the way she left it now, so she could pretend they were inside; Gogo reading books, Espie serving tea to her monkey and the other animals.

Linda entered the room and dropped to her knees. She tipped her head down—as though in prayer—and brought it down hard on the marble floor. "*Mea culpa,*" she said with a bang of her forehead. "*Mea maxima culpa,*" she said with the next. She was not aware of the passage of time until hands were on her arms, lifting her up. Detective Sanchez turned her around, took a handkerchief from his pocket—so very much like the one her father used to carry—and held it to her forehead. She was surprised to see it come away red, like he'd dipped it in a pot of finger paint. The kind that Espie liked.

"Mrs. Alonso," Sanchez said. "Where's your stuff?"

Linda did not answer.

"Okay, let's go," he said. "You have the right to remain silent..."

Linda did not hear the rest of what he said as they exited the house together. Linda looked to where Noelle had been but could no longer see her there. Sanchez opened the back door of the squad car, maneuvered her into the seat, and closed the door behind her, leaving her there alone. As they drove down Reef Road, Linda saw Noelle walking away. She did not even turn around to wave at Linda as she passed.

74

A WRITER'S THOUGHTS

The inevitability of the consequences that would unfold from Linda's father's long-ago murder of her aunt is finally becoming clear to Linda. She can now, I believe, see herself as the tiny cog she is, in a wheel much larger than herself. And she is probably becoming aware of the fact that her children will be—already are—equally miniscule cogs in that very same wheel.

None of us is terribly important. None of us is really at the center of much. Yet we all cast ourselves in the middle of stories we create in our minds. My mother's mind latched onto a narrative and could not let it go. Mine did likewise. Our stories featured the long-reaching arm of the law. The law of cause and effect, of the intergenerational ties that bind us like handcuffs to the past.

But this is not an idea original to my mother or to me. Let's examine the Good Book for a few examples of the story we are merely rehashing.

The Bible says in Exodus: *For I the Lord your God am a jealous God, visiting the iniquity of the fathers upon the sons to the third and fourth generation of those that hate me, and showing mercy to thousands of those that love Me and keep My commandments.*

The Bible also says in Numbers: *The Lord is long-suffering, and of great mercy, forgiving iniquity and transgression, and by no means clearing the guilty, visiting the iniquity of the fathers upon the sons to the third and fourth generation.*

And let's look at what the Bible says in Deuteronomy: *You shall not bow yourself down to them, nor serve them. For I the Lord your God am a jealous God, visiting the iniquity of the fathers upon the sons to the third and fourth generation of those who hate Me, and doing mercy to thousands of those who love Me and keep My commandments.*

And Jeremiah: *Ah, Lord Jehovah! You have made the heavens and the earth by Your great power and stretched out arm. Nothing is too great for You. You show loving kindness to thousands, and repay the iniquity of the fathers into the bosom of their sons after them.*

Pretty repetitive, but you get the point. And you don't need to confine your admonitions to the Abrahamic religions. Let's take a look at the classical world of Greece and Rome. Euripides says, *The gods visit the sins of the fathers upon the children.* Horace says, *For the sins of your fathers, you, though guiltless, must suffer.*

And hopping up to Elizabethan times, let us not forget the Bard. Shakespeare says, in *The Merchant of Venice*, *The Sins of the father are to be laid upon the children.*

You need more? How about *Mystic River*, the novel by Dennis Lehane, which says, *There are threads in our lives. You pull one and everything else gets affected.*

Indeed.

So, while my mother did not live to see the murder of her best friend avenged, I would like to think I played my part in finally making that happen. I like to think my mother rests easier in her cold, hard grave. I like to think Noelle Grace Huber—the girl I never knew, the girl whose photographic image is indelibly etched in my brain, the girl for whom I am named—rests a little easier, too.

Linda is just one thread in the story that began—or seemed to begin—on December 10, 1948. I am just another thread. Diego, Miguel, Noelle, the children—all of us are threads in a tapestry we cannot even see. We certainly can't unravel it or reweave it or make any sense of any of it. What happened to Diego and Linda's children? What will happen to Michael Collins and his family? To Linda?

I don't know. And isn't that the point? Mysteries are not always neatly solved.

Are tragedies preventable? Could anyone have stopped this from happening? Are there enough metaphorical sage sticks that could have been burned in the proverbial House of Huber to cleanse them of their sins? You might say that I helped Linda along on the road to perdition. Sure. But we human beings have free will. And we exercise it badly all the time. The serpent offered Eve the apple.

But she took the bite, didn't she?

75

A WRITER'S THOUGHTS

I t is Thursday, December 10, 2020. Seventy-two years to the day since Noelle Grace Huber opened the back door of her little house and allowed death to enter. Eight months, give or take a few days, since the disappearance of Linda Huber Alonso's family.

Karma's a bitch.

Thanksgiving was strange for most of America this year, but it wasn't much different for me. Publix always sells a nice turkey breast that you can cook up for yourself and your dog. I do prefer the stuffing baked inside the bird—I am traditional that way—but it would be impractical, not to mention expensive, to cook and stuff an entire turkey just for us. Not that I am averse to wasting food. Bulimics are world-class food wasters. But, if only as an eating deterrent, I opted for the more dainty portion.

Cordie and I did not take a walk together after our Thanksgiving lunch. In the past six months, she has deteriorated to the point where she can barely make a turn around our tiny backyard. The thought of her absence from my life fills me with a dread not too dissimilar from the dread I used to feel from my mother's presence. Even acknowledging such thoughts makes me feel sad and sorry for my mother. After all, she did not mean to turn out the way she did. She did not mean for her friend to get murdered. She did not mean to have the type of personality or circumstances or genetic predisposition to be one of those people who just could not get over something and ruined everyone's life in the process. December 10, 1948, did not happen directly to her. She was merely collateral damage. So, why the hold on her? And why the hold on me?

We ate early that day, Cordie and I—around one—and I cast about for something to do with the rest of the afternoon. Since I couldn't bring Cordie anyway, a bike ride seemed the best option. I washed our Thanksgiving dishes, walked Cordie around the yard, got her settled into her bed (she can no longer jump up to mine), and went outside.

I brought a mask, though it is no longer mandatory in Florida. Our governor is leaving that decision up to us. In fact, the wearing of a mask has now become suspect. A mask-wearer can be seen as a vaguely hostile and liberal-leaning naysayer. Even worse, a *virtue signaler*, that worst-of-the-worst sort of sanctimonious goody-two-shoes-show-off. "Look at me," that mask says, "I follow rules. I toe the line. I'm better than you." I try to stay out of all that political mud, but mud has a way of splattering on everyone even remotely in its vicinity. Collateral damage.

I began my outing by cycling south, in the direction of Worth Avenue. I couldn't remember if the Christmas tree next to Tiffany was up this early in the season, but I thought it might be nice to see it. It is big and fake and plays Christmas carols and it comes as close as anything can to put me in the spirit of Christmas in Florida.

Midway there, I lost my enthusiasm in a sputtering fizzle. So I turned around to go—I thought—home. My desultory mood could not be shaken, even by a giant plastic tree. Maybe I would stop, I reasoned at that juncture, at Publix, to pick up some ice cream. That always made me feel better before it made me feel worse. And then I remembered that Publix was closed. Which made me feel worse than I already did.

So I did not go home. Instead, I rode my bike toward the tip of the island of Palm Beach and, slowing down, turned the front wheel onto Reef Road. And there it was, the house I knew to be Linda Alonso's, smack in the middle of the block. Unoccupied now. For sale by the bank.

I don't go up to Reef Road much anymore. I don't find it terribly compelling. Worse than that, I find it depressing. In fact, I could go ahead and lump thoughts about Reef Road and its inhabitants into the same category as thoughts about my dog dying or spending time with my dead mother.

But I did go up to Reef Road that day. Call it nostalgia. It was Thanksgiving, after all. I don't know if I feel thankful or not for the way it all played out. I don't know if you could say I had any undue influence on Linda and what she did. I have lived long enough to know that I don't know much of anything. I have also lived long enough to know that blame is in the eye of the beholder.

I still have a task or two to complete. I leave my beloved Cordie in the care of my neighbor, the one with the little girl. Cordie likes them, as much as she likes anyone who is not me. I board a plane for Pittsburgh, a commercial airline on which we all wear masks—N95s, if possible—and sanitize around our seats. No food or beverages are served. Everyone sits in silence.

I come home to Pittsburgh. Not to my family; I have no family left. My mother is dead. And, it turns out, so is my father. I learned that from a Google search some years back. Maybe my cousins, Becky and Joe. But I haven't seen them for half a century, so there would be no purpose in that. Our business, whatever it was as a family, was finished long ago. I have other business to attend to.

I check into a Comfort Inn. I try to make a joke to the receptionist about the irony of the name. Who said we were at the end of the age of irony? Graydon Carter? Spalding Gray? Was it after 9/11? I think so, but I can't call the facts to mind. The receptionist is not interested, anyway, so I make my way to my room.

I find the nursing home, a memory care facility. Normally, these places are very secure, but this one is neither fenced nor gated. They don't let just anyone in to see their patients, but I have no intention of going inside. I wait until the patients are taken outside. One patient in particular. I have seen a fairly recent photo of Linda's father from snooping around her house the night she and Diego dumped Miguel into the ocean.

The old folks are never alone; an attendant is always with them. But I have decided on my tactic. I get out of my car and cross the parking lot. I approach Matt, who is in a wheelchair, and the large, uniformed man who is pushing it.

"Matt!" I call out. "Happy Anniversary!"

The men turn to me.

Matt looks blank.

The attendant says, "Can I help you?"

"I'm his sister, Noelle."

The attendant looks at him and back at me. I am more than thirty years younger than Matthew Huber, Jr., and I hope I don't appear to be the same age. But an older woman is an older woman and I guess the attendant can't tell the difference between a woman who is fifty and one who is a hundred and fifty. Plus, I am wearing a mask.

"Oh, hey!" he said. "I didn't know Matty boy had a sister. I'm Dwayne."

He does not hold out his hand for shaking. We do not do that anymore.

"Yep," I say to Dwayne. "I'm Noelle. Noelle Huber."

"Well," he says. "What kinda anniversary?"

"It's a special one Matt and I share," I say. "Something that happened in our childhood."

"Noelle?" Matt finally chimes in. Just in the nick of time.

"Oh," Dwayne says. "Well, that's nice. Want me to leave yinz together for a bit? I can go over there," he points to a bench, "and have a smoke. We're not supposed to smoke near the residents. Gets them too excited."

"Sure," I say, taking hold of the wheelchair handles. "Thank you. I won't keep him long."

Dwayne moves off to satisfy his craving. I am surprised at how easily he has abdicated his responsibilities.

The day is the color of steel, which is fitting for the town we are in. The town where we both grew up. It must have snowed a week or so ago, for the roads are lined with dingy black mounds of it, icy and crusted all around. I glance at the cars parked along the path. The windshields have that road salt coating I remember so well from my youth. That film that is impossible to see through and streaks when you use your wipers and find you're out of fluid.

I do not miss living in Pittsburgh.

Huber smells like an old man. That oily head smell they get from not washing their hair often enough and that mothball smell from his clothing. From my vantage point behind him, I can see that his hair is, in fact, dirty; it hangs down too long and bends at odd angles where it hits his collar. Flakes of dandruff speckle his navy woolen coat. They don't take good care of him here.

I take a breath to speak. But, before I can, Matthew Huber, Jr., has something to say to me.

"Noelle?" he rasps. Then he clears his throat twice before continuing. A nervous tic or an old man's phlegm, I'm not sure which. "Is that you?"

Just then, my attention is drawn upward as a sudden gust of wind whips up a pile of old leaves in a swirling funnel. Just as quickly, it stops, and the leaves drop straight from the sky, as suddenly inanimate as they had been briefly full of life. I put my hand on his shoulder, ignoring the dandruff.

"Yes," I say. "It's me."

"I..." he begins. "I didn't mean for things to happen the way they did."

"I'm a writer, Matt. Did you know that?"

He is silent.

"I'll be sending my manuscript to my editor in a week or two. It's nearly finished. I've called it, *The Wife.*"

Still nothing. Maybe he had a brief burst of awareness that departed, like that sudden gust of wind. I turn his wheelchair off the path and head for the woods beyond. Away from the eyes of Dwayne, which are glued to the screen of his phone as he sits on the bench and smokes. Away from this place. Away from the past and the present and all the entanglements I have not been able to shake since the day I was born.

"Anyway," I continue, "my editor thinks I've been writing it this past year. But you know what, Matt? I've been working on this book my whole life. I'm glad to finally be finishing it. Do you know the most gratifying moment for a writer?"

Matt says nothing as his wheelchair bumps over the stones and roots that replace the smoothness of the path we just left to enter the covering of trees. His body slips a little to the left and I reach down to right him.

"Matt?" I say. "Are you going to guess, or do you give up?"

Nothing.

"Okay then, I'll tell you if you don't want to guess." I hang on tightly to the handles of the wheelchair as we clatter down a slope toward a stream. "The most gratifying moment for a writer, Matt?" I stop and move around the wheelchair and crouch down to face him. "It's when she types the words, 'The End.'"

EPILOGUE

A WRITER'S THOUGHTS

spoke a little too soon. *The End* was not actually the end. Although is it ever?

Allow me to travel backward with you just a couple weeks. Before I traveled to Pittsburgh to complete my business with the Huber family; before I turned in my novel; before I exited the carnival ride I had jumped on the day I was born; I had another trip to take.

I had a hunch about Diego, from everything Linda had told me. Florid tales of gangs and fingers and treks across borders just seemed a bit exaggerated. To me, anyway. Linda, I realize, bought it wholesale. Maybe she doubted the veracity of his stories once he had gone. Once she had handed her children over to him. But in the year of their affair, I know she believed him.

Suffice it to say, I did not.

To be truthful, I had a little bit more than a hunch. I knew that Señora Alonso had died. Google is a treasure trove of information. The official cause of death was COVID-19, but the obit waxed long about the miraculous return of her firstborn son—the namesake of her dear, departed husband. So she may have died happy that a new Diego Alonso was in the pipeline. But I am guessing that she croaked when she saw the adult Diego appear, the one she'd thought she'd gotten rid of decades before. Cancer hadn't killed her in all those years, but the return of her husband's bastard son surely did.

But I did not think Diego would stay in Argentina. My gut told me San Miguel de Allende. So I took a little trip to Mexico before I went to Pittsburgh. I couldn't very well go after Pittsburgh because, by then, I was going to be in as much trouble as Linda. I snuck this little side trip in right after Thanksgiving. The borders—post-COVID—had reopened in October. And I only needed a few days.

I flew into Mexico City, then I took a three-hour bus ride. The village was as charming as Linda had said. I checked into a cute hotel and I wandered around the town. It was chock-full of Americans. It took a couple days. But I found him.

I watched him from a café. There he was with Linda's children, Gogo and Espie. And also with a woman. I saw no other child. I suspect he made the whole thing up about the little girl. I suspect he had no offspring named Gabriela, aka Messenger of God. I suspect he came looking for his brother so that he could reclaim his inheritance. How much of what unfolded did Diego Alonso actually plan? Did he intend to kill Miguel and take his kids? Sleep with and throw over his wife? Or was he merely an opportunist? I could not begin to say.

I did not speak to him. What good would it have done? It wasn't as if Linda could care for her children anymore. Where else would these children go? And, as I said, they looked happy.

So, that was it. I tracked him down. He is alive and living with Linda's children in that lovely little town. And I am sure he has buckets of money from the death of Señora Alonso. And he has a nice-looking woman by his side. A woman who must not ask too many questions about the provenance of brand-new children.

Have those children escaped the wheel of destiny that chained their forebears? Will they be able to grow up free of their family's generational scars?

I don't know.

But I got out of that town to give them a chance to try. I'm not a monster.

ACKNOWLEDGMENTS

The road to *Reef Road* has been long: a lifetime—or many lifetimes—one in particular cut far too short. While this is not a true story, it takes its inspiration from a true crime.

Thanks abound, but I would like to start with Sean Byrne. Many years ago, when I told you of an unsolved crime that has haunted my family for generations, you helped to find some answers.

Thank you to the Pittsburgh Police Department, the University of Pittsburgh archives, and the technological wizards who have uploaded years of newspapers into the ethers so that writers like me, sitting at home in the middle of a pandemic lockdown, can access a world of living history with a touch of our fingers.

Thank you to my fabulous agent, Beth Davey, for your wisdom and guidance, and to my publishing team: Anthony Ziccardi, Megan Wheeler, and Maddie Sturgeon. You have given me the freedom to write the books I am called to write. Thank you to my talented PR and marketing team: Emi Battaglia and Kathie Bennett, Susie Stangland, Kelsey Merritt, Allison Griffith, Justin Loeber, Devon Brown, and Karen Mender. It is your creative vision and deft and graceful tag-teaming that bring my books to the right readers, and I am truly blessed to have had each one of you touch this particular book and its entry into the world.

Thank you to Barbara Ellis, Heather Steadham, and Mary Cantor for your editorial wisdom and sharpened red pencils. You have made my books infinitely better.

Thank you to Cassandra Tai-Marcellini and Becky Ford for making my books so beautiful to behold.

Thank you to Kara Feifer and Meryl Poster for your commitment, passion, and perseverance.

Thank you to my steadfast group of beta reader friends and family: you never say no: Chuck Royce, Alexandra and Cody Kittle, Tess Porter, Kathy Goodrich, Cyndy Anderson, Susie Baker, Linda Munger, Iliana Moore, Hilary Hatfield, Leigh and Yolanda Rappaport, Nimfa Timber, Tim Lewis, Heidi and Lew Pearlson, and Susana Arauz.

Thank you to my writing group for your insights, honesty, companionship, and some Wordle distraction: Becky Ford, Melissa Devaney, Icy Frantz, Claire Haft, and Katherine Pushkar.

Thank you to the one and only Captain Kirk Reynolds for answers to all my boating questions, no matter how peculiar. And thank you to Iliana Moore and Marta Pero for guiding me through Argentina physically, linguistically, and culturally.

Thank you to the masterful writer and friend, Luanne Rice. You are an endless source of inspiration. And thank you to a growing list of author pals who make this solitary work so convivial, in particular: Zibby Owens, Hank Philippi Ryan, Mary Dixie Carter, Megan Collins, Virginia Hume, Wendy Francis, Katie Mahon, Joan Hill, Rea Frey, Annabel Monaghan, Wendy Walker, Mitch Giannunzio, Joani Elliott, and Brian Cuban. Writers are simply the most generous people I have ever had the privilege to meet.

Thank you to all the independent bookstores and libraries, book reviewers and book bloggers, bookstagrammers and TikTokkers. Thank you to the Pulpwood Queens—all of you but most especially Kathy Murphy and Mandy Haynes, to the book fairies of Canada who leave books to be found by passers-by, to the friends who throw book parties, to the people who show up at those parties, and to the whole world of readers who love books and do everything they can to share that love with others.

Finally, thank you to all the citizen detectives out there. You work hard to crack the code to horrific violence. And sometimes, just sometimes, justice is served.